The

Lopez

Affair

MORE BY THIS AUTHOR

Historical Fiction

The Testament of Mariam

This Rough Ocean

The Chronicles of Christoval Alvarez

The Secret World of Christoval Alvarez
The Enterprise of England
The Portuguese Affair
Bartholomew Fair
Suffer the Little Children
Voyage to Muscovy
The Play's the Thing
That Time May Cease

Oxford Medieval Mysteries

The Bookseller's Tale
The Novice's Tale
The Huntsman's Tale
The Mercahnt's Tale

The Fenland Series

Flood
Betrayal

Contemporary Fiction

The Anniversary
The Travellers
A Running Tide

The

Lopez

Affair

Ann Swinfen

Shakenoak Press

For

Tanya

With Much Love

Chapter One

$\mathscr{I}$t was only later, much later, that I came to realise how those many broken fragments fitted together, and how they would lead to an act of appalling injustice and cruelty, which became known as the Lopez affair. On that sunny summer afternoon, I could not have suspected that I would myself become entangled in the brutal battle already being waged between the great men in Elizabeth's England.

The stableyard at Walsingham House in Seething Lane was rich with the aromas of hay and sun-warmed horse. I leaned out over the half door of Hector's stall to watch the two children riding their ponies in demure circles around the yard. The girl, who must be nine years old now, sat astride with confidence, displaying an innate ease around horses. Her brother – or, to be accurate, half brother – was much younger, not long breeched. He looked frightened, clutching a handful of his pony's mane, tangled amongst the reins, and every tense line of his body betrayed his panic at being thus mounted so high above the ground on an animal which he clearly found terrifying. Harry, the chief stable lad, had a firm hold of the leading rein, and kept his hand comfortingly against the small of the child's back, but nothing seemed to reassure him.

You would never suppose that little Lord Robert was the son of that boastful and swaggering dandy, the Earl of Essex.

The children's mother, Countess of Essex – though I still thought of her as Frances Walsingham – walked over to me.

'Do you think Robert will ever overcome his fear of horses, Kit?'

I smiled at her.

'He is not yet three, is he, my lady? Plenty of time yet.'

'Elizabeth was never afraid.'

'Some children have a natural affinity for horses.'

'Aye, and some are naturally fearless.' She smiled wryly. 'Sometimes I think Elizabeth is a little too fearless. Do you remember that time at Barn Elms, when you snatched her from under the hooves of another horse?'

'Aye, my lady, I remember.'

We were both silent, remembering. Her father and my employer, Sir Francis Walsingham, had still been alive then. Lady Frances had already lost her first husband, Sir Philip Sidney, but had not yet been married to Essex. I could only observe this second marriage from a distance, but I was certain it was not a happy one. All of London knew of the Earl's wanton habits.

The little boy still looked terrified.

'He's very young to be riding,' I said tentatively, although I had not been any older when my grandfather had first put me up on a pony back on his estate in Portugal.

Lady Frances grimaced. 'The Earl is determined that he shall grow up manly, a very warrior. Even while he is still a small child.'

Her voice was bitter. I had noticed before that she always referred to Essex as 'the Earl', never as 'my husband'. And it was perhaps all too obvious that she continued to live, with the children, at her mother's home in Seething Lane, not at Essex House in the Strand.

'I am sure that Lord Robert will overcome his fear, given time. That is a very quiet pony.'

She smiled. 'Aye. He used to be mine, until I outgrew him. He must be more than twenty.'

We watched the children a few minutes longer. The Lady Elizabeth was cantering gently round the perimeter of the stableyard now. She had a good seat and looked happy. I turned away, unhooking the lower half of the door and stepping outside.. It was time to return to my lodgings. After finishing my day's work at St Thomas's Hospital, I had crossed the river for a brief visit to my horse Hector, for I had had no opportunity to ride him for more than two weeks. The stable lads exercised him when they had the opportunity, but he fretted if left too long in his stall.

'Dr Alvarez? Kit?' Lady Frances seemed suddenly awkward.

'Aye, my lady?'

'Would you . . . could you take a look at my daughter?'

I did my best to conceal my surprise. The Walsingham family had their own private physician; they had no need of the services of a physician from St Thomas's like me, whose role was to care for the poor and needy of Southwark. I did have a few private patients, but the Walsinghams and Essexes were not among them. Ruy Lopez, I knew, was Essex's physician. However, Sir Francis's daughter and I had known each other for many years, ever since we were quite young, and by calling me Kit, she was – probably intentionally – drawing attention to that.

'Certainly, my lady, if I can be of any service to you.'

When Elizabeth had been helped to dismount by one of the stable lads, and had given her pony an apple from her pocket, she ran across to us, her eyes bright and her cheeks flushed. One of the Countess's waiting women stepped forward, but Lady Frances shook her head.

'Take Lord Robert back to the nursery, Mistress Godliff,' she said. 'Lady Elizabeth will come with me and Dr Alvarez.'

The little girl skipped ahead of us as we made our way into the house and up the backstairs, which I had climbed so many times when I had worked here with Thomas Phelippes, deciphering new codes and transcribing the intercepted letters of England's enemies. And indeed

3

devising some new form of spurious information to be slipped into the courier service of the king of Spain, in order to create confusion and outwit his many attempts to kill our Queen and invade our country.

Lady Frances led me along the familiar corridor, past the office where I had worked with Phelippes, which now stood deserted, with the door ajar. Past the gloomy portraits of past Walsinghams, until we reached the family's portion of the house, which I had very rarely entered.

'This way,' she said. 'We will go to my private apartments.' She turned to her daughter. 'Elizabeth, go and take off your riding habit and put on a light summer gown, then come to Mama's parlour.'

The child nodded and ran off, while Lady Frances led me into a pretty room, not very large, with windows facing south and providing a view over the rooftops of lower buildings to the river beyond. Now, at the height of summer, the Thames was crowded with ships, from the small one-man wherries and the larger long ferry which carried passengers down to Gravesend, up to tough little coastal traders bringing coal down to London from the north of England, and the great merchant ships come from the Mediterranean, or the coast of Africa, and even those fast ships carrying a full complement of cannon, belonging to the privateers who harried the Spanish treasure ships along the shores of the New World.

When we were alone in the room, Lady Frances told me to close the door, then turned to me, looking curiously hesitant.

'Kit,' she said, 'we have known each other for many years. You were even a witness at my marriage to the Earl.'

I nodded, mystified as to where this could be leading. 'Indeed, my lady.'

'My father . . .' she hesitated, and cleared her throat. 'Before he died, my father told me something of your history.'

Unaccountably, she blushed, and I found myself going suddenly cold. Sara Lopez knew who I was, but only three other friends had known my true identity: Sir Francis Walsingham, Dr Hector Nunez, and my companion in Muscovy, Pyotr Aubery. All three were now dead. All of them men I had liked and admired. But with them gone, I thought my secret safe. Except, except, from my personal enemy, Robert Poley, who had tricked me into Walsingham's service.

Just what had Sir Francis told his daughter?

'My lady?' I hoped that by seeming perplexed, feigning lack of understanding, I might forestall what I feared she was about to say.

She looked down. 'I know that your true name is Caterina Alvarez, and that . . . you are no more a man than I am.'

She glanced up and I saw that she feared she had made me angry. Instead, my mind churned with conflicting emotions. I had known Frances Walsingham a long time, as she said, but never closely, for her rank was far above mine, even when she was Lady Sidney. Now that she was the Countess of Essex, our worlds scarcely touched.

'I would never reveal what I know to anyone,' she said, hastily and apologetically. 'Not even my mother knows.'

'Nor your husband?' I spoke through gritted teeth.

Of all men in the world, I dreaded my identity being discovered by Essex. Then I faced what I had been trying to shut out of my mind. That one other man who knew my identity. Poley. I had not seen him of late, not since he had been implicated in the murder of Christopher Marlowe earlier in the year, yet he had lingered like a dark cloud on the horizon of my life ever since I was sixteen. Robert Poley. It was folly even to allow my guard against Robert Poley to slip for a moment. I might be of no account to him now that he served the Cecils and we no longer both worked in the intelligence service of Walsingham, but times might change. Or he might reveal my identity from mere spite.

'Nay,' Lady Frances said. 'Certainly not my . . .' She

hesitated, and swallowed painfully on the words. 'My husband.'

She walked to the window and stood looking out, her back to me.

'My father did not reveal your secret to me carelessly, Kit. He believed that some day you might need a friend. Instead . . .' her voice caught. 'Instead, it is I who am in need of a friend.'

Before she could say more, the door opened and her daughter came in, followed by the waiting woman.

'Thank you, Mistress Godliff. That will be all.'

As soon as the door had closed behind the waiting woman, she held out her hand to the child.

'Come, my sweet. I want Dr Alvarez to examine you, where you were hurt the other day.'

The child looked at me anxiously, then hung her head. 'I didn't do anything bad, Mama.' Her eyes filled suddenly with tears.

'Of course you did not, my pet. Now, lie down here, and lift your gown. You are not bleeding any more?'

The little girl shook her head, but she had flushed with embarrassment. I examined her quickly. She was but nine years old, too young to bleed. What I found would not have surprised me amongst the sad waifs of Southwark, but here in Walsingham House I was shocked, although I tried not to show it. It was not as I had momentarily feared. The child had not been raped. But her back bore the marks of a recent beating, a vicious beating, which had drawn blood.

The weals were beginning to heal, but still looked angry, so I applied a salve of cooling herbs and spoke cheerfully of how the pain would soon be gone.

Once the child had been sent off to her lessons, Lady Frances motioned me to a chair and ran a trembling hand over her face. She was wearing loose sleeves, not those of the tight fitting cut favoured by ladies of rank, who never undertook any task more demanding of movement than needlework. As her sleeve fell back, I saw that her arm was ringed with bruises, as though it had been held hard by a cruel hand.

'That was a violent beating the child received,' I said carefully. It was not my place to comment on how parents might discipline their children, and I knew that many believed that beating was the only way to ensure obedience. This, however, had gone beyond anything I had seen except amongst the most brutalised families in Southwark, cowering under the hand of a drunken and violent man.

'It was done without my knowledge,' she said. She drew a deep breath, and flushed with shame. 'It was done by the Earl, with his horsewhip.'

'Essex!' I was too horrified to use his title. 'And with a *horsewhip*? But surely . . . his own stepdaughter . . . your child.'

'She means nothing to him but an encumbrance. You would think, since she is Philip's daughter . . . he has always professed his great love of Philip Sidney, but it seems not to extend to his child.'

Suddenly she began to weep, great silent tears welling up and spilling down her cheeks, which she made no attempt to check.

I did not know what to say. I had expected nothing like this. But the most urgent matter was that the child should be protected from further harm.

'Forgive me,' I said hesitantly, 'but I understand that the Earl lives mainly at Essex House on the Strand?'

She nodded, drawing out a fine linen handkerchief and wiping her eyes. 'Aye, and we live here, at home, with my mother. He comes, of course, whenever he pleases, to exact his matrimonial rights. That is, whenever he is not occupied with one of his whores, or at Court, or crossing political swords with Lord Burghley and his son in this endless struggle for power.'

I thought of Thomas Phelippes, employed now by Essex, reluctantly working away at the Customs House, trying to build an intelligence service as successor to Walsingham's great work which had kept England and our Queen safe for so many years. Phelippes's great mistake had been his failure to offer his services at once to the Cecils after Walsingham's death. Instead, Robert Poley had wormed his way into their favour, buying his place (so Phelippes and I both believed) with the secret files and code books which had been stolen from our office here during Walsingham's very funeral at St Paul's.

'Certainly you must keep the child safe from any further beatings,' I said tentatively. 'But that may be difficult, if the Earl is constantly about the house. She seems to be bearing it stoically.'

She smiled through her tears. 'She is a courageous child. She has learned to be. Of course, she cannot remember her own father, she was too young, but her grandfather filled his place, until this second marriage of mine. She was disposed to look on the Earl as her father, but he was indifferent to her from the start. Now, of late, he has become cruel. She is so afraid of him. During the day she wears a brave face, but at night she wakes up screaming from her nightmares.'

'Then I think you must separate her from him completely,' I said. 'More of this and he could do her permanent harm. Suppose I recommend that for her health she should spend some time in the country?'

'I should hate to part with her.'

'It may be necessary, for her safety. Is there not one of the Walsingham properties well away from London, where she could go?'

'The Earl likes to visit them regularly. As my mother and I are my father's only heirs, he believes that all the property is now rightfully his.'

I recalled that Essex had risen, like his father, from a relatively modest gentry family. The great properties he now possessed in his own right were largely the gifts of the Queen. Little wonder that he snatched greedily at the Walsingham inheritance.

'Francis Mylles,' I said.

'Master Mylles? My father's principal secretary?'

'Aye. Did he not purchase one of your father's

country manors, when Sir Francis was turning some of his landed property into coin before his death? To provide for you and Dame Ursula? Why not send the Lady Elizabeth to Francis Mylles and his wife? She has known them all her life. He is a good, kind man. She would be safe in his home. The Earl would have no cause to go there. If he beats the child merely because he finds her an encumbrance, a mote in his eye, he is unlikely to go in pursuit of her.'

'Aye,' she said slowly. 'That might serve. Indeed, I think it might.' She sighed. 'Oh, but I shall miss her! It is such a comfort to me, to see her grow into a fair young maid. Philip would have been so proud of her.'

'Indeed he would.'

I had only ever seen Sir Philip from a distance, for he had been killed not long after I had first been drawn in as a code-breaker in Walsingham's service, but I knew that he had been not only handsome and courageous, but a fine poet, a man of intelligence and tenderness. To be tethered now to that strutting popinjay Essex must be a constant torment to Lady Frances.

'The Earl does not beat his son?' I asked, nervous that I might be venturing too far into private matters.

She shook her head. 'Not yet, though I have seen him clout Robert on the head. I think he believes all boys should be brought up as hardened warriors, like King Arthur's knights of old.' Her mouth twisted in a grimace. 'He seems to think the days of knightly chivalry are still with us in our modern world of cannon and muskets. He has little interest in matters of intellect and culture.'

I nodded, remembering Essex during the Portuguese expedition. As the army had begun its despairing retreat from Lisbon, Essex had ridden up to the gates of the city, challenging someone to come out and meet him in single combat, to fight for the honour of Queen Elizabeth. As he rode to join the rest of the shambling, starving remnant of our army, he had smirked complacently, assuming that no one from the Spanish garrison had dared to face him.

But from within the city we had heard the sound of

mocking laughter.

'You needs must keep a watch on Lord Robert,' I said. 'Blows to the head in a child so young can lead to permanent damage.'

'I shall indeed watch as best I may, but Essex is my son's father and may overrule me.'

She sighed again. She was very pale and drawn. I thought that a time on Francis Mylles's country manor could do her own health no harm.

'Do you wish me to write a note advising that the Lady Elizabeth should be sent into the country?' I asked. 'Or will you leave that to your family physician? I believe it is Dr Lopez.'

She twisted her fingers together. 'I should prefer it from you, Kit. You have a name for treating children. Dr Lopez is an excellent man – we are fortunate to have the services of the Queen's own physician – but matters are somewhat strained of late. Dr Lopez has been the Earl's physician for many years, but now, in this struggle with the Cecils . . . it seems Dr Lopez is their man.'

I shook my head in despair. Until his death, Dr Nuñez had been physician to the Cecil family, but now, like Essex, they too employed Dr Lopez. On the other hand, both physicians, who were Marranos like me, had also been merchants, dealing primarily in spices and other costly goods, imported to England through the Mediterranean. This had made them useful allies of Sir Francis Walsingham, their captains and mercantile agents providing eyes and ears for his intelligence service, while their ships also carried secret despatches and intercepted those of Spain and France. Now that England was being torn apart, and our security placed at risk, while Essex and the Cecils fought for control of the new secret service, Ruy Lopez was in an unenviable and ambivalent position. Physician to both parties, he had, so it seemed, allied himself with the Cecils' intelligence network. As Phelippes should have done.

'Certainly I will write a letter, advising country air

for the Lady Elizabeth,' I said. 'Do you but provide me with paper and ink.'

She gestured toward a small writing table placed beneath the window, where I could see a pile of heavy-laid paper, and an inkwell, and a flat box containing uncut quills. Her sleeve fell back again as she moved her arms, and I caught sight of those bruises again, but for the moment I said nothing.

With the small penknife I carried in my medical satchel, I trimmed a quill and quickly wrote the required advice, urging that the child should have plenty of exercise, including walking and riding and archery, and should be given a wholesome diet of fresh country food, none of the elaborate dishes which I was sure would be served up when Essex was in residence. Walsingham, who had suffered from many internal complaints, had always been abstemious in his diet, as I was sure his own family would be still.

There was sealing wax and a small silver burner for melting it. As I drew out the seal ring I wore on a chain round my neck, Lady Frances smiled.

'Did Arthur Gregory make that for you?'

I smiled in return. 'He did.'

'I miss it, you know. Oh, certainly I was never a part of my father's work, and he rarely spoke of it to my mother and me, but it was exciting to know that here, in this house, so much was happening, to out fox our enemies.'

'He was a great man, Sir Francis,' I said. 'Few in England realise how much their safety over all these years was secured by him.'

'Do you ever see Arthur Gregory?' she asked. 'He had a little boy, I remember.'

I was surprised by this. 'Why, my lady, he is employed in the Earl's own intelligence work, not far from here, at an office in the Customs House, along with Thomas Phelippes.'

She shook her head. 'I know nothing of that, only that the Earl employs the Bacon brothers, Anthony and Francis.

And I know of this great rivalry of the two parties, locked in combat like a pair of rutting stags. The Earl hates Sir Robert Cecil. They have been sworn enemies ever since boyhood, when the Earl was taken in by Cecil's father after his own father's death. Lord Burghley was only Sir William Cecil then. He was the Earl's godfather.'

I nodded, but said nothing as I pressed my seal ring into the blob of soft wax before it could harden. It was a tangle indeed. Burghley was Essex's godfather. The Bacon brothers were his son Robert's cousins, yet now they were working for Essex, Robert's deadly enemy. It was no surprise that Cecil and Essex hated each other. Cecil, thin, small, pale, crippled since childhood, but with a brilliant mind – what must he have thought of Robert Devereux, Earl of Essex, this cuckoo introduced as a boy into the family nest – large, handsome, athletic, but stupid.

Francis and Anthony Bacon were the greater puzzle. Why had they thrown in their lot with Essex? Perhaps they felt they could not compete with their brilliant cousin within Lord Burghley's party, but must seek their future elsewhere. The mothers of Robert Cecil and the Bacon brothers were sisters, two of the gifted daughters of Anthony Cooke, tutor to the Queen's brother, King Edward. Their father had ensured they were educated as well as his sons, and they were famous still as amongst the most talented and learned women in England, next after the Queen herself. The sisters had belonged to a close-knit family, and Francis and Anthony, clever like their cousin, must surely see through the arrogant boorishness of Essex. But, then, Essex had the Queen's ear, and might be able to do much to advance them. How glad I was that this was not my world!

As I returned my penknife to my satchel, I took out a small pot of salve.

'My lady,' I said, 'this is a salve of pounded arnica root, sovereign against bruises. Will you allow me to treat those bruises on your arm?'

At my words, she blushed a fiery red, drawing the

loose sleeve down over the exposed arm.

'It is nothing,' she said.

Greatly daring, I said, 'You told me you needed a friend. As a friend, I can treat the bruising and say nothing, as I shall say nothing about the beating your daughter has suffered.'

She hesitated, then she nodded. 'You are right, Kit. I am foolish to refuse your help.'

She turned back both sleeves and held out her arms to me. Both were ringed with black bruises, beginning to turn yellow at the edges. Someone had gripped both her arms in a vicious hold. Probably she had twisted, struggling against it, which had made the bruising even worse.

I spread the salve lavishly over the bruises on both her arms.

'This is best used at once, before too much of the blood gathers under the skin,' I said, 'but it will help to disperse it even now, though more slowly. I will leave this with you. In case you should need it again.'

Her eyes were cast down, watching my fingers smoothing in the salve, but I saw the colour rise again from her neck to her cheeks. She was wearing a small ruff, not over elaborate, the sort worn by ladies of quality in their own homes by day, unlike some of the elaborate affairs affected, even at home, by a few of the merchants' wives who lived in Goldsmiths' Row on Cheapside. At Court Lady Frances would don one of those larger elegant ruffs in fashion amongst the aristocracy. Although I believed she did not often attend Court.

The Queen had disapproved of Frances Walsingham's first marriage, to Sir Philip Sidney, whose rank had been certainly higher than Sir Francis Walsingham's, despite the spymaster's importance in the governing of England. When the Lady Frances had later been married in haste – and in some secrecy – to the Queen's favourite, Robert Devereux, Earl of Essex, it was said that the monarch had been incandescent with fury. Since then, it was widely rumoured that the lady had not been welcome at Court. In my own mind I was sure that it had been no love match. It was certainly none such on Lady Frances's part, for she had wept at her wedding, and from all I had seen it was not on Essex's part either. Nay, Essex had married her for political reasons, hoping to step into his late father-in-law's shoes as Principal Secretary to Her Majesty. His anger that he had still not achieved that aim might well lie behind his harshness to the child Elizabeth. And also, I suspected, to his wife.

For I saw now, appearing above the edge of her small ruff, the mark of further bruising on her neck. Just for a moment, I had a flash of memory. I was standing in the filthy kitchen of a mean farmhouse in Portugal, gazing in horror at my sister Isabel. She too had just such bruising on her neck, the marks of a man's fingers which had come close to throttling her.

It was not my place to make any comment now on the relations between husband and wife. Just as Dr Lopez must remain discreet in his treatment of the Queen, so I would keep silence about what I had observed here today, but that did not bar me from providing medical help.

'If you will remove your ruff, my lady,' I said quietly, 'I will salve the rest of the bruising.'

Her colour deepened, but she said nothing. Instead she began to fumble with the many pins holding the ruff in place. At last she had freed it, and laid it aside. She would need the help of her waiting woman to replace it, for I had not the skill. I had not worn a full ruff since I was a child in Portugal, and then my own waiting woman had secured it for me. These days I never wore one, just the frilled collar of my shirts, which did duty as a substitute.

The bruises on her neck showed the clear imprint of a man's fingers. The thumbs had come close to her windpipe. Too close. I set my mouth grimly as I spread the arnica salve gently over her neck, where I could feel the faint pulse beating.

I replaced the stopper in the jar and set it down beside the discarded ruff. Then I looked her squarely in the eye.

'That was a near thing, my lady.'

She nodded, tears welling in her eyes, but she did not speak.

'It seems that you too need protection.'

'I must endure,' she said dully. 'I have no other choice.'

'It is monstrous.'

'No worse than many women must face.'

Not for the first time, I was thankful for my male disguise. Even were I to return to my woman's estate, no one could force me to marry a brute and a bully, for reasons of state or inheritance. I knew that Sir Francis had agreed to the marriage because he wanted to secure a safe future for his daughter and granddaughter, but had he really taken Essex's measure? Had he still lived, he would never have tolerated this. But women even of Lady Frances's rank had little redress against an abusive husband. In law, she was his property. He might treat her however he wished.

'Perhaps,' I said slowly (for I was treading on dangerous ground here), 'perhaps you should accompany your daughter into the country? It would give you some respite.'

She shook her head. 'He would never permit it. I will have some difficulty even arranging for Elizabeth to go if he decides to refuse. Me, he would never permit. Besides, there is my son. I need to stay with him. And I am again with child.'

She was right, of course.

'Then I suggest you make some provision to protect your throat, my lady. At least a thick starched collar beneath your ruff.'

She gave me a wan smile. 'I think I am safe enough now that I have told him I am with child. The Earl wants more sons. A single boy cannot be sure to secure his line.'

This, too, was true. For men of the Earl's rank, a solitary heir was no security for the future. Many eldest sons had failed to live long enough to inherit from their fathers. The Queen's own father, the late King Henry, was a younger son, whose brother had perished in his youth. Essex would hope for a whole quiverful of sons.

As I made my way out of Walsingham House, down the backstairs and through the stableyard, I turned over the uncomfortable discoveries I had made about the Essex marriage. Although I had never suspected that the Earl was violent toward his wife and stepdaughter, I found it did not surprise me. I had never known anyone so totally self-obsessed and arrogant. He would not hesitate to use violence against anyone who – for so much as a moment – stood in his way. And the woman and girl who formed part of his property he would regard as his to use as he wished. I had heard it whispered that Essex was even becoming overbearing with the Queen herself. For a time she might tolerate it. But I think, in the end, he would go too far.

Once across the river in Southwark, I made my way swiftly to St Thomas's. I had left my dog Rikki with the gatekeeper Tom Read longer than usual, for I had gone straight to Seething Lane after visiting one of my recovering patients in a wherryman's cottage on the river bank. Rikki jumped up enthusiastically to greet me, while Tom's old wolfhound Swifty raised his head and thumped his tail.

'I am sorry, Tom,' I said. 'I meant to be back long before this.'

Tom looked up from his supper – a thick pottage from the hospital kitchen. On a side plate was fresh bread, awaiting honey from a pot provided by an admirer of his amongst the hospital bee keepers.

'Rikki is no problem, doctor,' he said. 'And do not let him play the beggar with you. He has had a good bowl of scraps already.'

'Do you hear?' I said. Rikki cocked his head innocently, tongue hanging out as if in hope of a second supper.

As we set out for my lodgings, however, he ran ahead cheerfully, turning aside only once to chase a neighbourhood cat up one of the spindly trees which grew between the street and the river.

'Have a care,' I warned. 'Harm that puss and Bessie Travis will string you up by your paws.' Bessie Travis kept the nearby whorehouse and was a figure to be reckoned with in our neighbourhood. I recognised the cat as one of the three or four who made their home in that nest of Winchester geese.

It was a soft summer evening, such an evening as I would usually have chosen to make my way to the Lion, the inn close to the Rose playhouse, where the players were wont to gather to eat and drink after the day's performance. Tonight, I knew, they would not be there. Ever since the murder of Christopher Marlowe in the early summer, the players had been grieving and subdued. Marlowe had often made himself unpopular, for he was arrogant and quarrelsome, often flaring up, ready for a fight, yet he was of their company, though a playwright, not a player. The murder had touched them too close.

I knew another side of his life, one not truly understood by the players. For, like me, Marlowe had served Walsingham, although not as a code-breaker. I knew a little of his work. He had been sent on missions abroad, sometimes to infiltrate Catholic groups which were planning attacks on the Queen. It was dangerous work, occasionally also undertaken by Robert Poley, though in the latter's case there was the possibility that he was a double agent, serving our enemies, whoever would pay him the most. I had guessed that the risks had drawn Marlowe to the work just as much as the purses of coin, for he was a man who lived always on the knife edge of danger and seemed almost to feast on it. Yet the money must also have attracted him. Despite his talents he came from a humble family. His fine clothes, his arrogant air, I realised now, were in some sense an attempt to claw his way out of that modest life. He had tried to seduce my friend Simon into his spendthrift ways, to his harm. It was easier to forgive him, now that he was gone.

The true facts of Marlowe's death were hidden, but I

suspected that he had come to know too much and could not be trusted to keep silent. After Walsingham's death he had worked for Lord Burghley and his son. Like Robert Poley, like Ruy Lopez. Had the Cecils decided he was too dangerous to remain alive? I shivered. I cared nothing for Poley, but Ruy was married to my friend Sara, and I did not want to see her in danger, should Ruy, like Marlowe, prove an expendable pawn in the political game of chess being played out between Essex and the Cecils.

Why could not these men of power lay aside their differences and work together for the safety of England? How futile – and ultimately how dangerous – was their quarrel over who should maintain the network of intelligence and agents now that Walsingham was dead. Three years had passed, and still it was unresolved.

Rikki ran ahead of me up the stairs in my lodging house, but I stopped to knock on Simon's door, the room below mine.

'Come in.' His voice sounded dispirited.

He was sprawled on his bed, with his shoes on, some loose pages of a play script strewn across his lap.

'You are late home,' he said. It sounded like an accusation.

'I went to Seething Lane after I finished at the hospital, to see Hector, then the Lady Frances asked me to physic her daughter.'

'Do they not have their own physician? Dr Lopez?'

'Aye.' I had not meant that to slip out, so I prevaricated. 'I expect he is busy. It was nothing. Just some salve. Are you learning a new part? Have you eaten?'

'Aye and nay. 'Tis a poor thing. We are still waiting for Will's new piece and must make do with this rubbish in the meantime. In this good weather we need to fill the playhouse every day, for there is no talk of a winter season this year.'

He swung his legs round to the floor and yawned.

'And I have not eaten. You spoke of collops of mutton.'

'Aye. Come up to my room. I left them there before I visited a patient on my way to Seething Lane. I have enough for the children too.'

'You cannot feed those four hungry mouths all the time, even if you are now earning a full physician's pay.'

He often teased me about what he called my lame ducks, though I had grown accustomed to it and no longer paid it any mind. Tonight he simply sounded tired and discouraged.

'Mostly they eat in the hospital,' I said, 'but the butcher gave me extra today. He has not forgotten that I cared for his child during that false accusation of plague.'

We followed Rikki up the next flight of stairs to my small room, and while Simon climbed the ladder to the garret, where the four children who had once been street beggars now lived, I set to lighting my fire and frying the collops in a little saved bacon fat, with some onions and a few chopped carrots. The carrots I had bought cheap, for they were somewhat withered, but stirred in with the rest they would help to bulk out the meal. The weather was too hot to be leaning over a fire, and I was wiping the sweat from my forehead when Simon returned with the children.

He fetched a loaf from his own room and soon we were all eating hungrily, Simon and I sitting at the table, the children cross-legged on the floor. It could hardly compare with the food served at the Lion, but we all wiped up the last drops of gravy with our bread, and finished with some small early apples Katerina produced proudly from her pockets, windfalls from the hospital orchard. They were hard and somewhat sour, but left us feeling satisfied. I thought Simon seemed less downhearted, now that he had eaten. There was a time when he had been a close friend of Marlowe, even shared lodgings with him and Thomas Kyd. It was not easy for him to shake off the memory of the man's brutal killing. Truly, none of us could.

'And have you worked hard today?' I asked the children.

The two older ones, Katerina and Matthew, were

employed at the hospital, she in the laundry, he as one of the boys who ran errands and did any odd jobs that were needed. The twins were too young to find employment there, but followed the others about and helped, unpaid.

'I am learning to iron sheets,' Maggie said proudly. 'You must be careful not to scorch them. You spit on the iron to see if it is hot enough, but if it smokes when you put it to the sheet, then you must let it cool.'

'I see,' I said gravely. Are not the sheets very large and heavy?'

'Katerina helps me,' she admitted. 'But soon I shall be strong enough to manage by myself.'

There was some truth in this. When I had first know the little group of beggar children they had been gaunt and starving, but two years of food and now a roof over their heads, had transformed them. No violent beatings with a horsewhip for them, I thought, and although they had been kicked and punched often enough in the past, they were safe enough now, a little family with a home of their own, even if it was no more than a small attic room.

Soon after we had finished eating and scrubbed the greasy bowls clean, I chased the children off to their beds. I knew they found it entertaining that anyone should bid them to bed, having for so long been responsible themselves for finding some sheltered outbuilding or doorway to sleep in, but they went obediently enough. Simon and I sat a little longer with a cup of ale, looking out of the window as the sun sank, crimsoning the waters of the river, and candles began to shine out from windows across in the City.

'So, you are now at the beck and call of the Countess of Essex,' he said. 'I did not know you knew her well.'

'Not well,' I said. 'But indeed I have known her these many years, ever since I began to work for Sir Francis.'

'I remember when we stood in the freezing wind watching the funeral procession for her first husband,' he said.

'Aye.'

'The child was very small then. How old is she now?'

'About nine, I think.'

'And does the countess wish to retain you as her personal physician?'

'Oh, not at all. It was just a small matter.' I would have liked to share what I knew with Simon, but I must respect the Lady Frances's confidence.

'She is unhappy,' I said. 'Essex is a brute.'

'Aye, well,' he shrugged. 'I suppose even great riches and a place at Court cannot buy you happiness.'

'Very true,' I said. 'They cannot.'

Chapter Two

*I*s it not strange, the way life may continue with little change, following the same path for weeks upon end, and then, as if Fortune's Wheel had suddenly spun crazily about, everything is tumbled awry? My life had brushed that of Frances Walsingham from time to time, but no more than that. Now I possessed uncomfortable secrets about her life, while she possessed the dangerous secret of my true identity. She sent me word, in a carefully written letter, that her daughter, accompanied by a waiting woman, two armed attendants and two grooms, had left for Francis Mylles's manor. She gave no hint as to whether Essex had made any objection to the arrangement. Even if he had, it seemed that our plan was able to go ahead.

As to whether she herself was still suffering abuse at Essex's hands, I could not tell. I hoped that the possibility that she might be carrying the second son he hoped for would persuade him to keep his fists to himself. Before I left Walsingham House I had hinted that she should point out to him possible danger to the unborn child.

Although I had, for the moment, no further dealings with Lady Frances, I could not quite dismiss her troubles from my mind. Then a second disaster burst upon my world. Not a disaster for me, but for a friend. And it was one which seemed insoluble.

Peter Lambert and I had arrived at St Bartholomew's hospital at about the same time, nine years before, in 1584. My father had been employed there as a physician to the poor of London ever since our arrival two years earlier, his post having been found for him through the good offices of Dr Nuñez, on whose merchant ship we had travelled to England. The post had also provided us with a small house in Duck Lane. When I was fourteen, my father had arranged to employ me as his assistant at the hospital and one of the first people I came to know there was Peter Lambert, a boy of about the same age.

Peter was an orphan, a street urchin, who had somehow managed to find a place as a servant in the hospital. He had shown himself quick-witted, able, and trustworthy, and by some lucky chance he had been noticed by the hospital's chief apothecary, Master Winger. By the time I arrived at St Bartholomew's, Peter was already beginning his training as an apothecary, and while I was there, we often worked together. A few years ago he had married Master Winger's daughter Helen, and they had a son. Although I rarely saw him now that I lived south of the river and worked at St Thomas's, we had remained friends. He was one of those people I felt were moving ahead with their lives, while I – trapped in my male disguise – must bid farewell to thoughts of marriage and children.

It was with some astonishment, therefore, when I was leaving St Thomas's about a fortnight after my disturbing encounter with Lady Frances, that I found Peter standing outside the gatehouse, apparently waiting for me.

'Peter?' I said. 'Are you free of your duties so early that you can come all this way from the City?'

I looked at him more closely. His face was haggard, his clothes somewhat unkempt. Not the neat, composed young man I knew.

'Are you ill?' I said.

'Aye,' he said. His voice cracked as he spoke. 'Aye, Kit, you may say that I am ill. Ill of a fatal disease, perhaps, and no hope for me. Or for my family.'

There was a wild look in his eye, which I did not care to see. They were the words a man might use if he were struck down with the plague, but clearly Peter was not so afflicted.

'Come with me,' I said briskly, seizing him by the elbow and setting off toward the nearest ale house. The food and drink would be better at the Lion, but if the players had begun to drift back there, I thought it better to talk to Peter alone. He came with me willingly enough, and we said no more until we were seated in a quiet corner with our cups of ale before us and two small pies. I had recognised them as coming from our neighbourhood pie shop, which did not eke out the contents with meat from dubious sources, so they would be safe to eat.

Peter pushed the pie about on his plate with his finger, but did not pick it up. He did, however, take a deep draught of his ale.

'Now,' I said, 'what is all this tale of fatal illness? You have not come to me, I think, as a physician but as a friend.'

He put down his cup and buried his face in his hands. I could see that they were shaking.

'I spoke,' he said, 'as your play makers would have it. Metaphorically. But it will end in fatal illness, either on the scaffold or from starvation. And what will become of Helen and the boy then?'

'The scaffold!' I stared at him, not trusting my ears. 'Come!' I reached across the table and shook him by the shoulder. 'What dreadful crime have you committed, that the shadow of the scaffold should loom over you? It is not a matter for jest.'

'I? I have committed *no* crime, but that will not save me, for I am accused of one, and thrown out of Bart's. And out of our cottage – just at the end of Duck Lane, near where you used to live – that came with my position as apothecary. We are given notice to leave within this fortnight, and where shall we go?'

For a moment, I was speechless. Peter had no family to whom he could turn, but Helen's father, Master Winger, was high in his profession and could surely help them, both with a roof over their heads and with a defence against whatever strange charge had been made against Peter.

Then I remembered that Master Winger was no longer at St Barthomew's, but had recently assumed a position as personal apothecary to Lord Strange, the patron of Simon's company of players. Lord Strange had been suffering from some recurring illness and had taken himself off to his country estate, away from the sicknesses carried on the summer air in London. He had carried off his entire household with him. Master Winger could be reached eventually, but perhaps not quickly enough.

'Now, gather your wits together, Peter,' I said, 'and tell me exactly what has happened.'

I signalled to the potboy to bring us more ale, for I saw that Peter had drained his cup.

'And eat your pie,' I added, 'for you look in need of it. When did you last eat?'

He shook his head, as if someone had clouted him in the ear. 'I do not remember me.'

'Well, you may eat and talk at the same time. As your physician, I order you to eat.'

He gave me a weak smile, and took a small bite of the pie. Then, as if he was unaware of what he was doing, he finished it while he unfolded the story.

'A fellow was brought into the hospital a few days ago. Nay, it must have been more than a week ago. Carried in unconscious by the Watch, who had found him lying injured in the street during their night-time patrol. He had been badly beaten, and I suppose left for dead, for he had lost a great deal of blood, but Dr Temperley physicked him and reckoned he would live. He also bled him twice in the first day, though I will swear that weakened him. He had little enough blood left.'

I tightened my lips and nodded, but said nothing. It was Dr Temperley who had taken my father's place at the hospital after he died while I was away in Portugal. Temperley's younger brother had been given my position as his assistant. Temperley was a physician of the old school, who believed repeated bleeding was a sovereign remedy in every manner of illness. Brought up by my father in the more enlightened practices of modern Arabic medicine, I used it only with the greatest of care, but I thought this was not the issue here.

'In spite of the bleeding, the man began to recover,' Peter said, 'and since we are short-handed at present, Dr Temperley decided that the patient could be left to my care. He would check on his progress once a day. That was well enough for two or three days.'

I nodded again, glad to hear that Peter was being given more responsibility, though I suspected that it owed something to Temperley's known practice of keeping strict hours and never remaining in the hospital beyond them, no matter how many patients were in need of care.

'Something went wrong?' I said. 'And you have been held responsible?'

'Aye.' His mouth twisted in a travesty of a grin. 'You could say that something went wrong. The man died.'

'Delayed result of the beating, I expect. It sometimes happens. There may be internal injuries which are not evidenced at first, to the spleen, perhaps . . .'

'Nay. It was nothing like that. He was poisoned. And the poison was in the febrifuge medicine that I had given him.'

There was a desperate look in Peter's eyes.

'He had begun to develop a slight fever on the third day he was with us, and Dr Temperley instructed me to dose him with a mild febrifuge tincture, nothing unusual. In fact there was plenty already made up in the stillroom, and other patients had taken it, with no harm done. None to him either, the first two days. It was on the third day of the fever that it was poisoned.'

'But why should you poison a patient?' I exclaimed. 'It is absurd.'

He shrugged. 'After he had regained consciousness, we learned who he was. One Josiah Gurdin, from Lord Burghley's household. The almoner sent them word, and a man came to see him. I did not learn his name. It was evening and I was helping the nursing sisters settle the other patients for the night. This man sat with our patient for a short time and left before I could speak to him. I had wanted to ask whether his lordship wanted Master Gurdin sent back to Burghley House, now that he was much recovered.'

It was not the apothecary's role to settle the patients for the night, but it seemed that more tasks than ever had been loaded on to Peter's shoulders.

'And he was from Lord Burghley's household? This visitor?'

'That is what I thought at the time, but later his lordship's steward denied that anyone had come from the Cecils.'

'And what happened then?'

'I gave Josiah his febrifuge medicine before leaving him for the night. He complained that it tasted bitter, but I made nothing of that. As you know, some of the febrifuge herbs have a bitter taste, *Tanacetum parthenium* for one. I went home to Helen, but I was summoned later, very in the early morning, and found the patient suffering from paralysis of the limbs. He could barely speak, could barely move his lips or tongue, but he kept gasping "Poison. Poison" until he could no longer breathe. He died before dawn.'

He shivered. 'It was terrible, Kit.'

I nodded. It is always terrible when a patient dies before your eyes, but if this man had been speaking of poison . . .

'But how?' I said. 'How did he ingest poison?'

'The cup which had held the febrifuge tincture was still beside the bed. I smelled it and tasted a drop from the dregs on the tip of my finger. I said "hemlock" aloud, just as Dr Temperley and the superintendent appeared.'

'It must have been this nameless visitor,' I said reasonably.

'That is what I said. It is what I have been saying ever since. But they do not believe me. It seems I was the only person to notice the visitor. It was late, getting dark. Just a few candles left burning. He did not stay long. There were only two of the nursing sisters there and they were at the other end of the ward. They say they did not see the man. And then, when Lord Burghley's steward said that no one from the household had visited the hospital . . . Everyone believes that I am the only person who handled the medicine. And it certainly contained hemlock.'

'The symptoms you describe are definitely those of hemlock poisoning,' I said thoughtfully. 'And hemlock is not difficult to obtain. There is water hemlock as well, also poisonous and a common weed. I have seen it growing in marshy ground near the Fleet. Some people even mistake it for water parsnip, with fatal results. You will have common hemlock in the hospital stillroom.'

'Aye, for use in treating sprains, but never to be taken by mouth. Dr Temperley and the others argue that I could easily lay my hands on it.'

'By why should you do so? This man was a stranger, you did not even know his name at first. Why should they suppose you would want to kill him?'

He spread out his hands despairingly. 'They do not believe I had anything against the patient himself. It is that–' He swallowed uncomfortably and looked down.

'I have had a few fallings out with Dr Temperley and his brother of late. They have been careless in a few cases, and I have had to cover their mistakes. And their excessive use of bleeding has seriously weakened some of the women in childbirth. I suppose I have spoken out of turn, and should not have done. Dr Temperley has rebuked me before this, and he is now saying that I killed this patient to fasten the blame on him for the bleeding, and that if he had not arrived at the hospital in time, I would have destroyed the evidence of the hemlock. But I had cried it out aloud, what I had discovered, in front of several of the nursing sisters and other patients. I concealed nothing!'

I was silent for a few minutes. I knew of Dr Temperley only by repute and had little reason to like him. He and his brother had usurped my father's place, and mine, at St Bartholomew's, resulting in a desolate period in my life, until a position had been found for me at St Thomas's. I knew his reputation. He was entrenched in the most outmoded practices and regarded new discoveries in medicine with suspicion. He was not dedicated to the care of his patients as my father had been, and as I hoped I was, but I did not believe that he was an evil man.

Nay, I think all this trouble arose from the quarrels between Peter and this man. Peter was clever and conscientious. In other circumstances, he would have made a fine physician and he had always worked well with my father and me. I knew that Master Winger thought highly of him. But he could be outspoken and rebellious. I knew that he had once treated a wounded soldier secretly, that he might not be captured by the City officers. He had probably spoken out of turn, as he had admitted, and too critically of a man who was, in a sense, placed in authority over him.

Yet surely Dr Temperley could not seriously believe that Peter would poison a man simply in order to damage the physician? It was madness even to conceive such an idea. Everything seemed to hinge on this mysterious visitor who had been seen by no one but Peter. There are always people coming and going about a hospital, but this seemed to have happened late in the evening. Probably no other visitors would have been about, most of the physicians and apothecaries gone home, the nursing sisters anxious to finish their tasks for the day. Yet someone else might have seen this man. The gatekeeper. One of the servants.

'This visitor,' I said, 'would you recognise him again? Can you describe him?'

Peter pulled a face.

'That was what they asked me when I said Josiah had had a visitor. But they were in the darker end of the ward, and I was paying no particular mind. We were lifting an incontinent patient to a clean bed and stripping the wet sheets. I only glanced that way briefly, because Josiah had been left in my charge, and I wanted him to take his medicine and go to sleep. That was all he needed to recover from his injuries.'

'You should not have been making beds, Peter. That is a task for the nursing sisters.'

He shrugged. 'As I said, we have been short-handed and I do not mind lending my aid when it is needed. There has been a summer rheum going about amongst the sisters, and that evening there were only two working on that ward instead of the usual four. I thought it only right to lend a hand. I realise now, of course, that if I had not, if I had stayed by Josiah, this man could not have interfered with his medicine, as I am sure he must have done, else how could the hemlock have found its way there? The flask of febrifuge tincture in the stillroom, from which I had poured it, was untouched.'

I nodded. 'From everything you say, it must be this visitor who brought the hemlock with him. Can you remember nothing about him? And how did the patient, this Josiah, seem? Were they friendly? Or was he afraid of the man?'

Peter screwed up his eyes as if he tried to see again what had happened that night.

'It was certainly a man. What age I am not sure, but not old. He did not move like an old man. Not very young either, for he bulked in body more solidly than a youth. A man in the prime of life, I would say.'

He opened his eyes again, and seemed surprised that he could remember so much. 'I think he was dark haired, but I cannot be sure. In that shadowy corner any but a flaxen-haired man would probably look dark.'

'And your patient's reaction?' I prompted.

'He seemed neither afraid nor glad, I think. Their heads were together, speaking softly, but nay, I am sure he was not afraid. Poor fellow! Yet I do not think it could have been a close friend. That was not how it seemed. I was *sure* it was someone come from Lord Burghley's household, sent to ascertain how Josiah Gurdin fared. Someone he knew, but perhaps not well. Then it was so strange when his lordship's steward said that no one had been sent.'

'Perhaps no one was *sent*,' I said, 'but someone could have come of his own will, without the steward's knowledge. And then, when word of the poisoning was sent to Burghley House, he took care to keep silence.'

'Aye,' he said slowly. 'So he would.'

'That would mean there is someone in Lord Burghley's household who wanted your Josiah Gurdin dead.' I thought for a moment. 'I suppose he need not have come from Burghley House. Someone else might have learned Gurdin was in the ward at Bart's.'

'I do not think so,' he said slowly. 'We had but sent word to Burghley House that morning. I do not think anyone else was told. We knew of no family.'

'Then the visitor would seem to have come from there. Unless, of course–' I paused. 'Whoever inflicted the original beating might have decided to finish the work. If Gurdin was found lying injured near Bart's, and there was no word of a dead body found the following morning, his attacker might easily deduce he had been taken to the hospital.'

'Aye, I suppose that might be. He was found not far away, I believe, on the edge of the Smithfield grounds.'

'So there are two possibilities – either his original attacker or someone from Burghley's household, who came to the hospital without the knowledge of the steward. Unless the steward is choosing to not to tell all he knows.'

'If it was the man who first attacked Gurdin,' Peter said, 'would he not have seemed frightened when the man appeared at his bedside?'

'Aye, if he recognised him. But if it happened in the night – and it can be very dark around Smithfield at night – perhaps he did not see his attacker, or attackers, at all clearly.'

We were hardly any further forward. Out of all the thousands of men in London, most would be in the prime of life, and with any colour of hair but flaxen. If the visitor had indeed come from Burghley's household, and if Peter could identify him – which seemed unlikely – there might be some chance of fixing the blame for the killing where it truly lay. But if the man were indeed the attacker, or one of the attackers, who had given Josiah Gurdin the original beating, then he would have slipped back amongst the crowds of anonymous villains who roamed the streets at night, to steal a purse, or even nothing more than a man's shirt.

Yet I did not believe in such a random killer. A lowly pickpocket would never run the risk of pursuing his victim into the hospital, where he might be recognised, even though he had taken care to come after dark, and slip quickly away. Nay, this was a killing with purpose behind it.

'Did Lord Burghley's steward say what role Gurdin held in the household?' I asked. 'A servant? A clerk?'

Peter shook his head. 'I did not see the boy who brought the message. There was no written letter. I do not think Master Gurdin's occupation was mentioned at all, though it may have been.'

'What manner of man was he?'

He frowned. 'Quiet spoken, but well spoken. Not a lower servant I would say. But not a learned man either. Nay, not well lettered enough to be part of Lord Burghley secretariat, I am sure. A somewhat colourless man. Nothing remarkable about him.'

Colourless and unremarkable. That, certainly, suggested something to me.

'I wonder,' I said, thinking aloud.

'What?'

'Nothing.' My thoughts were too cloudy to trouble Peter with them. Best to remain practical. 'You are secure in your house for two weeks, you said?'

'Aye,' he said bitterly. 'Of their generosity. They know that Helen is with child again.'

I smiled. 'But that is good news, surely! What you must do, at once, is to write to Helen's father. I am sure he will return to London once he hears what is alleged against you.'

'That was partly why I came to see you,' he said. 'We do not know where Lord Strange has gone, and Master Winger with him. Since you are acquainted with Lord Strange's Men, I thought you might know.'

'Aye, I do. Master Burbage was there but last week.'

I took out a sheet of paper from my satchel, tore off the end and scribbled the address with a charcoal stick.

'Be sure you tell him everything and urge him to come back at once. In the meantime, all you can do is to keep a cheerful countenance, for Helen's sake.'

'I have little enough to be cheerful about. Even if I am not tried for murder, I shall never work as an apothecary again. And I may be arrested at any time.'

'Do not despair, Peter,' I said, with more conviction than I felt. 'Once it is proved who was the real murderer, I am sure St Bartholomew's will take you back, aye, and apologise as well. All is secure for this two weeks at least.'

I hoped that what I said was true. Peter and Helen might have the house for the two weeks, but he had the right of it. There might be an attempt to arrest Peter before then. At least the courts would not be sitting in mid summer, although the inquest would be held without delay.

'There is another reason I sought your help,' Peter said hesitantly.

'Aye?'

'I know that you no longer work in the intelligence service, now that Walsingham is gone, but–'

'Aye?'

'Do you not still have friends in that world?' he said. 'I wondered . . . if this man Josiah Gurdin worked for Lord Burghley . . . and someone was anxious to kill him . . . anxious enough to risk coming into the hospital, where he might have been caught . . .'

I saw that Peter had been making the same deductions as I had. A colourless and unremarkable man, this Josiah Gurdin. Despite his desperate fear, there was nothing wrong with Peter's brain.

'You think Josiah Gurdin might have been working for the Cecils' intelligence service?' I said. 'That he was one of their agents?'

'Aye, that. Or else he was one of Essex's agents, planted as a spy in the Burghley household.'

'Either is possible,' I agreed. 'I had the same thought myself. It does not look like a street brawl. Such a thing would not be carried through to the end by means so devious as hemlock.'

'Do you think you might be able to discover? I thought . . . if it could be shown that Gurdin belonged to that world, perhaps Dr Temperley and the superintendent would begin to believe me.'

They might. Or they might be even less likely to risk involvement in such dangerous matters, I thought, but did not say.

'Certainly I can try to find out,' I said. 'Thomas Phelippes and Arthur Gregory now work for Essex. The only former Walsingham man I know of, who now works for the Cecils, is Robert Poley. He is not to be trusted, nor would he be willing to reveal any privy matters to me. Most of the other agents from Walsingham's day are dispersed now, save for a few Thomas Phelippes makes use of, from time to time. However, I will see what I may do.'

I drained the last of my ale, and picked up the crumbs of pastry off the trencher with a damp finger.

'I could wish you had managed a better look at this visitor, though I realise you had no reason to do so. Everything must depend on that. If somehow you could view the members of Lord Burghley's household, perhaps you would recognise him simply by some manner of his walk, or the shape of his head.'

'If it can be managed,' he said, 'I will surely try.'

'Of course,' I said, rising from my stool and brushing a few fragments of pastry from the front of my doublet, 'the man may be none of Burghley's. He may be Essex's man.'

After Peter had left, promising he would send a letter by some means to Master Winger the next morning, I made my way thoughtfully in the direction of my lodgings. Rikki had sat quietly under the table all the while we had been speaking, sensing that these were serious matters, but now he ran ahead, stopping from time to time and looking over his shoulder, urging me to keep pace with him.

I had intended to go directly home, but after Peter's worrying tale, I decided to walk further up river to the Lion, to see whether any of the players had decided to resume their practice of eating and drinking there after the day's performance at the Rose. The story of this poisoning and the accusation against Peter had left me worried and unsettled. Cool reason must argue against Peter's guilt, but if no one else had seen this nameless visitor it was easy to understand why Dr Temperley and the superintendent had so readily jumped to their unreasonable conclusion. Perhaps a time for calmer reflection would persuade them of the unlikelihood of Peter's guilt, but one could not be sure.

I hoped that Master Winger would be able to return quickly to London. It would need Lord Strange's permission, and his lordship might still be ailing and need the attentions of his apothecary. In the meantime, was there aught I could do, to help? The more thought I gave to the matter, the more convinced I was that Josiah Gurdin sounded like an agent in Lord Burghley's service. Experienced agents did not drawn attention to themselves – unremarkable, unnoticeable, these were the best attributes for an agent. Quiet spoken, intelligent but not learned or scholarly. He sounded like the best agents I had known in Walsingham's service. Marlowe's swaggering demeanour was one of the things which had made him less suitable for the part, despite his cleverness and his zest for danger. It had probably helped to bring about his end.

But who had silenced Gurdin?

If he was a loyal agent of Lord Burghley, the most likely murderer was one of Essex's men, intent either simply to weaken the Cecils' growing network of intelligence or else because Gurdin himself had been working to weaken Essex. If that was the case, I could hardly take Thomas Phelippes into my confidence.

Of course, perhaps Peter's suggestion was right, that Gurdin was one of Essex's men, planted in Burghley's household. If that had been discovered, the assassin would himself be one of the Cecils' trusted men.

Or perhaps Gurdin was a double agent, working for both sides, in which case he could have been eliminated by either.

With all these possibilities floating through my head, it had begun to spin.

What a pass we were come to, that the two rival intelligence networks in England were working against each other, when all their efforts should have been directed against our common enemies from without – the Catholic agents trained in France or the Spanish Netherlands, or the agents of King Philip of Spain. How it would have grieved Walsingham to see the bulwark he had built to protect England and the Queen disintegrating in this internal warfare.

I supposed there might be one more possible explanation for the murder of Josiah Gurdin. Perhaps he was a worthy agent, working for England's safety, and had discovered one of the Catholic priests who came with the Pope's blessing, not merely to spread their faith but to seize any chance to assassinate the Queen, assured that by so doing they would be fulfilling God's will. Such a man, with such a purpose, would take any measure to protect his anonymity.

But Josiah Gurdin had not seemed frightened by his visitor.

Nay, I could make no sense of it.

Hardly noticing where my steps were taking me as I turned over all these possibilities in my mind, I realised that I had reached the Lion, Rikki running ahead of me to greet a group of my friends who were seated about an outside table, with flagons of ale. A serving wench was laying out bowls, and a potboy followed behind her with a deep cooking pot from which steam rose. Its rich aroma was wafted on the breeze to awaken a hunger which had I realised had scarcely been touched by the small pie at the ale house. Guy Bingham shifted along a bench to make room for me.

'You come mostly timely on your cue, Kit,' he said. 'Is not beef with onions your favourite dish?'

I smiled at him. 'It is, and I find I am mighty hungry.'

'You are late come from the hospital,' Simon said, leaning across the table to fill a cup of ale for me.

'Aye. A friend came to see me as I left. Peter Lambert, from St Bartholomew's.'

'The apothecary?'

'Aye.'

Guy squinted at me sideways. 'You do not seem to have welcomed his visit.'

I was undecided. Had Peter spoken to me in confidence? I thought perhaps I had best not speak of it before the whole group gathered about the table, though I might discuss it privately later.

'He has had some trouble at the hospital,' I said, taking my spoon out of my scrip and dipping into the bowl Guy passed to me. 'And wanted to share it with me. I am sure it will soon be resolved.'

Both Simon and Guy knew me well enough to guess that I was keeping the whole truth unsaid, but they would not press me. More happily, I was glad to see the players back here at the Lion after the dark days following Marlowe's murder. It was rarely spoken of, but it still cast a long shadow and no doubt would continue to do so for months to come.

Despite the apparent return to normality, we were a somewhat subdued gathering, and did not linger over our meal. When we had all contributed our share to the reckoning, Simon, Rikki, and I retraced our steps to the Atkins house, as the rest of the company dispersed. While the repairs continued to be carried out at the Theatre, north of the City in Shoreditch, the company was playing at the Rose and most had moved to lodgings south of the river. The Rose, being the newest playhouse in London, had many devices unknown in the Theatre. Cuthbert Burbage had been discussing improvements to the Theatre with his father, but ever since the disputes with the landowner of the ground on which it stood, they were reluctant to spend money on the building, lest they be forced to abandon it.

'So,' Simon said as we climbed the stairs. 'What is Peter's trouble? It must be serious, if he came all this way to tell you of it.'

He opened the door of his room and motioned me in. Rikki, who regarded this room as much his own as my room, immediately jumped on the bed, turned around twice, and curled up to sleep.

'I must train him not to do that,' I said absently.

''Tis no matter. He does no harm.'

I sat down on the bed beside Rikki and ran his silky ears through my fingers.

'I do not think he would want it bruited abroad,' I said, 'but I do not think he would mind my telling you. For one thing, he wanted Lord Strange's address.'

Simon raised his eyebrows at this.

'He needs must write urgently to his father-in-law, Master Winger, seeking his help.'

'The apothecary, who used to be at St Barthomew's? I remember that he gave evidence at the inquest on the death of Master Wandesford, supporting your diagnosis.'

'Aye, he did.' I had forgotten that Simon would have seen him then. 'I was able to give Peter Lord Strange's direction, so that he might send a letter to Master Winger.

Of course, we cannot know whether Lord Strange will give Master Winger leave to return to London.'

'I have always heard that his lordship is a kind and reasonable man,' Simon said, 'though I have never met him myself. He has attended some of our performances, and we have played a few times at his house, though I have never spoken to him.'

'Hmm,' I said. I knew that great men, when ailing, liked to keep their physicians and apothecaries close about them.

'I think that was not the only reason came to see you.'

'Nay, it was not.'

I clasped my hands about my up drawn knee, and told Simon as briefly as possible, what had happened at St Bartholomew's to the patient Josiah Gurdin. When I reached the point when Peter was accused by Dr Temperley and the hospital superintendent of administering the hemlock, he let out a low whistle.

'They accused him of murder?'

'Aye. And he has been banned the hospital and told to quit the hospital cottage within this two weeks.'

'But he has not been arrested?' Simon put his finger on a crucial point.

'Not yet. It may be that they think they need more proof that Peter added the hemlock to the febrifuge tincture. He is adamant that the patient had a visitor, though no one else seems to have noticed him. Perhaps they wish to make certain of this before they act. They must know how trustworthy Peter is. Even Dr Temperley, who does not care to be criticised by him.'

'Perhaps also they are waiting to speak to a man of law, before making an accusation in haste, which must be retracted later.'

I nodded. 'That too may be true.'

'Does he want you to bear witness to his good character?'

'I would happily do so, if anyone cares for my opinion. It was something else.'

I chose my words carefully. 'From his demeanour, and his position in Lord Burghley's household, Josiah Gurdin seemed to us both to be a possible agent in the Cecils' service. That might explain why someone was so determined to finish what the beating had failed to achieve.'

Simon drew a deep breath. 'I thought all that was put behind you, Kit.'

'I no longer work in the intelligence service, of course, but Peter hopes that I might have friends still so employed, who might be able to throw some light on the murder of this man. But it is difficult. Impossible, even.'

'Why? I am afraid I do not follow you.'

'You must know, simply from the rumours on the street, that there is this terrible rivalry between the two intelligence services, that of the Cecils and that of Essex, run by Anthony Bacon.'

'Aye.' He frowned. 'But why should that make your enquiries impossible?'

I suppose I could not expect Simon to understand the labyrinthine manoeuvrings these men engaged in. I would not confuse the matter with all the possibilities which had occurred to me, but keep it simple.

'If Gurdin was an agent for the Cecils, his murderer may have been an agent for Essex. The most senior man I know who is still in this work is Thomas Phelippes. Who works for Essex. I cannot very well go to Phelippes and say, "Tell me, did you order one of Essex's men to murder this man Gurdin of Lord Burghley's? And if so, will you persuade him to confess, so that my friend Peter Lambert is not arrested for a murder he did not commit?" You can imagine how Phelippes might react. Indeed, Essex might order him to arrest *me*.'

'Ah,' Simon said, 'I see. That does make it awkward. Do you think that is what happened? That an agent of Essex's inflicted a beating on Gurdin, leaving him for dead, then came to the hospital, talked to him briefly, seemingly with no fear on Gurdin's part, then slipped the hemlock into the medicine?'

'Put like that,' I admitted, 'it seems unlikely. If Gurdin knew this nameless man as an agent of Essex . . . even if he did not recognise who attacked him at Smithfield in the dark . . . then he might have shown some alarm when he arrived at St Bartholomew's. Peter would have noticed that, I am sure, even though he was busy at the other end of the ward. He was keeping an eye on his patient, wanting him to take his medicine and sleep, as soon as his visitor left. Aye, I am sure he would have noticed if Gurdin was alarmed.'

'Of course, he might not have known him.'

'He might not. There are other possibilities.'

I recounted briefly the other thoughts I had been turning over in my mind, about who or what Gurdin had actually been, and what the identity of his murderer could be in each case. At the end, Simon was looking as baffled as I was.

'So what do you propose to do?' he asked at last.

I rubbed my temples. It was growing late and my head was beginning to ache with sheer fatigue.

'I cannot decide. If Master Winger is able to return quickly to London, I am sure he will take matters in hand. That may free Peter from suspicion – or may not – although it will not solve the murder of Josiah Gurdin.'

'There will be an inquest, will there not?'

'Of course, there must be. We must not forget that. And they will hold it quickly in this hot summer weather. Jesu! The inquest jury might rule that Peter is guilty, and he will be arrested, to go for trial before the next assize, which I suppose will be in the early autumn. A great deal will depend on who serves as coroner. If it is a cautious man, he may instruct them that more evidence is needed, but if he is one of these coroners who pride themselves on a reputation for settling on a guilty party at once, Peter will be in trouble.'

'He will. It seems to me the first thing to do, even before Master Winger comes, is to discover whether anyone else saw this visitor at the hospital. If that can be established, then at once Peter's assertion that there was such a man must be believed.'

'Aye,' I said, grasping at any shred of hope, 'and it will at once weaken any case against Peter. The most likely person to have seen the man is the gatekeeper. Peter said there were only two of the nursing sisters on duty in the ward that evening, and it was past time for most people to be about, but there would have been a gatekeeper on duty.'

'Do you know him?'

'Nay, he is a new man since I worked there, but there is no reason he should not be willing to say yay or nay, whether he saw this man. There cannot have been many coming in at that time.'

'Why do you not go and ask him tomorrow?'

'I will! That is one thing at least I can do for Peter. Best if he does not ask himself.' I felt some relief. My frustration (and my headache) were largely due to a sense that I could do nothing.

'But wait!' I thumped my fist into the bedclothes, disturbing Rikki. 'I cannot go tomorrow. It is the quarterly visit of the governors of St Thomas's. I must be there. We must all be present for the inspection. I shall not be able to go to Bart's until the following day. But it must be done before the inquest.'

'I could go,' Simon said. 'If the gatekeeper is unknown to you, it does not matter who makes the enquiry. I am free all day until the afternoon performance. No rehearsal tomorrow.'

'Could you?' I felt a surge of hope. I would have preferred to question the gatekeeper myself, but why should not Simon be as able as I to discover what we needed to know?

'I will tell you what Peter observed of the man, though it is very little, and might describe one man in every three in London.'

'Never fear,' Simon said cheerfully. 'We have established that few people would have come into the hospital at that time. Few strangers. Any unknown man might do.'

'Aye, you probably have the right of it,' I said slowly. 'Perhaps we can cause the first small break in this wall of accusation they are building against Peter. Jesu help us, for Peter needs every scrap of help.'

Chapter Three

Like St Bartholomew's hospital, St Thomas's had originally been part of a monastery, providing care for the poorer citizens of London who lived south of the river, as Bart's did for those to the north. When the monastic establishments had been banned, and largely demolished, in the time of the Queen's father, the two hospitals came close to ruin as well, but groups of charitable citizens had saved them just in time, so that their work might continue. I have often wondered what horrors of disease and death might have overwhelmed London, had they not done so.

Both hospitals were organised with a group of governors to oversee their affairs, a superintendent – generally some nobleman – and a deputy superintendent, who was in charge of day-to-day business. The role of superintendent was a sinecure, a source of income associated with very little in the way of duties. The duties of the governors varied according to their own interest and conscientiousness. And the deputy superintendent did most of the work.

In the light of this, the deputy superintendent at St Thomas's, Master Roger Ailmer, was generally known by all of us as 'Superintendent', an honour he merited more than the actual holder of the title. And when Peter had spoken of the superintendent at Bart's, I was certain that he meant the deputy superintendent.

Four times a year, the governors made an official inspection of St Thomas's, though those with a particular interest might visit at any time. Although I had only ever seen them on these rare occasions, and at a distance, it happened that I had come to know the governors of St Bartholomew's, who visited more often, once a month. One day my father had been summoned to attend Lord Burghley, which sometimes happened if Dr Nuñez was not available, and the elderly Dr Stephens had broken his leg, so that I had been left as physician in charge – to my alarm. During the visit, one of the governors, Sir Jonathan Langley, was seized of serious stomach pains and dizziness owing to food poisoning. I had treated him successfully, earning his gratitude and the appreciation of all the governors, something which had later stood me in good stead.

The governors of St Thomas's, however, were another matter. Two at least were known for their pleasure in finding fault wherever they might. Moreover, it was these men who had promised to keep my position for me when I returned from my mission to Muscovy, but had broken their promise. That I had later returned was no thanks to them, but to Superintendent Ailmer's determination to restore me to my position. It was therefore with some unease that I looked forward to these quarterly visits.

I reached the hospital shortly after dawn on the day of the inspection, for although I had ensured that the servants scrubbed every inch of my two wards the previous day, anything might have occurred during the night, especially in the lying-in ward, for babies take no account of other affairs when they choose to venture into the world.

To my relief, both the lying-in ward and the children's ward were clean and calm. The newest infant, born late the previous afternoon, was feeding contentedly, and none of the other mothers was on the point of giving birth. Should that happen during the visit of inspection, the governors would probably back away in horror, as they had done on one other occasion. The children's ward was more unpredictable. Most of the children had listened earnestly while I had warned them to be on their best behaviour when the gentlemen visited, but there was one scamp I could not rely on. He reminded me of Davy, the wandering acrobats' boy, who had been found near to death in a ditch, but was now training with Guy Bingham as musician, tumbler, and comic in the company of Lord Strange's Men.

My current problem child, Tommy Atgate, was just as lively and just as mischievous, now that he had almost recovered from a fall which had broken two ribs and dinted his skull. At any rate, his mother swore that it was a fall, but we had seen her bruises and black eyes often enough to have our suspicions on this occasion of Tommy's father, a great brute of a man who was a labourer at the Southwark brickworks. He was not one of their skilled men, making the fancy moulded bricks destined for fine manor houses, but one of those who dug and carried the clay for the talented artisans to work. He was in and out of employment, for he drank most of his wages and quarrelled with the other men. When he was out of work he took out his anger on his wife and children. I was surprised the brickworks took him back again, but he was mighty strong, and few men could do the work, or wanted to.

Not that Tommy's mother was in truth his wife, merely his woman, and I wondered she did not leave him. Yet she was by no means the first cowed and brutalised woman I had encountered in Southwark who stayed with an abusive man. Why did they endure such treatment? Why did they not simply leave? Perhaps they feared being reduced to earning their keep as one of the Winchester geese, though if Bessie Travis and her women were anything to go by, their lives were no worse, and sometimes better. Or perhaps these beaten women feared that the outraged man would pursue his escaped prey. I had heard of one woman murdered by the man she had left.

Now that Tommy was almost recovered, he could well cause trouble during the visit. I had hoped to send him home before this, but his mother had begged me to keep

46

him a few more days. I suppose his father was out of work again and terrorising the family at home.

'I think all is in order, Dr Alvarez,' Goodwife Margaret Appledean said, twisting her hands nervously in her apron. 'I cannot think what else we might do to prepare.'

I could see that the senior midwife was as anxious as I was about the visit, but I tried to reassure her by smiling encouragingly.

'Everything looks clean and fresh,' I said. 'The women have broken their fast?'

'Aye. Superintendent Ailmer had breakfast served early to all the patients, so that everything might be tidied away, in case the governors came early.'

I nodded. Six months before, two of the governors – including one of those excessively critical men – had arrived so early that the servants were still clearing away the patients' breakfast, and this had flustered them. One girl had dropped a tray, breaking several bowls, and they had demanded that she should be dismissed immediately. Superintendent Ailmer had complied, but he hired her again the following day. We had learned that lesson, so the early breakfast was no surprise.

'And the children's ward?' I nodded in the direction of the adjacent room.

'Goodwife Watson and young Alice both stayed over night,' she said. 'In case they were needed.'

'Most of the children are not seriously ill at the moment,' I said. Normally only one of the sisters stayed in the children's ward at night.

'I think they wanted to make quite sure. Just as well, for they caught that Tommy up to some mischief.'

I sighed. It would be like Tommy to destroy everyone else's hard work. I suppose his mischief making was some kind of reaction to his father's brutality. In the kinder atmosphere of the hospital, he knew he would suffer nothing more severe than a stern telling-off.

'I will speak to him,' I said, without much hope. 'And I'll stay in the children's ward until the governors arrive, but I will be here to support you when they visit the lying-in ward.'

The governors could surely find no fault with the children's ward. It had been freshly lime-washed just a few weeks before, the windows were open to let in the summer sun and a slight breeze which alleviated the heat which would build up later in the day, for there was the hint of a coming thunderstorm. There were posies of aromatic healing herbs dotted about. Alice was skilled at making these and replaced them every week or so. The beds had all been made up with fresh sheets. Money was always tight at the hospital, so that many of the sheets were turned or patched, but no one could find fault with their laundering. The children lifted clean, shining faces to me as I passed down the room, checking on their progress.

One small girl was sleeping quietly, her thumb in her mouth. She had been brought in nearly a week before with a festering sore on her leg. Initially a bite from one of the half wild street dogs which roamed Southwark, it was a common injury in London. It might have healed had her grandfather not undertaken to physic it himself, in some kind of distorted version of the doctrine of signatures, which teaches us, for example, that lungwort is sovereign for lung diseases, because the leaves resemble lungs, and eyebright for problems of the eye, since the flower looks up like a clear and sparkling eye. The old man had sworn that a dog's bite must be treated by smearing it with dog's turd. As a result, the wound had become seriously inflamed and infected, and the child delirious. She was over the worst, but sleep was the best remedy for her now, so I did not disturb her.

I arrived at last at Tommy's bed. We had placed him nearest to the chairs and table where the nursing sisters sat, so that he could be under their eye.

'Good morrow to you, Tommy,' I said cheerfully. 'Let me take a look at that pate of yours.'

He smiled at me angelically. One of the dangers of this imp was his strong resemblance to one of the young angels in a painting of the Nativity which graced the hospital chapel.

'Good morrow, Dr Alvarez.' He sat up straighter and inclined his head toward me.

The dressing had been removed several days ago, and I had snipped out the stitches yesterday. The blow to his head had broken and bloodied the flesh, but the skull underneath was not splintered, although I detected a slight dent. I pushed aside the fair curls, away from the shaved portion, and examined the injury. The scab was drying up, and there was no inflammation. It looked clean enough, though whether it would remain clean when he went home was another matter.

'That is doing well,' I said. 'Now lift your night shift.'

I felt his rib cage carefully, and he winced once, but declared that it no longer hurt. I thought he was probably putting on a brave face, for there was still considerable bruising, where his father had probably kicked him, but all was generally on the mend.

'Fine,' I said, pulling down his shift, and tucking the blanket around him, then I sat down on the edge of the bed.

'Now, Tommy,' I said, 'I believe you caused some disturbance in the night.'

He looked shifty, avoiding my eye.

'It was nothing,' he muttered. 'Goodwife Watson mistook.'

'Hmm,' I said. 'We shall ask her, shall we?'

I beckoned to the older sister, who came over and fixed Tommy with a stern look.

'Aye, Dr Alvarez? What shall we do with this keg of trouble?'

'I have heard that Tommy did not rest quiet in his bed last night,' I said, 'as he knows he must do, if that noddle head of his is to mend. What, exactly, was he about?'

Goodwife Watson sighed. "'Twas well past midnight, doctor. I heard the clock at St Olave's. All the children were asleep, and I told Alice she should get some rest on the cot, while I kept a watch, lest anything should be needed. All was quiet, and I daresay I dozed a mite, sitting in my chair. Then I heard something, just a furtive noise. I thought perhaps one of the children had need of the piss pot and did not want to disturb me.'

I nodded. 'But it was Tommy?'

'Aye, it was Tommy. I said not a word, nor stirred, but kept an eye on him. There was just the usual candle lamp burning, here on the table, but it was enough.'

'I *did* need the piss pot,' Tommy burst out, an expression of innocent indignation on his face.

'Do not interrupt, Tommy,' I said. 'Let Goodwife Watson finish, then I will hear what you have to say.'

'Aye,' the sister said grimly, 'he did need the piss pot. In fact, he was emptying *all* of them into just one. Then he carried Alice's chair over to the door, climbed up, and balanced the full pot on that ledge above the lintel.'

I frowned at Tommy, who had covered his mouth with his hand, but could not quite hide his grin.

'Tommy,' I said, 'that might have fallen on anyone. Suppose Alice had gone out to tell the servants to bring your breakfast – how would you feel if it had fallen on her?'

I knew that he was fond of Alice, who had nursed him tenderly through the worst of his pain. He flushed now.

'Nay, it would not. It was quite safe unless–'

'Unless what?' I asked.

He shut his mouth stubbornly.

Goodwife Watson fetched the piss pot, now fortunately empty, and set it down on the edge of the bed next to me. A long string had been knotted around the handle.

'And what is this?' I held up a loop of the string.

Tommy avoided my eye.

'He had run it along behind the beds to his own,' Goodwife Watson said, 'and when I caught him, he was climbing into bed, holding the end.'

'So he could make it tumble whenever he chose?'

'Aye.'

'Tommy,' I said, exasperated but doing my best not to laugh, 'why should you do such a thing? Who were you going to hurt?'

He slid down under the bedclothes until I could see little but the point of his nose. He mumbled something.

I pulled the blanket away from his mouth. 'What was that?'

'Those men that are coming today,' he said, suddenly fierce. 'Alice says they could close the hospital. Then what should we do?'

I realised that Alice had also been putting the fear of God into Tommy, but this time it had backfired.

'She is Sister Meadows to you,' I said severely. 'And how do you suppose knocking one of the governors out and soaking him with the contents of a piss pot would persuade them to keep the hospital open? I did not think you were so stupid, Tommy!'

Tears began to well up in his eyes. 'I wanted to show them that we would fight for St Thomas's, whatever they say.' His lower lip trembled, and I remembered that he could not be more than seven or eight.

'That is not the way to fight for the hospital.' I tried to sound less angry. 'We fight for the hospital by showing how *good* everyone is, how clean, how the patients get better . . . The governors would not close the hospital if they were displeased during the inspection, but they might not give us all the money Superintendent Ailmer needs. Do you see that silly pranks are the very last thing to persuade the governors that the hospital must be maintained, and even given a little more money?'

He nodded. The tears were running down his cheeks now.

'I'm sorry, Dr Alvarez,' he whispered.

51

'Very well.' I stood up. 'I am sure you will be as quiet as a mouse and as good as a cherub when the governors visit the ward.'

I leaned over and kissed the top of his head, though he did not deserve it.

'Best return that to the cupboard.' I nodded toward the piss pot, and winked at Goodwife Watson, my back to Tommy.

'Certainly, doctor,' she said with dignity.

As she stowed away the offending object, Alice came in, her arms full of wild flowers and rosemary which she had been gathering from the meadow where the hospital's bee skeps stood.

She smiled at me, clearly taking in what had been afoot.

'I have brought a few fresh blooms for the posies, doctor.'

'Excellent,' I said. '*That* is the kind of scent we want in this ward.'

Tommy, I noticed, had burrowed down under the bedclothes again.

As it happened, the governors' inspection passed off without disasters. They always began on the ground floor, before working their way up to my wards, so we had plenty of warning. First the kitchens, sculleries and storerooms, then the men's wards on the ground floor. By the time they reached us, it was near time for the midday meal, so I hoped the children would not become fretful with hunger.

In the lying-in ward, one of the women had, after all, gone into labour, but I thought we need not worry about the birth until after the governors had left. In the children's ward all was peaceful, and one of the gentlemen actually stopped at the bed containing a curly haired boy with the face of an angel.

'And why is this lad here, doctor?' he asked me. 'I see part of his head is shaved.'

'A bad fall, sir,' I said. 'Two broken ribs and a nasty gash in his scalp, but he is well on the mend now.'

He turned to Tommy. 'And how do you find St Thomas's, my fine fellow?'

I crossed my fingers within the wide sleeve of my physician's gown.

'It is a fine place, sir,' Tommy whispered, 'they have made me quite well and I shall be going home soon.' He gave an enchanting smile, which displayed his new front teeth, incongruously large against the baby teeth on either side.

'Excellent, excellent.'

The gentleman patted Tommy's arm and paced slowly out of the ward, followed at a respectful distance by me. I glanced back, and Tommy winked at me, the scamp!

The governors did not linger long in the adjacent ward, for the woman in labour had begun to shriek and writhe, so they backed away.

'Everything seems in excellent order, Dr Alvarez,' one of them said. To my surprise it was the same man who had demanded the servant's dismissal during that earlier visit. As they headed for the stairs, Superintendent Ailmer glanced back at me with a look of profound relief.

I went back to the woman who was moaning.

'Jess,' I said, 'are the contractions so painful?'

I was surprised, for this was her sixth. She lay back and gave me a gap toothed grin.

'Nay, doctor, there's barely a twinge yet. I thought if I gave them a good howl or two, they'd be off the sooner, and they was, wasn't they?'

I caught hold of the bed frame and began to laugh. There was no knowing what these Southwark folk would do in defence of their own.

I had been so caught up in the governors' inspection that I had forgotten that Simon planned to visit the gatekeeper at St Bartholomew's that day, but I remembered when I collected Rikki from Tom Read at our own gatehouse and started on my way home. It would have taken Simon quite a time to walk to Bart's, over beyond the City wall, beside Smithfield, then come back across the river for the afternoon performance at the Rose. He would have had no opportunity to leave word for me before going to the playhouse.

The actors were generally free at about the same time as I finished at the hospital, and it seemed they had resumed their practice of dining at the Lion. Most of them preferred to eat very little at midday, before the performance at two o'the clock. As I had come to know them better, I had learned, to my surprise, just how nervous they were before stepping out on the stage, even those who had spent a lifetime as performers, like Guy. He had once confided to me that, were he to eat a full midday dinner, he would be vomiting before a performance.

'I might be able to give you something to prevent,' I had said slowly.

He shook his head. 'Nay, a nervous stomach will reject everything, even your potions, Kit.'

'But how do you manage to perform?' I was puzzled. 'If you are so frightened that you vomit, how can you stand up before two thousand people and play your part?'

I knew that I could not do it.

He laughed. 'By some alchemy, as soon as I set foot on the stage, I am cured! You will find that is true of most of us, except perhaps Dick Burbage, who was carried on by his father to play the child in some piece or other when he was still a mewling infant. He had not had time to understand the terror of forgetting all one's lines before an audience, or playing the unintended fool some other way, like the rest of us who came to it later.'

As the result of this curious players' disease, they came to table in the evening with a roaring appetite, and loud with relief and excitement if the performance had been a successful one. If it had not – which was rare, for they were a talented company – they were equally loud, arguing about what had gone wrong. Generally, I believe, it was decided that it was the fault of the audience. Cloth-eared idiots, who had no understanding of the fine subtleties in the performances of Lord Strange's Men.

As I joined them this evening, I could tell while I was still yards away that it had been a good day, for their voices rang out cheerfully and they made room for me, grinning, on one of the benches.

'I have no appetite for one of your great dinners,' I said. 'I have already stayed my hunger.'

'Was not this the day of your dreaded inspection?' Will Shakespeare asked.

'Aye, and everything went so well that Superintendent Ailmer sent out for cakes and custard tarts to treat us all afterwards, staff and patients alike. So I will just take a sup of ale, and one of those early pears.'

Dick Burbage tossed me a pear across the table, so I sat eating it and quietly listening to their gossip. I had slept little the previous night. That and my early start, together with worry about the inspection, had left me too tired to say much. Simon, who was seated opposite, but three places away, caught my eye and nodded, but I was not sure what that meant. Was it merely a greeting? Or did he mean he had managed to speak to the gatekeeper at St Bartholomew's? And if so, had he learned anything to the purpose?

I needs must wait until we were walking back to our lodging, since, for the moment, I had no wish to discuss Peter's disturbing story with the wider company.

The meal seemed to continue longer than usual that evening, although perhaps it was no more than my own fatigue which made the time drag, but at last the players began to yawn and stretch, and count out their share of the reckoning. I put down my coins for the pear and the two cups of small ale I had drunk, and stood watching the river flowing swift and silver under the moonlight until Simon had settled with the others.

We had been sitting outside, as we usually did in summer, for the inn parlour could become mighty stuffy in hot weather, although it was a welcome spot on a cold winter's day. This evening, however, I could sense again that coming change in the weather. There was a heaviness in the air which pressed against my temples, and the very trees hung listless as though they too could feel the oppression. The weather had been too hot and too dry for long enough. We needed a good English downpour to clear the air. I smiled to myself. I was becoming as true a native as my current company, looking forward to rain. In Portugal we had accepted the unrelenting sun of summer as the natural order of the world.

Simon was free at last and we began to walk along Bankside with Christopher Haigh and Will. Guy was behind us, chivvying young Davy towards bed and explaining some new trick they were planning to include in their comic business. The hint of storm even seemed to have affected Rikki, for he did not run ahead as usual, but plodded along like an old dog.

At the Atkins house we bade the others good e'en, and climbed up to my room.

'I think Rikki needs a drink,' I said, 'in this heat. I should have asked for water at the Lion.'

I unlocked my door and poured water into Rikki's bowl, which he lapped up eagerly as Simon lit one of my candles. The summer evening should still have been light at this hour, but the clouds were building up, making it darker than usual.

'So,' I said, sitting cross-legged on the bed, 'how did you fare at St Bartholomew's? You did go, did you not?'

'Aye, I did.'

He sat down on the floor next to Rikki and began to scratch him behind the ears.

'I walked over to the City as soon as I was up.'

'Which was not very early, I daresay.'

He shrugged. 'About ten o'the clock. 'Tis a fair way, you know.'

'I know.'

56

'At first there was no chance to speak to the gatekeeper. There was a great deal of coming and going, goods being delivered, patients gathering in the old cloisters, waiting for the almoner to admit them, other patients leaving, a young man carried in between two friends with a badly gashed leg, bleeding like a stuck pig. They hurried to take him in, ahead of the others.'

I nodded. A normal day at either hospital.

'I must have waited at least an hour before all the hurly-burly subsided. I did not want to tackle the gatekeeper until he could give his full mind to what I wanted to know.'

'Aye. I should have done the same.'

'Finally, when things were quieter, I found him seated in his room in the gatehouse, with the door open for air. 'Tis a fine gatehouse, is it not? With that statue of King Harry atop it.'

I nodded again, wishing he would reach the point of his narrative, but he was clearly enjoying drawing it out. It was the player's blood in him.

'I'd thought to buy a flask of good beer on my way, so I introduced myself as a friend to you and to Peter Lambert, and invited him to partake of a sup with me.' He paused. 'I think he was a little suspicious of me at first. He said he knew Peter, but knew nothing of you.'

'It is a new man since I worked there.'

'So it seems. He has only been there a year.'

'Simon,' I said, unable to control my impatience any longer, 'what did he say? Did he see this visitor for Josiah Gurdin?'

'I think no one had taken the trouble to question him about that night. He seemed surprised that I should be interested.'

'As far as I can tell, from what Peter told me, Dr Temperley and the superintendent made up their minds to accuse him on the spot, and never cared to investigate further.'

'Aye, so it seems.'

Rikki laid his head on Simon's lap, and sighed. He was falling asleep, and if Simon did not make haste with his tale I would soon do the same, despite my anxiety to hear what the gatekeeper said.

Simon must have sensed that he had drawn the tale out too long.

'When he agreed at last to talk to me, he admitted that there *had* been one visitor late that night. Three nights ago, it was, the night Josiah Gurdin took ill and died.'

'Could he describe him?'

'Not very well. A man perhaps in his thirties, middle height, not particularly heavy built, but looked as though he might be strong. I asked what he meant by that, but he couldn't explain. One thing struck him as strange. The weather has been so warm, even at night, but the man kept the hood of his capuchon pulled well forward over his head, hiding much of his face.'

'So he would not recognise the man again?'

'I asked him that, but he wasn't sure.'

'Could he even know this was a visitor for Josiah Gurdin? He might have been anyone.'

'It seems he was the only stranger to come to the hospital that night. And besides, he asked where he might find Gurdin. He said he had been sent by his master to see how the man fared.'

'Did he, indeed! Yet Lord Burghley's steward said no one had been sent.'

'His master might not have been Lord Burghley.'

'I suppose he might not. Or he might simply have lied.'

'True. In any case, the gatekeeper said he did not stay long, not above a quarter of an hour at most. Bade the gatekeeper good e'en as he left, very courteous, but still kept his hood forward.'

'Why has he told no one of this?' I said. 'That is, I suppose he has not?'

'I asked him, and he has not. He simply shrugged and said no one had asked him. I told him he must go to the superintendent and tell him everything he could about this visitor. Even if it is not much, it does back up what Peter said, that there *was* a visitor, even if no one else inside the hospital saw him.'

'Do you think he will go to the superintendent?'

Simon shook his head. 'I'm inclined to think not. He is one of those fellows who likes to keep his head down and away from trouble. Backing up Peter might annoy those in authority, and he would not want to risk that. He must already have heard what Peter is accused of. I cannot imagine it has remained a secret. He could have gone to the superintendent with his information before this.'

'He must be made to tell.'

I got up from the bed and went restlessly to the window. When I leaned out I could see that the gathering clouds had now completely blotted out the moon. There was that hushed, waiting stillness that often comes before a storm breaks. Even as I watched, there was a distant flicker of lightning down river, probably near Gravesend.

'I do not suppose you heard when the inquest is to be?' I asked.

'Aye, I did. The gatekeeper knew *that*, so I am sure he knew everything about the charges against Peter, though he did not admit it. The inquest is tomorrow at noon.'

'Where is it to be held, did you learn that?'

'At St Bartholomew's.'

'I cannot go,' I said. 'I am needed at the hospital, and you could not get back to the Rose in time for the performance. I must send a message to the coroner, that the gatekeeper has important evidence about a visitor that night.'

'Aye,' he said, 'best make sure he is obliged to speak out.'

'What is the man's name? The gatekeeper?'

'John Broughton.'

'I'll write this minute,' I said, sitting down at my table and drawing a sheet of paper toward me. 'I will give it to the Atkins boy to take to the Guildhall first thing in the morning. Whichever coroner is to conduct the inquest, a clerk at the Guildhall will find him.'

Simon eased Rikki off his lap and stood up.

'I will leave it with you, then. The existence of this nameless visitor cannot prove Peter did not administer poison, but it does prove that he is telling the truth – that such a man did come to see Josiah Gurdin – and it muddies the waters. The hospital authorities cannot now point the finger and say no one else had access to Gurdin's medicine.'

'Aye, it certainly helps. Thank you for that, Simon.' I smiled at him

He grinned back. 'I would not see Peter unjustly accused, any more than you would, Kit. I should have liked to leave word with Peter about what I had learned, but I did not know which house in Duck Lane was his, and there was no time to make enquiries. As it was, I had to take a wherry back over the river, to reach the Rose in time, else Master Burbage would have skinned me.'

'Flaying would not suit you. Aye, leave it with me.'

I removed the top of my ink well. It was nearly empty, but there should be just enough for a short letter. I began to trim a quill as Simon gave Rikki a final pat and wished me goodnight as he slipped away.

Already I was turning over in my mind how best to frame my letter to the coroner. He might wonder indeed why a physician from another hospital and a player from Lord Strange's Men had any business with the case of the poisoning of a member of Lord Burghley's household in a ward of St Bartholomew's hospital. My letter would need careful wording.

It took me a long time to write, and I made several false starts, so that I had barely enough ink to finish. It was done at last. When I had sanded the ink to dry it, I folded the letter neatly, and sealed it, pressing my engraved ring into the wax. Although my seal would mean nothing to the coroner, any seal adds an air of importance to a letter, which a mere blob of wax does not.

I had been so absorbed in my task that I had not noticed the rising wind until I looked up and saw one of the shutters swinging back and forth. Outside the darkness was unbroken by any light of stars or moon. I laid down my letter and went to the window to close it and fasten the shutters, when a blinding flash and a tremendous crack of thunder seemed to explode in my face and sent me cowering back. Rikki jumped to his feet and began to bark.

'Hush!' I said, leaning down to stroke him reassuringly. ''Tis only a thunderstorm. It startled me.'

Then a second flash, following after barely a pause, made me jump again. The hairs bristled on Rikki's neck and he barked again, facing the window, determined to repel the intruder. I closed the window and the shutters, and drew my thin curtain, but it could not altogether shut out the light and the noise. In the hope of calming the dog I hurried to change into my night shift and climb into bed. Rikki jumped up beside me, and we curled up together, trying to allay our alarm. Overhead, I heard someone moving about. The children in the attic would have felt much nearer to the crash of thunder than I did, but I knew better than to go up and comfort them. Having spent most of their short lives living on the streets in all weathers, they had their pride and would have scorned it.

The storm seemed to last a long time, though that was probably deceptive, but it meant another disturbed night. When I finally crawled out of bed the following morning, it was to find the storm had been followed by a steady downpour. Be careful what you wish for! The storm had certainly cleared the air, but the fine summer weather had been replaced by a dreary leaden grey which felt more like November. It would be beating down the crops in the fields as well, making for a poor harvest.

I found Jos Atkins in the kitchen at the back of the house, gloomily eating lumpy porridge while his mother stood over him. Indeed, it did not look appetising, but many of the waifs I saw in the hospital would have been glad of it.

'I would like Jos to carry a letter for me,' I said to the landlady. 'To the Guildhall. Can you and Goodman Atkins spare him?'

Jos looked at me hopefully. His mother kept him busy about the house and he also worked with his father, who was employed from time to time as a carpenter on the docks. He had received no formal schooling, but he could read a little, slowly, and often ran errands or carried letters for me and the other lodgers.

'Aye,' she said. 'There will be nothing doing for him with my man in this weather. He shall take it for you when he has eaten his porridge.'

I laid the letter aside on the coffer where she kept her linen, not risking it amongst the sticky dishes on the table.

'Here is a silver ha'penny for you, Jos,' I said, 'and a penny for your mother, for giving you leave from your chores.'

I knew that normally Jos would be required to hand over his earnings to his mother, but I hoped that by this stratagem he might be allowed to keep the ha'penny for himself.

'Terrible weather,' I said, nodding to them as I went out.

Hunched in my hooded cloak, I made my way to the hospital with a reluctant dog, who would have preferred to remain dry and warm in my room, but I encouraged him with promises of comfort in Tom Read's gatehouse. As for myself, I could not avoid the puddles, the water standing several inches deep along the street, for the earth was so hard packed and dry that it absorbed the rainfall only reluctantly, so that I arrived at St Thomas's not only with sodden shoes but with hose wet and muddy to the knee.

Rikki safely delivered, I found that Jess had gone into labour during the early hours, with the babe promising arrival before long, so I soon forgot my wet feet until we were able to present her with a son, who squalled with a pair of lungs to match his mother's.

'Mary be praised,' Jess said. ''Tis time we had another boy, with our four maids and the only lad Jacob, who will never be strong enough to take an oar in my man's boat.'

'This one seems strong enough,' I said, winding the flailing limbs in a swaddling blanket. 'Give him a year or two and he'll make a fine wherryman.'

I'll swear the babe gave me a knowing look, as if to say he might aim higher than the waterman's trade.

Once all was calm again in the lying-in ward, I squelched my way to the children's ward, where Alice was reading to them from a book of fables, the one about belling the cat. Had Tommy been one of the mice, I reckoned he would have volunteered for the task. In a few years, the army might hold a future for him. England did not have a full standing army, for neither Queen nor Parliament could afford the expense, but there were certain permanent troops, guarding the Channel ports and other places of strategic importance, like the Tower. Only when invasion threatened, or we provided help for our allies, such as the people of the United Provinces, was an army recruited. I had an old friend, Andrew Joplin, who might find a place amongst his troopers when Tommy was old enough. It would at least provide an escape from his father.

'Dr Alvarez!' Goodwife Watson stared at the trail of water and mud my shoes had left across the clean floor. 'Have you been in the river?'

'As near as,' I said. 'Bankside is awash after the storm. Have you not been outside this morning?'

'Nay, what with the inspection and then the storm, me and Alice both spent the night here. You'd best let me have those shoes to dry by the fire.'

I could hardly go about the hospital in nothing but my wet stockings, but indeed my feet and legs were beginning to feel chilled. It would help no one if I caught a rheum or worse, so I gave her my shoes. She stuffed them with rags and set them close beside the fireplace to dry. Someone had

had the good sense to light a small fire to drive away the chill and the damp from the ward.

'Can you ask one of the servants to make up a fire in my office?' I said. 'I will be working there if I am needed.'

She bustled off to see to it, and I withdrew to the tiny space I called my office. It was barely more than a cupboard, but it had a table and chair, a few hanging cupboards, and a narrow slit of a window. The lad Eddi came in with a bucket of firewood, kindling, and a strike-a-light, and soon had my small fire lit. The fireplace was on a miniature scale, but the space was so small it soon warmed up. My hose would dry quickly.

I set about my records, which were behindhand. Unlike many of my colleagues, I kept case notes on all my patients, a practice I had learned from my father. While the other physicians thought it a waste of effort, I knew that I learned a great deal from writing everything down, from symptoms to treatment to outcome, lessons which could prove valuable in similar cases. I always scribbled rough notes at once, and wrote them up more carefully in a ledger whenever I had the time. My father had hopes of one day producing a medical text, based on the lectures he had delivered while a professor at Coimbra and his practical experience at St Bartholomew's, but he had never lived to write it. I had no such aspirations, but my records were useful to me, and where they could be helpful I shared them with the midwives and nursing sisters.

As I wrote, my wet hose began to steam in the warmth of the fire, and I started to feel less chilled. Before long, Goodwife Watson brought me a mug of hot spiced ale, fussy like a mother hen, but I was glad of it.

'Your shoes will be dry soon, doctor,' she said. 'We cannot have you falling ill!'

I smiled and thanked her. I knew that several of the older nursing staff, including the senior nursing sister, Mistress Maynard, regarded me as a young man who needed mothering. Sometimes I wondered wryly whether they would be quite so caring, had they known I was a girl.

Probably not. Young women were expected to make the best of things, whatever life might throw at them, whereas young men were to be cosseted and cherished.

Still, I might as well enjoy the mothering. I clasped both hands about the beaker until it was cool enough to drink and surveyed the notes I had written up.

I had treated a number of poisoning cases in the past, generally food poisoning. If it could be caught quickly, it was extremely unpleasant but not usually serious. Only if the sufferer was already weak might the results be fatal. I had known a few cases of poisoning by *belladonna*, both accidental and intentional, and an unusual attempt to poison the Tsarevich of Muscovy with a rare mushroom, which had been circumvented by having his food tasted by a servant, with fatal results.

In my own experience, I had not encountered poisoning by hemlock, although it is perhaps one of the most famous – or notorious – of all poisons, having been employed by the ancient Greeks as a form of execution. It was used on the philosopher Socrates. As a result, anyone who had studied the classical authors, or the histories of Greece and Rome, would know of the properties of hemlock. I was uncertain how easy true hemlock might be to obtain in London, as it was not a herb I had ever used myself, despite its sometimes use for sprains. Water hemlock, though not quite the same, was easily found, as I had mentioned to Peter.

In fact, it seemed a curious choice, though the effects, slow paralysis, might not have been noticed during the night in a busy hospital. They might have been taken as a delayed result of Josiah Gurdin's head injuries, for injury to the brain can sometimes have these unforeseen and delayed effects. And as far as I knew, there was no antidote, unless perhaps immediate vomiting and purging might succeed in clearing the body of the poison before it could do any harm. Yet the very nature of its slow insidious progress would, in most cases, rule that out.

I laid aside my notes and propped my quill in the ink pot. My small window looked down over the main courtyard of St Thomas's which, at this time of day, was busy and full of people coming and going about the business of the hospital, or of the many workshops, surviving from monastic days, which shared the same grounds – the printing shop, stained glass workshop, leather workers, and others – not to mention our vegetable and herb gardens, flocks of sheep and goats, and a small dairy herd. Yet, like St Bartholomew's on the night Josiah Gurdin was killed, all would be very quiet at dusk.

What Simon had learned from Bart's gatekeeper confirmed that there had indeed been a visitor for Gurdin that night, but his description of the man was so general that it could apply to thousands in London. Had the man indeed come from Lord Burghley's household, with or without the steward's knowledge? Or was the 'master' of whom he had spoken someone else altogether? Or perhaps did not even exist?

Peter could never be quite clear of suspicion in this matter of Gurdin's death unless the true murderer could be found, and in that case it would be much easier to find him if it were known just who – or what – Josiah Gurdin was. Could he have been, as I had suggested, one of the agents working for the Cecils? Or could he have been a spy of Essex's, introduced into their household?

I turned back from the window and sat down again at my table. Setting aside my case notes, I drew a fresh sheet of paper toward me and wiped the excess ink off the tip of my quill.

There was one person who belonged neither to the intelligence service organised by Essex, nor to that of the Cecils. Yet a man with years of experience in intelligence work, and who knew every corner of London like no other. A man who had retired to establish a poultry business which he found mind-numbingly tedious.

I would seek the help of Nick Berden.

Chapter Four

I should need to see Nick Berden myself, rather than send him a message about the murder which had been laid at Peter Lambert's door. Besides, I always felt that discussing some affair of intelligence work with Nick cleared my own thoughts. I would walk over to Poultry after I finished my work at the hospital today, and hope that the persistent downpour might have abated somewhat by then.

However, there was one letter I could send, and the sooner the better. I was not certain whether Peter would be summoned to the inquest. Even if no formal accusation had yet been made against him, he would probably be called upon to tell what he knew about the condition of the patient Josiah Gurdin and the contents of the febrifuge tincture he had administered. He would also want to assert again that Gurdin had been visited shortly before taking his medicine. And although I had despatched word of the gatekeeper's evidence to the coroner, it was possible it might not reach him before the inquest at midday. If I sent a message now to Peter at St Bartholomew's, he would at least know that there was another witness who had seen the nameless visitor. If the gatekeeper John Broughton had not been summoned, Peter could request his presence.

I quickly wrote a letter setting out briefly what Simon had discovered, sealed it, and sent for Eddi to carry it to St Bartholomew's.

'To save time, Eddi,' I said, 'here is the fare to go and return by wherry. It will also save you getting quite such a wetting,'

'Aye,' he said with a grin, 'it do be pouring down like a flood tide out there.'

'And,' I said, adding another coin, 'this is to buy yourself a hot pie at Pie Corner, against the chill. Go to Goodman Quiller's shop. His wife has a light hand with the pastry.'

'You did live thereabouts, did you not?'

'Aye, when I worked at Bart's. Now, be sure you put the letter directly into Master Lambert's hand yourself. If you cannot find him at the hospital, his house is in Duck Lane. Anyone at the hospital will be able to direct you.'

'I'll be certain sure to do that, doctor. 'Tis urgent, is it?'

'Aye. It concerns evidence to lay before an inquest at midday, so you will need to make haste.'

'Wings on my heels, doctor,' he said unexpectedly. He must have been visiting the playhouse lately.

Apart from the arrival of Jess's son, all was quiet in my two wards for the rest of the morning, after the worry and disruption of the governors' inspection on the previous day. Eddi returned before noon, saying that he had found Peter lurking about St Bartholomew's, awaiting the inquest.

'He opened your letter at once, Dr Alvarez,' he said, 'and mighty glad he was, too. Sent you his grateful thanks and went running off somewheres, saying there wasn't a moment to lose.'

'Good,' I said. 'Thank you, Eddi. It may be that we have been able to prevent summary injustice, though the mystery is not solved.'

He looked baffled, as well he might, but I did not chose to explain the case to him, not yet.

Once all the patients were settled and awaiting their supper – which was served in the late afternoon – I donned my shoes, which were dry now, though a little stiff, put on my hooded cloak, and set off for the City. Rikki was somewhat perplexed to find me heading for the Bridge instead of along Bankside to my lodgings, but the cooler weather after the storm seemed to have revived him and he ran ahead, stopping now and then to rescue some fallen scrap of food left behind by one of the street vendors, or to raise his leg impudently against the fine carved timbers of Nonesuch House.

It was no longer raining, but the streets were still awash. The kennels which ran down the centre of most of them were intended to drain away rainwater, but they often became blocked with rubbish, despite the street men engaged to clean them, and they were overflowing now across the cobbles. I must have appeared to be performing some strange dance, dodging about to avoid the worst of the standing water.

Once we drew near Poultry, Rikki knew where we were bound and ran ahead, so that I found him already making himself comfortable in Nick Berden's office by the time I reached it. Nick was clearly doing his accounts and not enjoying it, for there were streaks of ink on his cheeks and even in his hair, where he had run a despairing quill as he tried to make his numbers balance.

'Ah, Kit!' he said, throwing down his quill in relief and crossing to the court cupboard where he kept his ale mugs. 'The very person! You are clever with figures. I never foresaw, when I set up as a poulterer, how much of my time would be spent sending out reckonings – which are never paid on time – and trying to decide from my accounts whether I am making a profit or feeding London at my expense.'

I accepted the cup of ale he handed me and raised it to him in a silent pledge.

'The Court is still failing to pay its debts to you?'

He shook his head in despair. 'I do not think they have paid me a tenth of what they owe since I set up in business. When I worked for Sir Francis, at least I could count on regular wages. Now . . . !' He spread his hands expressively in a gesture of hopelessness. 'Now I think perhaps I should take up spiery again.'

'Indeed?' I had glanced down at the ill-written and blotted pages of his accounts, but now I looked up. 'And which intelligence service would you favour? Essex or the Cecils?'

He sat down on a stool and stretched out his legs. 'Ah, there's the rub. Which? Essex I do not trust, but Thomas Phelippes is there and he is the best man Walsingham ever employed. Barring yourself, of course.'

I grinned. 'Of course.'

'The Cecils, now. 'Tis my belief the Cecils will prevail in the end, but they made a mistake in not catching Phelippes before Essex did. Do you reckon, Kit, that they were behind the theft of all our files, during Sir Francis's funeral?'

I pulled up another stool and sat down.

'I do not know if they were behind it, but I am certain it was Robert Poley who stole them, and took them to Lord Burghley, to buy his way into their favour. He would have known where everything was kept, and would not scruple at breaking the locks.'

'Hmm.' He took a swig of his ale. 'An expensive bargain for them, if the files came with Poley attached. A treacherous bastard. A double agent, I've always suspected.'

'I have heard that he flourishes under the Cecils.'

'Aye, he will probably serve them well, until someone else offers him a larger purse of coin. He's a cunning bastard, I'll grant him that. Look how he insinuated himself into Babington's group of traitors, when they were bent on murdering the Queen and setting up the Scots woman in her place. They believed he was a treasonous papist like them.'

'They did,' I said. 'Or at least that is what Babington believed at first. Toward the end, I think he had found Poley out. I have often wondered–'

'What?'

'Babington nearly gave it up, did he not? He was in two minds. I think in his heart he had realised that it was an evil thing to do and wanted to disentangle himself, but it was too late.'

It came to me suddenly as a shock that when Babington had gone to the scaffold, he was but two years older than I was now. I shivered.

'He may have wanted to,' Nick said, 'but he was too deeply mired by then, that's true. And that was not the only time Robert Poley has managed to pass for an ally of England's enemies. Probably because he *is* one, in truth, when it suits him. The man has loyalty to no one but himself.'

'Perhaps one day it will catch up with him,' I said grimly.

'However,' Nick said, 'you did not come all this way to Poultry to talk of Robert Poley, though if you were to lend me your aid with these b'yer lady accounts, with your gift for numbers . . .?' He grinned at me hopefully.

'I know little of accounts, Nick, but I can check your figures. In return, perhaps you will help me with a puzzle of my own.'

'Aha, I thought so! And you are dipping your toe in spiery again, I'll be bound.' He rubbed his hands together in gleeful anticipation.

'Show me your troublesome figures first,' I said, 'and then we may talk of it with a clear head.'

'That seems a fair bargain, though I think I shall come out of it the winner.'

He pushed his untidy pages over to me, and I clicked my tongue reprovingly.

'No surprise that you make mistakes, Nick. Is this a five or an eight? And this, is it a ten? Or a one followed by a blot?'

Between us, we went through four pages of scrawled and near illegible items sold, with their prices, and a mere two pages of monies received. It was clear that many of Nick's customers were in arrears with their payments, and it seemed that the richest and grandest were also the most remiss.

'Your most profitable item seems to be the eggs your women sell on the street,' I said. 'At least they take payment when they hand over the eggs.'

'Aye, that's very true.'

'While your ducks and geese and capons supplied to the royal palaces are largely unpaid for.'

'True again.'

'So why do you not concentrate on eggs?'

'Because it raises the reputation of my business to be able to say that I supply Her Majesty. The very words bring in custom.'

I shrugged. 'I am no merchant, Nick, but it is clear you are making a loss at present. How long can this continue?'

He sighed. 'No long, I suppose.'

'You need to warn the palace stewards, or the Master of the Royal Kitchens, or whoever is responsible for paying you. Could not one of your former . . . agents . . . be somewhat persuasive?'

The group of men Nick had used in his work for Walsingham included some formidable fellows. Not anyone I should choose to cross.

'Hmm.' He looked thoughtful. 'Perhaps, if it were done discreetly. Aye, 'tis an excellent suggestion. I know the very fellow.'

I laughed. 'They must lack employment these days, your men.'

'They survive, although I know some of them miss our former work. Now, enough of this.'

He knocked the newly written pages into a neat stack and weighed them down with a smooth pebble. 'What is your real reason for coming to see me? Shall we adjourn to an ordinary and discuss it over supper?'

I agreed. Leaving one of his women servants to shut up the poultry for the night, we made our way to a nearby ordinary, where we could buy a light supper and take our time over a mug or two of beer.

Once we were settled, I leaned forward over the table we had chosen in a retired corner.

'One of my friends at St Bartholomew's, an apothecary called Peter Lambert, has been accused of poisoning a patient. It is manifestly false, the man was a stranger, and Peter is no poisoner, he is careful and meticulous in his work. But the patient was a man from Lord Burghley's household, had been beaten and left for dead in the street. From what I have learned, I think he may have been one of the Cecils' intelligencers. And it would not surprise me were it to prove that he was a victim of this violent rivalry between the Cecils and Essex.'

'Indeed!' He raised his eyebrows. 'Has it come to killing each other's men?'

As we ate our supper, I laid out for Nick every scrap of information I had about Josiah Gurdin, about the nameless visitor, and about the reluctant evidence of John Broughton.

'So you see,' I concluded, 'there is very little to go on, in order to identify this visitor, though in all likelihood he was the murderer. Just why, is a matter for conjecture. The simplest answer is that he is a man of Essex's, but it may be more complex than that.'

'Aye.' He began to trace patterns with the tip of his knife in a puddle of spilt beer on the table. 'There are other possibilities.'

'That is what I thought also. Gurdin might have been an Essex spy introduced into Lord Burghley's household, and unmasked.'

'Indeed. In which case the visitor might be a man of the same household, sent to dispose of him. Or Gurdin might have been a papist spy, in which case someone from either party could have killed him.'

'Although usually,' I said slowly, 'Lord Burghley and the rest prefer to make a public spectacle of the arrest of a papist spy, in order to demonstrate their vigilant care for the nation's safety.' I paused. 'Unless they hope to turn an enemy agent through bribery and threats into one of their own.'

'In which case they would not kill him.'

'They would not.'

We both sat sipping our beer as a serving maid carried away our used trenchers, and, at Nick's request, brought another flask of beer. I shook my head when he offered to refill my mug.

'I shall fall asleep if I drink more,' I said, 'and I still need to walk back to Southwark.'

I shifted on the bench. Rikki had fallen asleep on my feet and they were growing numb. 'Of course, we may be quite mistaken. Perhaps Josiah Gurdin was *not* an agent.'

'Someone wanted him silenced.'

'A jealous husband?'

'It might be.'

'Someone who owed him money, and could not pay?'

'An over elaborate killing in such a case, would you not say? More likely a knife in the back when he came out of hospital.'

I nodded. 'There is another possibility.'

I drank the last of my beer and linked my hands behind my head. 'Perhaps Gurdin *was* one of the Cecils' agents, and a loyal one, but he knew something. Knew too much. And the Cecils themselves had him silenced.'

'You are become very cynical, Kit,' Nick said.

'It has always been a dangerous world, this game of spiery and intelligence we once played, but since Sir Francis's death, it has become . . . I do not know how to put it . . . More vicious? More ruthless? Between them, Essex and the Cecils seem to be ripping out the entrails of England. Before, we worked for the safety of the State.'

'Then we are well rid of intelligence work. Even chickens are better!'

I laughed. 'Nevertheless, Peter Lambert cannot be fully cleared of this suspicion of murder until the real killer is laid bare. I do not know what happened at the inquest today, but even though it can now be shown that there *was* a visitor to Gurdin, does that mean anyone will attempt to find him? I wish we knew more. If we could but put a name to the man, perhaps then the city authorities would take note and Peter's name would be cleared.'

'And this is where you think I can help?'

'Perhaps? There is no one who knows every corner of London better than you do, Nick. I know there is very little to go on, but could you put the word about amongst your men – those who used to be your men – in case they might have heard some whisper?'

'I will do so,' he said, 'but do not build your hopes too high, Kit. If both these men, Gurdin and his killer, are agents of either Burghley or Essex, then they will have been very skilled at melting into the shadows. There are likely to be few traces of them on the streets.'

'That I know only too well,' I said, 'but I cannot think of anything else. I might call on Thomas Phelippes. I would not ask him outright, but I may manage to learn something of the men in Essex's service, from him or from Arthur Gregory. I accounted them friends in the past, when we worked so closely together, though I have seen little of them lately.'

'Nor have I.'

The clock on one of the nearby churches struck seven, reminding me I had another task this side of the river, before I returned home. I got up, laying down coins for my share of the meal.

'Stay and finish your beer, Nick. I will make my enquiries, and if I learn anything, I will send you word.'

'I shall do the same. Shall we meet again in a week, and lay our heads together?'

'Aye. Let us hope we have learned something by then.'

I caught up my cloak, whistled to Rikki, and bade Nick good e'en.

My other errand to the north of the river was in Seething Lane. My horse Hector had had little exercise of late, and a horse confined too much to the stable will grow stale. The stable lads exercised him when they could, but their first duty must be to the horses belonging to the household. Now that Essex kept a number of his mounts at Walsingham House – no doubt to save himself trouble and expense at Essex House – the stable staff had even less time to look after my horse.

One of the young boys was sweeping the yard clear of scattered straw when I arrived. It must have been spilt when the horses were being bedded down for the evening with fresh straw. I found Harry and the other senior lads in the snug tack room, where they had a small stove for warmth in winter, used also for brewing up hot mash for the horses, or warming a poultice for a sprain. It also served for the lads' own cooking, as it did now, for a savoury aroma of bacon and beans was drifting out to meet me as I leaned over the half door.

'Dr Alvarez!' Henry jumped up. 'Come you in-by and take a bite of supper with us.'

The lads had never shown deference to my calling, either as physician or code-breaker, a fact which both amused and pleased me.

'Nay, I thank you, Harry,' I said. 'I have supped already, though not so well as you, I suspect. I called by only to say that I plan to take Hector out for a long ride on Sunday. It is time he stretched his legs. I wanted to be sure he is fit, and does not need the farrier before then.'

Harry came over to the door and leaned out beside me. 'Had the farrier last week. Hector's feet are in good trim. I rode him out for a short while, day before yesterday, but he is needing a good day's exercise. I'll check him over for you, but I reckon he's fit enough. Likely he'll be in a tearing hurry to get out of the city.'

'Likely he will. I'll be round early on Sunday. Have your supper. I'll just take him an apple, then I'll be off over the Bridge.'

As always, Hector seemed glad to see me, accepting the apple courteously, lipping it up gently from my palm with his velvet mouth, then blowing a juicy breath into my ear by way of thanks. I ran my fingers through his mane, then down his silky neck. Some might think his dappled and pied coat ugly, but beneath it he had the build and beauty of his Arab ancestry, combined with his English strength and endurance. As always, my heart gave a little lift as I thought, amazingly, that Hector was mine! Sir Francis's gift had been beyond belief. Indeed, I could hardly believe it even now.

However, it would be dusk soon, and I did not want to waste my chinks on a wherry if the gates on the Bridge were closed. I had already spent enough today, sending messages and supping with Nick, so I gave Hector a final stroke, urged Rikki out of the nest he had made amongst the straw, and bolted the stable door for the night.

As I turned around, I nearly collided with Lady Frances.

'Oh,' I gasped. 'Forgive me, my lady!'

'Nay,' she said. ''Twas my fault, Kit. I saw from the house that you had come into the stables and I was waiting for you.'

'For me?' I felt a tremor of worry. I was not sure that I wished to be involved in the affairs of the Countess of Essex any further.

'Aye. As I came into the yard I heard you telling Harry that you mean to ride Hector into the country on Sunday, so what I intended to ask you may prove no difficulty after all.'

'Which is?' I spoke politely, but with reserve. What could she possibly want, that involved my ride on Hector?

She looked at me anxiously, biting her lip.

'Could you take your ride into Hertfordshire? It is not far, I think. An easy ride there and back in the day.'

'Hertfordshire?' I was puzzled.

'Master Mylles's manor,' she said. 'I have heard nothing since Elizabeth was taken there, save for a short note from Master Mylles when she first arrived, saying that she was safe. Sent back with the armed men who went as a guard on her journey. Nothing more. I had thought she would write to me. Indeed, she promised . . .' Her voice trailed away, and even in the fading light of evening I could trace the lines of tension and fear on her face.

'I am sure there is no need for worry,' I said. 'Children so quickly become caught up in new places, new experiences. I am sure the Lady Elizabeth never meant to cause you concern. She will be taken up with her new friends – do the Mylleses not have children themselves? And she will be outside all day in this fine weather, riding her pony, or playing at *jeu de mail* or trying her hand at archery.'

'You probably have the right of it.' She assayed a tremulous smile. 'I am no doubt concerned without cause. Blame it on a mother's foolish whim. Though my own mother, too, is worried.'

'Then set your worries aside,' I said firmly. 'I can easily ride that way on Sunday. I can call on Francis Mylles as an old friend, for we worked together in your father's time. It will seem quite natural. And I can find some reason to speak to Lady Elizabeth. Perhaps you would like me to carry a letter from you? And I will see the waiting woman as well. Mistress Godliff, is it? She should have written to you herself, to set your mind at rest.'

Her face lit up. Frances Walsingham was not a beautiful woman, but when she smiled she gained a kind of beauty, and reminded me of Sir Francis on the rare occasions when he relaxed from his wearisome toils.

'I cannot thank you enough, Kit! And, aye, I should like you to carry a letter, and perhaps her favourite poppet, which I do not think she meant to leave behind. I will give them to Harry, so you may have them to hand if you want to make an early start on Sunday.'

'And if I may, I shall try to persuade Lady Elizabeth to set pen to paper and write you a few lines,' I said.

'Children do not know how much worry they can cause, simply by inattention.'

She gave me a curious look. 'You speak almost like a mother.'

My smile was somewhat tight, for this was a condition I could not aspire to. 'I have charge of the children's ward at St Thomas's, my lady. I spend most of my day in the company of children of every sort.'

'Of course. I had forgot. That was why they sent you to Muscovy, was it not? Because the Tsar wanted a physician who was accustomed to treat children.'

I looked away. 'Aye. One child I managed to help. The other was murdered.'

She gave a gasp, pressing her fingers to her lips. I was instantly sorry. I should not have worried her with talk of murdered children.

'I did not know!'

'It was the little Tsarevich. A fine little boy, who might have made a fine Tsar one day, without the madness of his father or the simple mindedness of his half-brother. But he stood in the way of Boris Godunov, a man of overwhelming ambition, who clearly hopes to make himself Tsar one day.'

'Poor child. Poor boy. To be caught up in the cruel battles of ambitious men.'

She spoken with feeling, and I nodded. A woman married to the Earl of Essex understood all too well the dangers of being close to an ambitious man.

'Fortunately,' I said firmly, 'Lady Elizabeth has no claim to any title an ambitious man might want. She is quite safe.'

Lady Frances gave a grim smile. 'Nay, she can merely be married off to secure some politic alliance. My son, however, is a different matter.'

I had no answer to this. I wished I had bitten my tongue, rather than mention the little Tsarevich, but whenever Muscovy is mentioned, his image leaps into my mind.

She turned away. 'I must not keep you, Kit, for no doubt you want to reach home before nightfall. I thank you with all my heart for going to Hertfordshire for me.'

I bowed as she walked slowly away toward the backstairs of the house.

Back at my lodgings in Southwark, I found Simon in his room, idly looking over the script for another new role, but he was glad enough to set it aside and hear all that I had done that day, the messages I had sent, and my discussion with Nick Berden.

'But you have not heard the outcome of the inquest?' he said.

'I have not. I hoped perhaps Peter might have sent word, but Goodwife Atkins says there has been no message for me. I hope that does not mean he has been arrested, despite what you learned from the gatekeeper.'

'Surely not. But perhaps he has been so caught up in the business that he could not write.'

'Perhaps.' I leaned out of Simon's window, which gave on to the same view as mine, but lower down. Mine was the better, for I could see over the roofs of all the houses to the river and the City beyond. 'I suppose it would be foolish to hope that he has been taken back to his duties at Bart's. I wonder when – and indeed if – Master Winger will come back to London. He is most highly respected. With his support, and the evidence about Gurdin's visitor, it is to be hoped that Peter will be able to resume his employment. Helen is with child again. They will need his earnings. And their house, too.'

'You may hear tomorrow,' Simon said. 'And I like your plan of asking Nick Berden to set his men to find out what they can about the man who visited Gurdin, and probably murdered him.'

I turned and leaned my back against the window frame. 'There is little enough to go on, Jesu knows. The description might fit thousands of men in London. But they will start by learning what they can about the Burghley

80

household, what is to be known about Gurdin himself, and whether in truth anyone was sent from there to the hospital, despite the denials of the steward.'

'It will be more difficult to enquire into any men of the Earl's following,' he said, 'for I think you have said that he does not maintain such a household as the Cecils.'

'Nay, his household is all for pleasure and show. His intelligence service, if it deserves the name, is conducted at secondhand, through Anthony Bacon, who passes it down to Thomas Phelippes, who, as you know, is based at the Customs House, a goodly distance from Essex House. The Earl does not want his private life sullied by too close contact with the likes of Phelippes, and certainly not with any man Phelippes employs. They, in turn, will be employed much as Nick used to run the men under him, living their own lives quite separately from the intelligence service.'

'Much more difficult to trace, then.'

'Much more difficult, though I might try to see whether I can learn anything from Phelippes. Yet even he might not know . . . He works with the usual intercepted letters, breaking codes, despatching agents on intelligence work . . . I think if Essex wanted someone eliminated, he might not do it through Phelippes.'

'So it will hardly be worth asking,' Simon said.

'I do not expect to learn anything very much to the point,' I said, 'but I shall see what I *can* learn, nevertheless.'

Simon went to the food cupboard hanging on the wall and took out a wooden dish containing two apple turnovers. 'Goodwife Atkins gave me these. She has been using the early windfalls from the garden.'

I raised my eyebrows. Our landlady was not usually so generous. Perhaps the silver I had dispensed that morning had warmed her heart.

'Quite good,' I said, biting into the one Simon passed to me. 'I have eaten better pastry, but they are well filled.'

I brushed the crumbs from my mouth and the front of my doublet.

'On the way home I called at Seething Lane.'

'Admiring your fine steed?' He grinned. Like me, he was astonished that I owned such a valuable piece of horse flesh.

'Indeed. And making sure that he would be fit for a long ride on Sunday. He needs the exercise, but I wanted to be sure that he did not need shoeing.'

'All was well?'

'Aye. I shall take him out into the country for the day. Would you like to come as well?'

He looked startled. 'I? But I have no mount.'

'You could hire one. Would you not enjoy a day out of London?'

'I suppose I could.' He considered. 'You are just going for the pleasure of the ride?'

'That was what I first intended. But now it seems I have a mission as well. Do you remember Francis Mylles, who used to be principal secretary to Walsingham?'

'I met him once or twice.'

'He bought a small manor from Sir Francis, when he was turning some of his property into coin, not long before he died. It is in Hertfordshire, not a long ride.'

He looked at me curiously. 'Why do you wish to see Master Mylles? He cannot help in this matter which must concern today's intelligencers. He has put all of that behind him.'

'Nay, it is a different matter altogether.' I paused, then added thoughtfully, 'Though perhaps it may not be.'

'You are talking in riddles, Kit.'

I sat down on the bed and leaned forward, my elbows on my knees.

'I intended merely to go for a ride in the country, but Lady Frances overheard me talking to Harry – the head stable lad at Walsingham House, you remember.'

'What has Lady Frances to do with it?'

'She has sent her daughter, Lady Elizabeth, her daughter by Sir Philip Sydney, to stay at Francis Mylles's manor for a time, and asked if I might direct my ride there, to see how she is faring. She misses the child, and has had no letter from her.'

He looked at me shrewdly. 'I think there is more to this that you are not telling me, Kit.'

I opened my mouth, then closed it again, and shook my head. 'It is not mine to tell, Simon, not without word from Lady Frances. I have recommended a period of clean country air for the child, that is all you need to know. On Sunday I shall take the mother's letter and a doll to Lady Elizabeth, and persuade the daughter to write a sentence or two in return. Otherwise, the day is free for a pleasant ride in the country. That storm has cleared the air. It is no longer so hot. I should enjoy your company.'

He considered for a moment, then grinned. 'Aye, a day out in the country would be pleasant, before summer is at an end, and there is little to do of a Sunday, when the playhouse is closed. Mark you, a hired nag will hardly keep pace with your fine stallion.'

'Never fear,' I said solemnly. 'We will make regular stops, so that you may amble along and catch us up.'

He hurled the wooden bowl at me, but I ducked, and it fell harmlessly on the bed.

Sunday dawned bright and clear, but there was a fresh breeze blowing from the east, so it seemed likely that it would not be unpleasantly warm for our ride. I had bought a fresh loaf the evening before, and a lump of yellow cheese, and half a dozen small red apples of some early variety I did not recognise. When I banged loudly on Simon's door, expecting him to be still asleep, I was astonished when he opened it, fully dressed, combed and shaved, dangling a leather jack of ale from his hand.

I staggered back, my hand pressed to my head.

'A miracle! You are in the land of the live and waking.'

'Very droll,' he said. 'I *can* rise early when I must.'

'Let us be on our way, then. Tom has agreed to keep Rikki for me. He could run alongside, but it will be a long day and I might end by carrying him across my horse's withers.'

We went quietly down the stairs, not to disturb the other tenants, who would be enjoying their Sabbath rest from work, and walked quickly to St Thomas's, to leave Rikki with Tom. To him it must have seemed like any working day when I went to the hospital, and he settled happily in the gatehouse.

Across the Bridge, Simon headed for a nearby livery stable, where he had bespoken a mount the day before, while I made my way to Seething Lane. Harry had Hector ready saddled and bridled, tied up beside the mounting block.

'Lady Frances left these for you,' he said, handing me a flat packet and a larger parcel. ''Tis a letter for the maid, and her poppet with its clothes. And there is this for you.'

He reached into the front of his cotte and drew out a purse.

I stepped back, frowning. 'I do not want to be paid. I was planning this ride anyway.'

He grinned. 'I think she suspected that you would say as much. This is meant to buy you a meal at an inn, on the way there and back, and oats for Hector. She says there is an excellent inn at Abbots Langley, the White Hart. Not far before you reach Master Mylles's manor house, which is this side St Albans. Her family is known there, at the White Hart, from when her father owned the manor, and you are to mention that you are on her business, so that they treat you well. She would not presume, she said, to pay you for your services.'

I gave a reluctant grin. 'Very well. Simon Hetherington is coming with me, but I expect there is more than enough to feed us both.'

'The player? Aye, I saw him last fortnight in the new Henry Six play. I remember when he used to play women.'

'Not for some time!' I laughed. 'He is three and twenty now.'

Henry shook his head. 'How time do fly by!'

'Truly, it does.'

'Will you be wanting a saddle bag?'

I considered. I had brought the food in a knapsack, but I also had my satchel of medicines, and now with Lady Frances's letter and packet . . . 'Aye, a small one, and I will pack everything into it. 'Twill be easier to carry.'

Harry brought out a small saddle bag from the tack room, the sort which buckles behind the saddle, instead of hanging in a pair on either side of the horse's flanks. After he had secured it, I stowed away everything inside, with the knapsack of food on top, so that the bread would not be flattened, and we could stop to break our fast in an hour or two.

I mounted by the block, for Hector is a tall horse. I had been taught by the trooper Andrew Joplin to vault over his hindquarters, but Hector did not like it. As a sign of his displeasure he would keep his ears flattened back for some time afterwards. I waved a goodbye to Harry and, as I came out into the street, Simon rode up on his hired hack. It was a bay gelding, who looked sturdy and reliable enough. Quite handsome in his way, but I could see at once that he would not have Hector's gift of speed. Well, by inviting Simon to come with me I knew I would have to forego some of the wild galloping I had first had in mind.

We headed north and left the City by Bishopsgate, then turned west along the edge of Finsbury Fields, taking care to ride well clear of the butts. Sunday was a favourite day for young men to practise their archery and we were taking no risks, though it was early for many to be astir yet.

Leaving the spires and smoke of London behind us, we picked up the road to St Albans running northwest through farming country, where the hay was all gathered in, but the fields of wheat and barley were a picture of ruin after the recent storm.

'That augurs ill,' Simon said, jerking his thumb at a wheat field which looked as though some giant beast had first trampled the crop into the ground, then rolled in it.

'Aye.' I looked about me from the vantage point of a tall horse. On every side the fields showed the same devastation.

'I wonder whether the storm was as severe throughout England,' I said. 'It could not have come at a worse time, when the corn was too tall to withstand a battering but not yet ripe enough to harvest. If it is like this everywhere, there will be hunger in many homes this coming year. And starvation in some.'

Simon nodded seriously. 'It does look bad.'

England was fearfully at risk of famine, always at the mercy of dangerous weather. Too late a spring delayed the growth of crops. Too wet a summer meant mould and blight. Too little rain led to withered grains. And a bad storm shortly before harvest could destroy even an abundant crop.

I remembered studying Roman history with my father. The Romans could not feed themselves from their Italian fields, but their fleet brought in great cargoes of grain from their colonies in Asia Minor and north Africa. England had no such resource, but must feed herself. And that meant some years of famine and death. Come the winter, when the price of bread soared, we should be seeing its victims at St Thomas's.

We rode on for about an hour, mostly at a leisurely pace, though I had given Hector his head twice, riding ahead at full gallop, then waiting for Simon to catch us up on his slower mount.

'Did you not promise me breakfast?' Simon said. 'All this country air has whetted my appetite. There is a likely spot.'

He gestured ahead to a copse of beech trees just off the road, where a very small stream had kept the grass green even in the recent hot summer weather.

'Aye,' I said. 'Let's stop there. We can have our bread and cheese. I forgot to tell you that Lady Frances has given us the price of a good dinner at Abbots Langley.'

'I shall have no trouble eating both,' he said, turning his horse aside across the verge and down a slight slope to the copse.

We unsaddled the horses and hobbled them so they might graze. I brought out the knapsack with the food, the bread only a little flattened, and Simon unhooked the leather flask from his belt.

It was pleasant under the trees, where the grass was thick and cool, and I found my own appetite had been sharpened by the ride. There was no knowing whether the stream was safe to drink, but the horses seemed happy enough with it, while we slaked our thirst, passing the ale jack back and forth, and drinking directly from it. This always gives the ale a slightly odd taste as it passes over the leather lip, but I was too thirsty to care. The bread was still quite fresh, and the cheese, although hard, had a good flavour. We finished by eating two of the small apples each, and gave the rest to the horses.

I was sitting peacefully with my arms about my knees, listening to the silken rip of grass as the horses grazed, when I noticed that Simon had fallen asleep. He lay slightly curled to one side, with his cheek on his hand, a strand of his fair hair, worn rather long, fallen over his eyes.

Lying there, vulnerable, he reminded me of the boy I had first known, more than seven years ago now. I smiled, remembering how we had come close to quarrelling on that bitterly cold February day. He had insulted my competence as a physician and I had taken offence. Before the day was over, he had apologised and I had realised he was not the mawkish youth I had taken him for. Such a long time, and how much we had changed! Or perhaps we had not, beneath it all.

I knew every line of his face as well as my own, but looking now at his free hand, which lay loosely on the grass, I thought, *It is a man's hand. He is no longer the boy I knew.* And that disturbed me. I knew I had feelings for him that I must suppress, for if he knew me for what I really was, we could not be here, riding together companionably through the countryside. Indeed, were I ever to emerge from my disguise, it would be to enter the kind of prison which women inhabit. After my years of freedom, living as boy and man, it would be unendurable.

Simon's eyes opened, alert at once, as though he had not, in truth, been asleep at all. He smiled at me and there was a curiously knowing expression in his eyes which caused a quiver of alarm to run through me.

'Why are you looking at me like that, Kit?' he said.

'I was wondering how long you would lie there snoring,' I said briskly, 'when we need to be on our way.'

He smiled again. 'I was not snoring.'

I laughed. 'Can you be sure?'

Within a few minutes we had saddled the horses and were on the road again. But that curious sense of alarm stayed with me.

Chapter Five

*W*e reached Abbots Langley in good time for a midday dinner and had no trouble in finding the White Hart, which stood firmly in the centre of the single street running through the village. From its name, there needed no great intellectual effort to realise that the village had once been the property of the abbots of St Albans, who would have drawn the rents from its tenant farms, its mill, and any other trade, like the inn. With the abbots long gone – more than half a century, I suppose – I had no idea who owned the village now. Perhaps the Walsingham family had done so once, but I did not think the manor Francis Mylles had bought extended over so great an area. These days, it might be anyone. Men rose from nowhere under the Tudor family. Aye, and vanished back again into obscurity, often enough, even if they lived that long. Little wonder that those who sought the highest positions of influence in the land, like Robert Devereux, Earl of Essex, were ruthless in their pursuit of power.

Having mentioned our mission for Lady Francis, as she had bidden, we were treated royally at the inn, and dined so well that neither of us had much inclination to ride on further in any great hurry. We sat outside the inn for a while afterwards, idly watching half a dozen children playing with a ball made of an inflated pig's bladder, but at last I stirred and stood up.

'If you will fetch the horses, Simon,' I said, 'I will ask the innkeeper the best road to Francis Mylles's manor.'

He went off to the stable, where the two horses had been enjoying their measure of oats at Lady Frances's expense, while I went in search of the innkeeper. I found him serving beer and pasties to three old men, clearly local villagers, who eyed me with frank curiosity. I do not suppose there were many strangers who dined at the inn at Abbots Langley.

'Aye,' the innkeeper said, ''twas a manor of Sir Francis Walsingham's, once on a time, but 'tis another Francis holds it now.'

'Frances Mylles was Sir Francis's principal secretary,' I said, 'and also a good friend to him and to Dame Ursula. I am sure he will be a good neighbour to you.'

'He is that already.' The innkeeper beamed. 'Both he and his lady have dined here many times, and favoured us with their goodwill.'

By which I supposed that he meant that they had spent generously.

'Ride straight on your way through the village,' he said, 'then when you come to a ford over a stream, hard by a willow copse, you will see a lane off to your right. 'Tis mebbe half a mile down that lane you will come to the manor.'

I thanked him, gave him a few coins to treat the old men to a beer, and went out to where Simon was in the yard, mounted and holding Hector's reins. As we turned toward the village street, the innkeeper came to the door and called after us.

'There do be a great company there, nowadays, so I hear tell.'

'I wonder what he means by that,' I said.

Simon shrugged, kicking his horse to move a little faster. It had become clear during the day that his mount, though even tempered and willing enough, was inclined to be lazy.

'What counts for a great company in this rural backwater?' Simon said. 'Lady Elizabeth, her waiting woman, and a couple of servants? Probably the greatest wonder they have seen this ten years!'

I laughed. Simon was a Londoner to his very marrow. If he believed the southern part of Hertfordshire to be rural, what would he have made of the great wastes of Muscovy through which I had travelled? Or even the countryside of Portugal, across which I had ridden in search of my sister? By comparison, the road from London to St Albans – which, despite what he said, carried a fair amount of traffic, mounted and afoot – seemed almost urban.

We soon reached the ford and splashed across it, the water reaching not quite to the horses' knees. By the signs – fallen sections of bank and draggled grass – the stream must have risen higher after the storm, but was now subsiding again. The willow copse stood on the far side, and just beyond it was the lane leading off to the right.

'Does Master Mylles come from these parts?' Simon asked.

'Nay, I have heard him speak of family in Hampshire, and I think he has held office in the past in Southampton. Or was it Poole? I have only met his wife once. Mistress Alice. She comes from the Isle of Wight, I remember me. She is younger than he. When Sir Francis was selling some of his more scattered properties, Francis Mylles bought this one because it is quite near London. He still holds some government offices, though I am not quite sure what, so it was more convenient than returning to family lands away in Hampshire.'

As we drew nearer to the house, we could hear a medley of voices, old and young, interrupted with shouts and bursts of laughter. It seemed the innkeeper was right about there being a large company in residence.

The last part of the lane led through a tunnel of pleached lime trees, so that we came out from shadow into full sun, to be confronted by a modern house of timber and mellow red brick, standing on a slight rise beyond a garden. This occupied two broad terraces, that nearest the house filled with rose bushes, shrubs trimmed into neat topiary shapes, and a riot of summer flowers, while the lower terrace, nearer to us, was mainly a close mown lawn. It was here that the noisy company stood about in scattered groups, clearly engaged in a game of *jeu de mail*. It seemed I had been not far out when I had reassured Lady Frances about her daughter's pastimes.

This busy crowd could not be simply Francis Mylles's family, however. I knew that there were six children who had survived infancy, four boys and two girls, well spaced out in age, for the eldest boy must have been nearly of an age with me, while the youngest boy and girl would be about nine or ten.

But who were all these others?

'We have stumbled on a family gathering, it seems,' Simon murmured to me, reining in his horse.

'I think you may have the right of it,' I said, 'for although most of them are strangers to me, I do recognise that man, over by the clipped yew hedge. It is Thomas Fleming, Francis Mylles's brother-in-law. They married two sisters. Master Fleming is a lawyer, a man of some standing in the world of the law courts. Sir Francis sometimes had dealings with him. I suppose all these others must be his family.'

There seemed too many people to count. Mistress Mylles and another lady (so like her that she must be Mistress Fleming) were seated on a bench near the hedge, talking to Lawyer Fleming and watching the sport on the lawn in front of them. A gaggle of older boys and young women were wielding their mallets in what looked like a somewhat dangerous fashion, while the younger children dodged about, in and out amongst the players, getting in their way.

Then Francis Mylles, who had been standing with his back to us, turned and came striding around the edge of the lawn, neatly side-stepping a ball.

'Kit Alvarez, by all the saints!' he said. 'What brings you into Hertfordshire?'

I swung down from Hector and tossed the reins to Simon, who stayed where he was as I walked forward to Mylles. He clapped me on the shoulder and drew me toward his brother-in-law, without waiting for an answer.

'Thomas, are you acquaint with Dr Alvarez? He and I worked together for Sir Francis for several years. He is as clever a code-breaker as Thomas Phelippes, and a licensed physician as well.'

We made our bows. I had seen Fleming only in the distance before, but I now detected that air of wary containment you see in men of the law. On the one hand they will argue *this*, but when it suits, they will also argue *that*. Its opposite.

Mylles turned to me again. 'Are you but passing, on your way to St Albans, perhaps? Or have you come to see me?'

'I am always glad to see you, Francis,' I said, 'and it has been many months, but in fact I am come to see the Lady Elizabeth, on behalf of the Countess of Essex.'

'Well, as you can see, the child is there.'

He pointed to a group of giggling children, who were dancing about one of the young men, blocking his game. From his strong resemblance to Thomas Fleming, I thought he must be his eldest son, perhaps a little younger than myself.

'My friend Simon Hetherington and I are enjoying a country ride,' I said, 'and Lady Frances asked that I might deliver a letter and a packet to her daughter. She is worried that Lady Elizabeth has not written to her.'

He grinned. 'I know my wife has urged her to send a letter, but she has been caught up amongst all these young folk.'

'Master Hetherington,' he said, looking up at Simon, 'I will fetch a groom to take your horses. Do you both come inside out of this heat and take some refreshment.'

He crooked a finger at one of the younger boys. 'John, run and fetch a groom to the horses.'

With the minimum of fuss, the horses were led away to the stable and we were escorted into a small parlour overlooking the garden, Master Fleming accompanying us. We assured Mylles that we had recently dined lavishly in Abbots Langley, but nevertheless Mistress Alice came in, accompanied by a maid carrying a tray with a glass flagon of golden wine, its sides bedewed, and a plate of sweetmeats.

'Cool wine, in summer!' Simon said, as he took the first sip from a Venetian glass.

'Aye, we have a cold spring which bursts out from a rocky bank behind us here,' Mylles said. 'Some previous owner of the house, mayhap Sir Francis himself, contrived racks to hold wine flagons in a little basin beneath it.' He smiled. 'It is quite a luxury.'

I thought the whole house and grounds represented a state of luxury very different from the Francis Mylles I had known in Seething Lane, often as grey and careworn as Sir Francis himself.

'Living as Lord of the Manor suits you, Francis,' I said. 'You have grown ten years younger.'

He laughed. 'Aye, and plumper, too. But I still have duties in London, various offices which make demands on my time, yet I am here as often as I may be. Summer is usually free of those duties.'

'As I find also,' Thomas Fleming said, 'in between the law terms. Alice, my dear, will you not join us?'

Mistress Mylles shook her head. 'I have sent for Lady Elizabeth and her waiting woman, so that Dr Alvarez may speak to them. I will go and see whether the child has been made presentable.' She smiled shyly at me. 'I am afraid we let the children run a little wild in the country.'

I returned her smile. 'That is exactly what I hoped for, when I suggested to Lady Frances that she should send the child here. I am sure it can do her nothing but good.' I had brought the letter and parcel with me, and now laid them on the table. 'When I have given these to Lady

Elizabeth, perhaps you could ask her, and her waiting woman also, to write a few lines to the Countess?'

'That I will certainly do,' she said, going out with her maid and leaving the four of us to enjoy our wine. The maid shut the door behind them.

'Before the child comes,' I said, turning to Mylles, 'there is another matter on which I would like to ask your advice.'

I could hardly ask Lawyer Fleming to leave, but perhaps his thoughts might be useful.

'It concerns a strange case of a man murdered while lying as a patient at St Bartholomew's hospital, and his apothecary being accused of the crime.'

As briefly as I could, I recounted the story, calling on Simon to tell what he had learned from Bart's gatekeeper.

'And how can I help?' Mylles asked, when I had finished.

'I know you are no longer in the intelligence service,' I said, 'but I thought you might still know something of this Josiah Gurdin from the time when you worked with Sir Francis. I am certain that he showed all the signs of being an intelligencer. And perhaps you can throw some light on this tangle, for the more I think about it, the more confused I become.'

Mylles glanced briefly at his brother-in-law. *Why should he do that?* I wondered.

'And what is your interest in the case, Kit?' Mylles asked.

'Only that the apothecary accused of adding the hemlock to the febrifuge tincture is an old friend of mine. We worked together at St Barthomew's. When the soldiers were brought to us there after the disastrous siege of Sluys, Peter Lambert and I spend an entire night caring together for the injured. He even helped with an amputation, which was far beyond his responsibilities. I know he is innocent in this matter, and I want to see it proven.'

'Now that it is established there was such a visitor as the apothecary claimed,' Master Fleming said, 'then it would be difficult to make a convincing case against him. A good lawyer could soon direct attention elsewhere. What was the outcome of the inquest, do you know?'

'It was adjourned,' I said. 'I suppose that means a verdict could not be reached.'

'That is correct.'

'But, of course,' I said, 'until the true murderer can be found, suspicion will hang over Peter Lambert. He has still not been reinstated to his position at the hospital, although for the moment he and his wife and child are permitted to remain in their cottage, which belongs to St Bartholomew's.'

I turned to Francis Mylles. 'Since we were coming here anyway, I thought to ask you . . . Did you ever come across this Josiah Gurdin when you worked for Sir Francis? I did not. His name is quite unknown to me.'

Mylles glanced again at Fleming, then looked down at his glass, swirling the last of the wine around in it.

'Nay, I never heard of him in Sir Francis's time, Kit.'

'Ah, well.' I sighed. 'I thought it was worth the asking.'

'However,' he said, 'I have heard of him since.'

My heart gave a little jerk of surprise. Apart from Simon's discovery of another witness to the visitor, it was the first chink of light thrown on a matter wreathed in shadows.

'You have!'

'Aye.' He hesitated again. 'I have not entirely abandoned intelligence work, Kit. Some months ago Lord Burghley approached me about another affair, one of the Catholic agents Sir Francis had suspected of trying to enter the country. There had been a sighting of a man who might have been this agent, landing at Felixstowe. I had some dealings with his lordship then, and from time to time since. The man Gurdin was indeed one of his agents, your conjecture was quite correct.'

'And you are certain he was one of the Cecils' own agents, not some spy introduced into their household by the Earl of Essex?'

'Quite certain. Gurdin had been with them for a number of years. I believe even before Sir Francis's death and the Earl's attempt to take over his intelligence service.'

He drank the last of his wine and set down his glass firmly on the table.

'Thomas Phelippes has made a serious mistake,' he said, 'throwing in his lot with Essex.'

'That is also what I think,' I said. 'But I understand Poley forestalled him with the Cecils, and Anthony Bacon was most anxious to engage Phelippes in the service he was setting up for Essex.'

I paused, wondering whether I dared ask my next question, or whether it might be taken as an accusation of dishonesty on the part of the Cecils, but I decided to venture it.

'Is Lord Burghley now in possession of Sir Francis's secret files?' I said, then held my breath.

'Aye, so I believe.' He shot me a glance. 'I have not been told how he came by them, but I can guess.'

'So can I. Poley.'

He shrugged. 'Probably. However, that is all past history. We live in a different world now, and this struggle between the Earl and the Cecils is a danger to the State, and, I believe, to the safety of Her Majesty. Jesu knows, there have been plots enough in the past to assassinate her. If these lions are so intent on tearing each other apart, they may let their attention slip from their real business.'

'We are in agreement on that as well.' I grimaced. 'I wish we were back where we used to be. You and Thomas Phelippes should not be working against each other, and Nick Berden should not be selling poultry!'

He laughed. 'Nor he should! His talents are wasted amongst his chickens. But now let us think more carefully about this case you put before us. Master Hetherington,' he turned to Simon, 'tell us again *exactly* how this fellow, the

97

gatekeeper, described the man who came in the night to visit Josiah Gurdin in the hospital.'

Simon repeated what the gatekeeper had told him. 'Although it confirms that there was such a man,' he said, 'it is very little to go on. How can one hope to identify the right man from such a general description? I do not think it can be done.'

'Not easily,' Mylles agrees. 'And you say that Nick Berden is setting his men to find out what they can, Kit?'

'Aye, but like us he thinks it near impossible.'

'Hmm.' Mylles picked up the wine flask and shared out the rest between our glasses. I was glad I had eaten a substantial dinner to absorb the wine, for I had no wish to fall off Hector on the ride back to London.

'I think we may safely say that we have partially untangled your problem, Kit. I can speak for Gurdin being a trusted agent of the Cecils, no spy from outside, so that disposes of one of your theories.'

He held up his hand, and counted the possibilities off on his fingers.

'What remains? First, he was killed by one of Essex's men as part of the rivalry between the two factions. Second, he was killed by a papist agent, perhaps because he had a part in the arrest of one of their own. Third, he was killed for some reason in his personal life, in no way related to his intelligence work.'

We were all silent for a few minutes, then I said slowly, 'There is a fourth possibility.'

'And that is?'

'He was killed by one of the Cecils' own men because he had discovered something they did not want known.'

I swallowed uncomfortably. Had I gone too far? Now that it seemed Mylles was working for Lord Burghley?

He looked at me thoughtfully. 'That too is a possibility. I do not know what dangerous secret Gurdin might have discovered, but if he *did* . . . Well, it might come to that. The Cecils would need to have good reason to

98

do such a thing, but if they felt they had reason enough –
say, if they thought the Queen might be in danger – then
they would not hesitate. His lordship is grown more
cautious in his old age, but his son, despite his weak
physical appearance, is a man of determined and fixed
purpose. If necessary, he can be ruthless.'

I had heard this about Sir Robert Cecil, though I had
no experience of it myself.

'But . . . a trusted man of their own . . .?'

'If it seemed inescapable, aye.'

'It would account for one thing which has always
troubled me,' Simon ventured. Most of the time we had
been talking, he had kept silence, except when asked a
direct question.

'What is that?' Mylles said.

'The steward of the Burghley household said that no
one had been sent to the hospital to enquire about Gurdin or
visit him. Does that not strike you as strange? If he was a
valued member of that household?'

'Aye,' Mylles said. 'It does.'

Any further discussion of the murder and its ramifications
was brought to an end by the arrival of Lady Elizabeth
Sidney and her waiting woman, Mistress Godliff. The child
made her curtseys, then smiled happily at me.

'Dr Alvarez, I am so glad you told Mama I should
come to stay in the country! It is much better here than in
London.'

'And you are looking very well on it, my lady,' I
said.

Indeed, she had blossomed in the short time she had
been here. When I had seen her at Walsingham House she
had been somewhat pale, and thin for her age, but already
her face had filled out a little, and her eyes and skin glowed
with health. I wished I could send all my little Southwark
waifs to spend some time here in the clean air of the
country.

'Your mother is worried that you have not written to her,' I said. 'I have brought you a letter from her, and also this parcel. I would like you to write something in answer, however short, and tell her how you fare.'

I handed them both to her and she quickly broke the seal on the letter, although she did not read it at once. The parcel was wrapped and tied in a piece of canvas, which the waiting woman helped her to undo. Inside was a doll with a beautifully carved wooden head, dressed in a fine gown such as a lady at Court might wear. A whole bundle of clothes cascaded out of the parcel and fell to the floor, setting the child crawling about under the table to gather them up.

'Get up, my lady!' Mistress Godliff cried. 'That is most unseemly.'

Lady Elizabeth ignored her. 'I cannot find the other blue satin shoe.'

Simon crawled under the table to join her. 'Here it is, my lady. And is this her ruff?'

He stuck his head out from beneath the table, holding on the tip of his finger a pleated and starched ruff not much bigger than a walnut.

'Oh, I thank you, sir!' the child exclaimed, and promptly kissed Simon, who blushed.

'My lady!'

The waiting woman stooped and hauled her charge out from beneath the table. I grinned at Simon and winked, causing him to blush even more as he climbed back on to his chair.

'Mistress Godliff,' I said, 'will you take Lady Elizabeth to write a letter to her mother? We must be away soon. And you must write as well, for the Countess has heard nothing from you since you arrived here.' I did not trouble to conceal the disapproval in my voice, and the woman had the grace to look somewhat ashamed.

When they were gone, I turned to Mylles.

'I thank you for clearing at least one point about Josiah Gurdin, Francis.'

100

'I am afraid we have not progressed much beyond that,' he said. 'However, I shall keep my ears open. I should be in London again before long, and I shall make a few discreet enquiries, see what I can learn about Gurdin and his position in Lord Burghley's household, although, like you, I think it will be nigh impossible to trace the murderer.'

He turned to Fleming. 'And what say you, Thomas, as to the case against the apothecary? Do you think the hospital authorities are likely to pursue it?'

Fleming shook his head. 'Difficult to say. If this other man cannot be found, they might resort to such an accusation, merely to demonstrate their willingness to assign the guilt somewhere, in order to placate the Cecils.'

'And would you be willing to act for him? This Peter Lambert?'

Before Fleming could answer, I leaned forward anxiously. 'I am afraid Peter would be in no position to engage a lawyer!'

Fleming gave a small smile. 'We shall see. It is an interesting case. I should like to see what comes of it.'

I was not sure whether that meant he would be willing to take on the case without a fee, but I decided it would be best if I left the matter for the present.

'While we wait for the little maid to compose the letter to her mother,' Mylles said, 'let me show you the house and garden, if it would please you.'

I glanced at Simon, who smiled and nodded. 'I thank you, Francis,' I said, 'we would indeed be pleased.'

Thomas Fleming took his leave of us, as Mylles began the tour of the house. It was a substantial property, larger than I had understood when he had first told us in Seething Lane that he had purchased it, but it was clearly already a comfortable family home, filled with half finished needlework, and piles of books, and a scattering of children's toys, the very home I should have liked to live in myself. Before we had gone far, we were joined by a young dog, a black spaniel, who took considerable interest in sniffing my hose. No doubt the scent of Rikki lingered there.

I lost count of the number of chambers, but clearly there was room enough for the large family of Flemings to visit, as well as for the Mylles family. We did not climb up to the attics, where I assumed the servants had their quarters. There was a whole suite of rooms attached to the kitchen, which reminded me of the Fitzgeralds' house, where I had briefly posed as a tutor to the children.

Outside, we walked round the formal gardens, but avoided the grassy area, where archery butts had now been set up. Behind and to one side of the house were the usual outbuildings – stables and tack room, dairy, brewery, laundry, barn. In a small meadow four milch cows were grazing. Further away stood a group of three cottages.

'As you can see,' Mylles said, 'I have no land for farming, but should the adjacent property come up for sale when the elderly owner dies, I am considering buying it.'

'And give up your government offices to become a farmer?' I grinned at him.

'Aye, 'tis a difficult decision. I still feel a duty to serve Her Majesty, although the quiet life of the country appeals as well. I gave up one quiet life to serve in London.'

'And what was that?' Simon asked.

'I was sub-warden at All Souls College in Oxford. Indeed, I might have passed my years in academic study, had Sir Francis not persuaded me to join him.'

This was something I had never known about Francis Mylles.

'So you might have been Vice Chancellor of Oxford by now!' I said. 'And the learned author of many books!'

He laughed. 'That is uncertain. What I would have lost would be wife and children, so that I have never regretted my change of course in life.'

As we came back into the house through a garden door, the child Elizabeth ran up to me, holding out a folded and slightly crumpled letter. Her fingers were liberally stained with ink.

'Here is my letter for Mama, Dr Alvarez, and will you please tell her that I am very, very sorry not to have written before, but I have been so *busy*! And everything is quite in a whirl!'

I laughed. The child was well away from Essex and his whip. I hoped she could stay here a long while. Though I knew the separation would bear hard on her mother.

'I will tell her so, my lady,' I said. 'Best make sure you scrub all that ink off your fingers before you touch those fine clothes for your poppet.'

She made a face. 'Mistress Godliff has put them all away until I wrote my letter, but I shall say I must have them now, must I not?'

'Indeed you must. Your mother would wish it.'

I looked firmly at the waiting woman, who was eying me coldly. 'And you, mistress, have a letter for me to take as well?'

She held it out. 'It is here, doctor. And you may tell the Countess that the Lady Elizabeth receives the best of care at my hands.'

I inclined my head slightly. I was sure the woman did enough by her own reckoning, though there seemed little warmth in it. However, it was more than made up for by the boisterous kindliness of the rest of the household.

'It is time we were away,' I said to Mylles. 'Thank you for your hospitality and your advice on the matter of Peter Lambert.'

'It was little enough,' he said. He turned to Simon, 'And have you any new pieces at the Rose, Master Hetherington?'

Simon grinned. 'Will Shakespeare writes his plays like a man possessed. He scarce has the time to be a player these days.'

'Ah, with Marlowe gone, there is no one to rival him. When I am next in London, I shall pay a visit to your playhouse, to see what new is afoot.'

'Speak my name to the doorkeeper,' Simon said, 'and he will see that you have the best places, at the centre of the first gallery.'

'I shall do so.'

A groom brought our horses round to the front of the house and we mounted. Mylles laid his hand on my horse's neck.

'A fine fellow,' he said, patting Hector. 'I shall look you up when I come to London, Kit, and if I discover anything more, either from the Cecils or about the possible identity of the killer, I will write to you.'

Then, with a final wave, and circling well out of range of the archers, we set off on the ride back to London. I felt a sense of relief that Simon had been treated with courtesy throughout our visit, since players often met with rudeness and disparagement, for despite the rise in the popularity of the playhouses, and the Queen's own patronage, many people continued to regard players as no better than rogues and vagabonds. Working as he had amongst all conditions of men in Walsingham's day, I had expected Francis Mylles himself to receive us both with warmth and pleasure. I had been uneasy at first about Lawyer Fleming, but he too had spoken to Simon as to a gentlemen. I suppose lawyers also have to do with all manner of men. I knew that Simon, like my other friends amongst the players, was hardened to discourtesy, but I still found it offensive, and was glad none had marred our visit to the manor.

During the return journey we did not stop for a further meal at the White Hart, as Lady Frances had urged. It was still early, and we had dined so well that neither of us was hungry. However, about five miles from London we stopped at a village ale house for a drink and to rest the horses briefly, although they still seemed fresh enough, even Simon's hired hack. Adding together the miles there and back it was quite a long ride, but they had had two periods of rest and two feeds of oats, so it had not tried them unduly.

'I shall return my mount to the livery stables,' Simon said, as we made our way more slowly through the increasing crowds on the road near London. 'Shall you call on the Countess?'

'Aye, I must take her these letters. Best you do not wait, but go straight home without me.'

'I shall. We have neither of us been to church this Sunday.'

I nodded. It was an obligation for every good citizen who was not bedridden to attend church at least once of a Sunday. Those who did not were reckoned recusants, and therefore probably secret Catholics. Increasing fines were imposed, depending on their stubbornness.

'We will be in time for the evening service at St Mary Overy,' I said.

'Aye, I will see you there.'

When we reached the end of Seething Lane, I turned toward Walsingham House, while Simon continued on to the livery stable. In the yard I slid from the saddle with some relief. I had had little opportunity to ride of late, and I found myself somewhat stiff and sore. I should be all the more aware of it tomorrow.

'I will see to Hector,' Harry said, unbuckling the saddle bag and passing me my satchel of medicines and my empty knapsack.

'Nay,' I said. 'I know you have work enough of your own, with all those horses of the Earl's, as well as the family's own. How many does he keep here?'

'Six at the moment. Sometimes more. Once we had a dozen, which meant there were not enough stalls. We had to double up the ponies and also the carriage horses.' He wrinkled his nose. 'It do make for a fair amount of work. Mind, the Earl owns some very fine horseflesh.'

'I will rub Hector down and fill his manger,' I said. 'He has already had oats today. Is the Lady Frances at home?'

'Aye, she was asking if you was back, mebbe half an hour ago. Said you was to go up, and you know the way to her rooms.'

'I will so,' I said. 'I have a letter for her from her daughter.'

'You saw Master Mylles, then? How does he fare?'

I laughed. 'Very well indeed. Fine and sleek as any country gentleman, with a house full of guests. He's to be in London soon. I expect he will call on Dame Ursula.'

I knew that Mylles had spent time after Sir Francis's death helping his widow with her financial affairs and fending off spurious claimants for imaginary debts.

'I'll likely see him then. 'Tis strange not to have him about the place. He must have been with Sir Francis near thirty years, long before I came.'

'I learned today that he came here directly from a position in Oxford.'

'That's the place with the colleges? 'Twouldn't have suited him. He always had his head together with the master, seeking out spies and suchlike.'

I grinned. It had always been a marvel to me the way everything that went on within the house was known by the stable lads. Perhaps the stable lads at Burghley House might be our best source of information about the killing of Josiah Gurdin.

Hector was clearly glad to be back in his own stall, although I could sense that he had enjoyed his day away from London. I did not linger over rubbing him down and seeing that his manger was filled with clean hay. After I had drawn up a bucket of fresh water from the well in the yard, I gave him a final pat and made my way to the house.

The first part of the way was familiar: up the backstairs to my old office, and not far past it to the room Sir Francis had used. I noticed that the Turkey rugs on the floor were looking rubbed and even a little dusty, but I supposed no one often came this way, unless they used it as a route to the stables. Beyond this corridor I had only ventured once, when Lady Frances had led me to her rooms. On one other occasion I had entered the house by the front door with Dr Nuñez, when we had brought Sir Francis the despatch from one of the Nuñez ships, with news of the imminent arrival of the Spanish fleet.

The rest of the house was unknown to me, and this evening it seemed very quiet and somehow melancholy. I remembered it busy, with the coming and going of Walsingham, Phelippes, Mylles and Gregory, and all those whose work was based here, together with the arrival of agents bearing intercepted letters or full of information gleaned in a hundred different ways, honest and dishonest. It was like a hive of bees, where that information was gathered and turned into its essence like honey, as Phelippes and I decoded, Gregory carved his seals, and Sir Francis with the assistance of Mylles and Phelippes planned their projections. It seemed wrong that it should all have collapsed with Walsingham's death, like a house of dust.

Perhaps Sir Francis must carry some blame for this. Should he not have prepared a successor? I believed he had married off his daughter to Essex to secure her financial future, but I could not imagine he would ever have planned for Essex to take over the intelligence network. He had himself been appointed to the task many years before by Lord Burghley, so it would have seemed natural to have planned for the future with his lordship. Given Burghley's advancing years, for he was older than Walsingham, that future must lie with Sir Robert Cecil. He was the second son, but had always been trained up for service in government. His elder brother would inherit the title, but it was said that, although amiable enough, he had not a quarter of Sir Robert's intelligence.

Yet if anything had indeed been planned for the future with the Cecils, it would not have been necessary for all our secret files to be stolen. Walsingham must have left unfinished business behind. Poor man, he had been very ill those last years, valiantly working on through crippling pain. Service to the Queen had killed him as surely as any dagger thrust. Or a dose of hemlock in a glass of medicine.

Reflecting on this, I made my way, somewhat nervously, past silent rooms in the direction I thought I remembered Lady Frances taking me. Once, I caught sight of a man servant whisking away quietly down a staircase. At last I reached what I believed to be the door of the Countess's parlour and tapped hesitantly.

'Come!'

She was seated by the window, some needlework on her lap, but there was no needle in her hands, which lay idle on the arms of the chair.

'Ah, Kit!' she exclaimed, standing up. The crewel work slid unheeded to the floor. 'You have seen her? She is well?'

'Very well, my lady,' I said, handing her the two letters. 'Rosy as a ripe apple, and surrounded by playmates. Not only all the Mylles children. Francis Mylles's brother-in-law was also there, with his large family. Thomas Fleming.'

'I remember me. Fleming the lawyer. He helped Francis Mylles settle some of those claims on my husband's estate. 'Tis said he will make a judge one day.'

'You need have no worries about your daughter, my lady. She asked me to tell you that she was very, very sorry she had not written, but she has been very busy.'

Lady Francis laughed, but looked wistful. I fancy it made her sad that her daughter could be so merry away from her mother. I handed her the two letters.

'You saw Mistress Godliff, too?'

'Aye. She wished me to reassure you that Lady Elizabeth was receiving the best possible care.'

She smiled wryly. 'A very punctilious woman, but not very warm hearted. I am sure she will do the best by Elizabeth, according to her own lights, but she has not a natural affinity with children. Elizabeth misses her first nurse, who was very loving, but she died, sadly, two years ago.'

'I will leave you to read your letters, my lady,' I said, starting to back toward the door.

'Nay, stay a little, Kit. Please sit down. Once I have read the letters I would like you to tell me everything about the Mylles household and what you saw of Elizabeth.'

I did as I was bid, taking a chair a little withdrawn from hers, and watched her reading the letters. She did not at once seize her daughter's letter, as I had expected, but laid it to one side, carefully opening and reading the waiting woman's letter first. I smiled to myself. I saw that she was like me, always saved the most precious thing until last. It made me warm to her even more.

After she had read both letters, Lady Francis laid them aside on her work table with a sigh, and spent some minutes in silence, looking out of the window, before turning to me.

'And you say she is well and happy, Kit?'

'Indeed she is, my lady,' I said. 'There are more than a dozen other young people there at present, and although the older ones are near grown up, there was a rout of young ones playing together, and up to mischief too, I'll be bound. Mistress Godliff may be somewhat rigid and stern, but Mistress Alice is a kind, motherly soul, who understands that children need the chance to run about in the fresh air. I know some merchants' wives here in the City who are quite as formal as Mistress Godliff. For the sake of their health, I am obliged to urge that the children be allowed to spend as much time out of doors as possible. When there is a fine garden for such sport, nothing could be better for children. I could wish that the sad urchins I see in Southwark had the same, instead of the dirty alleys and cramped foul hovels they know as home.'

I bit my lips and lapsed into silence. It was not my place to rant about the conditions of the Southwark poor to Lady Frances, but she looked interested and concerned.

'I have never truly seen Southwark,' she said. 'Of course, I have often ridden through it when we have travelled to our home at Barn Elms, but I fear I have paid

109

little attention to the streets which lie just over the Bridge from here. That is remiss of me. Are the children very neglected and deprived?'

'Some mothers are so downtrodden that they are past caring,' I said, 'but there are others who do try to do their best for their children with very scanty means. It is the custom amongst the people there that the man should always have the best share of the food. The meat, if there is any. The women and children get by on bread and dried beans, or, if they are lucky, cheap offal from the butcher.'

'But the children need the nourishment!' she exclaimed. 'And if the women are with child . . .'

'They are almost invariably with child,' I said grimly, 'though many of the infants do not survive. You must understand, my lady, that it is not entirely selfishness on the men's part. If the man does not work, then the family will all starve, unless the women can find work as laundry maids or daily servants. And the work the men do is heavy work, in the tanneries and dyeries and brickworks. It needs strength.'

She shook her head sadly. 'I fear my life has been very sheltered and selfish. I have never even given thought to those folk across the river. I know that the unpleasant industries have long been banned from the City, because of their foul smells and the stinking effluent they produce, but I am ashamed that I had not thought about the people who must work there. Is there nothing that can be done?'

'There have been benefactors,' I said. 'Like Sir Richard Whittington, who endowed the lying-in ward for unmarried mothers. And even now good citizens contribute to the funds of the hospital and its almshouses. When the monastery was brought down, the benevolent works of the monks went with it.'

'I shall try to help. I will speak to our steward about making a gift to the hospital, perhaps especially for the children. Is there no help, no future for those poor mites?'

I smiled at her. 'Any help you can give will be welcomed by Superintendent Ailmer with open arms, my lady. We have just had an inspection by the governors, who hold the purse strings, but individual benefactions can come directly to St Thomas's, to do good. As for the children's future . . . 'tis an irony that the abandoned or orphaned often have the brightest hopes, for they have a good chance that they will be sent to Christ's Hospital, where they not only find a home but are educated out of the world of ignorance and poverty into which they were born. They are the lucky ones.'

'I see I have much to learn,' she said. 'Now that my daughter is safely out of the Earl's reach, I should not forget that there are other children who are suffering and hungry, not half a mile from my own comfortable home.'

'I fear such children will always be with us, my lady,' I said, 'but we can alleviate the suffering of a few of them.'

'Indeed, we must try.'

To my surprise, she rose and took both my hands in hers. 'Let the men fight over their tawdry triumphs of noisy power. There are quieter and better triumphs to be achieved by women.'

Chapter Six

*A*s I walked across the Bridge, hurrying a little that I might not be late for the evening service at St Mary Overy, I found my mind a whirl of confusing thoughts. It had been a strange day. Seeing Francis Mylles so firmly established in his country manor had forced me to recognise just how far things had changed since the old days at Seething Lane. Yet it seemed Mylles still had his finger in a pie or two. I had not expected to hear that he was now working, however rarely, for Lord Burghley. It made me very uneasy that he and Phelippes were now allied with the opposing camps in the internecine war over control of the intelligence service. How I wished that Phelippes were not working for Essex!

Then there was that odd exchange of looks with Lawyer Fleming. I was sure I had not imagined it. Was Fleming somehow also part of the Cecils' faction? Then I recalled a strange occurrence just a matter of weeks earlier, shortly after the murder of Christopher Marlowe. I had gone to see Thomas Phelippes, convinced that Marlowe's death had not been a mere accident in a brawl but deliberate murder by Ingram Friser, in which Robert Poley was also implicated. And I had found Lord Burghley and Sir Robert Cecil in conference with Phelippes, seemingly on most friendly terms. What lay behind that? I had been warned by them, in the most polite and reasonable terms, to let the matter of Marlowe's death rest. To let it be forgotten. A mere accident.

And Poley was employed by the Cecils.

For all I knew, so was Ingram Friser.

But was not Marlowe also?

According to Francis Mylles, Josiah Gurdin was a trusted agent of the Cecils. Like Poley. Like Marlowe. That is, if anyone was trusted in the corrupt world which the intelligence service – or services – had now become. Oh, Sir Francis, if you could only have kept Lord Death at bay a little longer!

And now I was finding myself embroiled with Lady Frances. It was inevitable, with my horse stabled in Seething Lane, that I should occasionally encounter members of the Walsingham and Devereux families, but I had not foreseen that I might become entangled in their affairs. For preference, I should have liked to keep as great a distance from Essex as possible. Instead I had found myself sought as an ally by Lady Frances in removing her daughter to a place of safety, well away from Essex. This unsought for alliance, it now seemed, unfortunately, had not ceased with the mere writing of a doctor's recommendation. I hoped fervently that Essex was unaware of my connection with his wife.

I could not have done otherwise than to make the recommendation, and I was glad to help both the child and her mother, but I was now sliding in too deep. Lady Frances knew my true identity. Having thought that Sara Lopez was the only surviving holder of my secret, apart from the odious Poley, I was now confronted with the wife of one of the most powerful men in England, who held my fate in her hands. One word from her could expose me to a charge of heresy for masquerading as a man. I believed her to be a good woman, and an honest one, but clearly she went in fear of her husband. If he should notice me, turn against me, seek to harm me . . .

I shivered.

Her last remark, about what women might achieve, had sounded an unmistakable warning in my head. Aye, it would be excellent if she should take an interest in the hospital, and even become a benefactor, but I felt uneasily that she foresaw some alliance between us *as women*. I must put a stop to that at once, for if ever the slightest hint should become public, I was finished. Somehow, I must keep myself at arm's length from her, physician to patient, but how to do that, without offence, I could not think.

The bell for evening service at St Mary Overy began to ring as I reached the southern end of the Bridge and I quickened my steps. Since my father's death I had been a back-slider from the Jewish services I had attended with him, and I had also stopped attending those informal meetings at the synagogue organised by Dr Nuñez, long before his own death. The legal obligation in England to attend church meant that my father and I had gone on Sundays to St Bartholomew the Great, and since I had moved south of the river I had gone either to morning or evening service at St Mary Overy, the parish church for my lodgings.

What had begun as a duty had become more a pleasure. These quiet Protestant services suited my own temperament in a way that neither the Jewish services nor the Catholic services in Portugal had done. Our Jewish services, both in Portugal under the Spanish invaders, and in London, had about them an uncomfortable air of intense secrecy and defiance, while I found the Catholic services we attended in Portugal as *novos cristãos* theatrically flamboyant, with their incense and chanting and strident colours.

The Protestant churches of London were mostly quiet, tranquil places, where I could go through the motions of the service while simply allowing my mind to grow calm and peaceful. They seemed to refresh my heart and soul as a draught of cold spring water refreshes an exhausted body on a hot day. Perhaps I was shallow, since my mind seemed to centre on this peace and quietness, when I should have been thinking about God, but my concept of Him was so confused by my tangled upbringing, that I was reluctant to plunge into deeper speculation.

114

I knew that Francis Mylles had leanings toward the Puritan viewpoint, but from what little I knew of them, I thought the Puritans overly severe and self-righteous, keen to ban all the simple pleasures from life. Mylles cannot have been too much committed to their doctrines, for it was evident that he attended the playhouse and did not scorn players like Simon, as any true blooded Puritan would have done.

I slipped into the back of the church with the last of the congregation, just as the bell for service ceased ringing. I could see Simon somewhere near the centre of the nave, while my nearest neighbour was one of the Winchester geese from Bessie Travis's whorehouse, for even whores must attend church. She was one of the younger girls, not more than fifteen or sixteen, and I noticed that she was praying earnestly.

When the service came to an end, I was filled with my usual calmness of spirit, which somewhat eased my earlier worries, and I waited quietly in the churchyard for Simon to emerge, since it took him longer to reach the door.

'So there you are,' he said, throwing a comradely arm around my shoulders. 'I wondered what had become of you.'

'After I saw to Hector,' I said, 'I took the letters to Lady Frances and she wanted me to stay and tell her about her daughter. As it happened we spoke more about the Southwark children. I think she may become a benefactor of St Thomas's.'

'That will surely be a good thing, will it not?'

'It will. It seems she has never realised the extent of poverty on this side of the river.'

'Hardly surprising. The rich have little cause to worry about those less fortunate than themselves. They lead an easy life, well protected in comfortable ignorance.'

'That is hardly the case with Lady Frances.' I felt myself compelled to defend her. 'Her life has been far from easy. She was only a small child with her parents in Paris when that bloody massacre of Protestants took place on St Bartholomew's Day. She and her mother had to make their escape to England through dreadful peril. Then she was married very young to Sir Philip Sidney, only to have him killed in Flanders and to miscarry her second child. And now she has been married off to that dangerous fool, the Earl of Essex, who mistreats both her and her child.'

I broke off. I should not have let that slip.

Simon slanted a sideways glance at me.

'Does he, indeed?'

'Forget that I said that,' I begged him. 'It was a matter of confidence which I should have kept to myself.'

'I have forgotten it already, although I had guessed for myself that something must lie behind this sudden removal of Lady Elizabeth to the country.'

We had turned aside to the hospital, so that I might collect Rikki from Tom Read. As always, he was delighted to see me, as if I had been away for a month, although I knew that he was far better fed on hospital scraps than on anything I could afford to give him at home.

As we walked back along the river and neared our lodgings, I said, 'Do you go to the Lion tonight? I own I am too tired.'

'Aye.' He laughed. 'I find I am aching from head to toe. I have not ridden so far since . . . since I know not when. And I must strut upon the stage tomorrow as if I were not on fire in every joint!'

'I have one onion left in my room. And there is some of the cheese and bread we took with us today.'

He tapped the ale jack which still hung from his belt. He should not have taken that into church. 'I'll go to the alehouse for this to be filled. And I have a pasty, though it may be a little stale.'

'So long as it is not rancid.'

'I bought it yesterday, and the weather has not been so hot of late.'

Combining our modest resources, we could contrive a scrappy supper, but it would suffice, after our lavish dinner at the White Hart.

'Fetch the ale,' I said, my foot on the lowest step to the Atkins house, 'and bring the pasty up to my room. I will fry the onion once I have a fire lit.'

In the end, having found I had some bacon fat, I fried pieces of the loaf along with the onion, for the bread was somewhat battered after a day in my knapsack. We layered slices of the cheese over the fried onion and bread while it was hot, and it was surprisingly good, with half a pasty on the side and washed down with the ale.

'Perhaps not such a feast as we might expect at the Lion,' Simon said, stretching out his legs as he drank the last of his ale, 'but it suited me well enough.' He laughed. 'By Jesu, that wine of Master Mylles's was very fine, was it not?'

'Aye.' I set the bowls on the floor for Rikki to lick, as a concession to his reproachful looks. I would need to heat some water to wash them before I went to bed. There was never time in the morning before I left for the hospital. Sometimes it can be trying, living in one room.

'It was an excellent wine,' I agreed. 'Francis Mylles is somewhat changed from the overworked secretary I remember from Sir Francis's time.'

'It was useful to learn what he knew about Josiah Gurdin,' Simon said.

'I suppose it simplifies the matter a little.' I shook my head. 'It still leaves open far too many possibilities. So many reasons he might have been killed. And no real hope of finding the killer.'

'Do you not think the coroner will press for an investigation? 'Tis not your responsibility, Kit.'

'I know it is not my responsibility, but I fear no one will take much pains to try to find the man. I agree with what you said to Mylles. It is very strange that no one from Lord Burghley's household came to visit Gurdin in the hospital.'

'Ah,' he said, 'but perhaps, after all, they did.'

I decided that the next day, after I finished at the hospital, I would call on Thomas Phelippes and see whether I might draw out some information from him about Josiah Gurdin and his possible killer. Knowing Phelippes of old, I suspected that he would be overburdened with work and would stay late, poring over intercepted letters and whatever foolish projections the Earl of Essex might be proposing.

I took Rikki with me, for he had always accompanied me to the office in Seething Lane, so I did not expect Phelippes to object. However, when I reached Phelippes's office in the Customs House, I was disconcerted to find not only Arthur Gregory there, as I had expected, but a very fine gentleman, unknown to me, wearing the most elaborate ruff I had ever seen outside the Court. The rest of his garments were similarly grand, and he turned on me a cold and calculating eye.

'My apologies, Thomas,' I said, starting to back away toward the door. 'I shall not disturb you if you are occupied with affairs.'

'Nay, do not go, Kit,' he said.

He turned to the gentleman. 'Master Bacon, may I present Dr Christoval Alvarez, of St Thomas's hospital? Also, of late, a code-breaker in the service of Sir Francis Walsingham. Kit, may I present Master Anthony Bacon?'

We bowed with stiff courtesy. I was conscious of Rikki at my heels, bristling a little with hostility about his neck, and I was glad I had kept on my long physician's gown, which always gave me confidence.

So this was Anthony, the elder by two years of the Bacon brothers. While the younger, Francis, had been quietly and methodically building himself a government and legal career here in England, Anthony had been living in France, where I knew he had served as one of Sir Francis's high-born overseas intelligencers. Some of his reports had passed through my hands, none of any very great significance, although I knew that he had cultivated the friendship of Henri, King of Navarre, who, at the time, was a possible heir to the French throne. Henri could be a valuable ally for England, since he was a Protestant. News had recently reached London, however, that Henri had converted to Catholicism, in order to secure the French throne, and thereby destroying any friendship with England and our Queen.

However, Anthony Bacon's comfortable life in France had come to an abrupt end last year, when the scandal of sodomy had engulfed his household, one of those guilty being Bacon himself. He would have gone to the fire as a convicted sodomite, had not Henri saved him, but his only hope for a future was escape to England. I had heard that he was now sharing his brother's chambers at Grey's Inn, where they had set up some kind of circle of *literati*, although Phelippes had told me that their intelligence service for Essex was also directed from there.

This, then, was the man who hoped to share with Essex the role of Sir Francis's successor. From what I knew of him, he was generally shrewd and intelligent, far more so than Essex, but like Essex he was vain, and his personal habits were not only vile and unlawful, but also dangerous. I eyed him warily. How deeply was he bemired in the struggle against the Cecils? It was unfathomable to me that he should align himself with Essex, when he was himself first cousin to Sir Robert Cecil.

'So,' Bacon said, looking me up and down, with a somewhat contemptuous curl to his lip. 'You are that Portigall refugee that Thomas Harriot thinks so clever.'

The sarcastic twist he gave to 'clever' was not lost on me. Of course he would know Harriot. These intellectuals in London clustered together like bees about a honey pot.

'Master Harriot was my tutor in mathematics when I was younger,' I said politely. 'He is too kind.'

'Hmph.' He sounded as though he gave little credit to Harriot's opinion of me, and turned away, dismissing me from his mind. 'Well, Phelippes, that is all for now. I leave the matter in your hands. You will report to me in . . . let us say two days' time.'

'It will take longer than that.' Phelippes spoke calmly, but I could see that he was holding his temper on a tight rein. 'For any meaningful outcome, it will take at least a week.'

'Two days for your first report,' Bacon said, ignoring him, 'then you may report again in a week.'

With a slight bow to Phelippes and quite ignoring Arthur and me, he swept out, donning a broad brimmed hat ornamented with a long curling plume as he went.

There was silence for a moment or two after the door closed behind him. Then Phelippes let out a long breath and Arthur smiled weakly.

'So that is Anthony Bacon,' I said, perching on a stool and laying my satchel of medicines on the floor by my feet. Rikki settled in his usual place in front of the fireplace, although on this summer's evening there was no fire. 'He is much as I expected. Only more so.'

Arthur smothered a laugh, and Phelippes ran his fingers up through his hair.

'Beggars cannot be choosers, Kit. A man must work for someone if he is to live.'

'A man might have done better to have chosen more carefully *who* he worked for. You should be with the Cecils, Thomas.'

He sighed. 'Too late. My lot is cast in with Essex now.'

Arthur and I exchanged a glance.

'Perhaps not forever,' Arthur said.

'Did I not find you in conference with Lord Burghley and Sir Robert, earlier this year?' I said. 'Were they seeking your services?'

This was really no affair of mine, but I hated to see him working for Essex. Or for Anthony Bacon either, who seemed cut from the same cloth, even if his lusts took a different turn.

'They wished to consult me about an old case of Sir Francis's,' Phelippes said stiffly. 'That was all. Arthur, is that seal ready?'

'Very nearly. I have but the edges to trim,' Arthur said mildly, and withdrew to his smaller office which opened off this main one.

'In the end, you know, the Cecils are bound to prevail,' I said. 'Essex has neither the mind nor the patience for intelligence work. He will be off after some new fashion any day now.'

Phelippes sat down at his desk and began randomly shifting his papers about, an uncharacteristic habit in so fastidious a man. 'Essex may not have a natural bent for intelligence work, Kit, but he knows just how important it is, and how much the Queen values it. Moreover, Anthony and Francis Bacon *do* have the talent for it. Anthony may dress like a cockscomb, but do not underestimate him, Kit.'

'Oh, I do not.'

I would be a fool to do so, for he came from one of the most powerful families in England, even if he held no noble title.

'I am always pleased to see you, Kit,' Phelippes said, 'but as you observe, I have a great deal of work in hand.' He gestured toward the usual piles of correspondence and reports. 'Unless you are here to help?'

I grinned. 'I am happy to give you an hour or two of my time, if in return you can cast some light on a problem of mine.'

'What is that?'

I turned over in my mind the best way to approach the matter of Josiah Gurdin. I could not come right out into the open and ask whether Essex had ordered the man's murder. I would need to work my way round it, crab like.

'I think you may have heard me speak of a friend of mine, from the time when I worked at St Bartholomew's,' I said. 'The young apothecary, Peter Lambert.'

I got up and went over to a table stacked with papers and began to sort them into those written in English, those in English with widely spaced lines (which meant there was a concealed message hidden between), and those still with their seals intact, which would be stolen despatches from England's enemies, awaiting Arthur's carefully unsealing.

'I remember you mentioning the name,' Phelippes said, 'but I have never met the man.'

'Nay, you would not have done. A patient has died in St Bartholomew's, and Peter was accused of poisoning him.'

'And did he?'

'Of course not! At first no one would believe Peter that the patient had a visitor shortly before he died. However, we have now established that there *was* such a visitor, seen by the gatekeeper.'

'We?'

I saw that I had caught Phelippes's interest, for he had stopped shuffling his papers.

'Simon Hetherington spoke to the gatekeeper, and I believe the man was then required to swear to it at the inquest, although I was not there.'

'And what has your friend the player to do with this?'

'Nothing,' I said, 'except to see an injustice avoided. Peter Lambert has been suspended from his position in the hospital, and his wife is expecting their second child. They live in a cottage belonging to St Bartholomew's.'

'I cannot see how I can help in this matter, Kit.' Phelippes looked genuinely puzzled.

'I had occasion, on quite another matter, to visit Francis Mylles yesterday, at his manor in Hertfordshire.'

'Indeed! Is he well?'

'Very well. Plump as a partridge.' I laughed. 'Every inch the lord of the manor, but I think he still hankers for the old days at times.'

'He does still hold some government offices, though I have not seen him these many months. Why were you calling on him?'

'It was another affair entirely, but I had taken my horse Hector out for a day's exercise in the country, and agreed to deliver a letter to the house. While I was there, I asked whether he knew anything of this man who was killed.'

'Why should he so?' Phelippes still looked puzzled, but curious.

'I had guessed that the man might be an intelligencer and thought Francis might have come across him in the past.'

'And had he?'

'Nay, he said he had not, in the past, but had done so more recently. I knew that the man was a member of Lord Burghley's household. And it seems Francis has, from time to time, offered some assistance to the Cecils.' I paused. 'Like you.'

By now Phelippes was beginning to look uncomfortable. 'This man was one of Lord Burghley's? Francis confirmed that? But, was he an intelligencer?'

'Aye.' I tapped the documents I had been sorting into neat piles and turned toward him, watching him closely. 'My instinct was correct. The man was an intelligencer. His name was Josiah Gurdin.'

Thomas Phelippes was adept at keeping his thoughts and feelings from his face, but I saw something, the merest flicker, in his eyes.

'Indeed?' He began shuffling those papers again, which did not fool me for a moment. He might not know Gurdin, but he had heard of him.

'So you see,' I said, drawing my stool a little closer to his desk and sitting down again, 'I thought you might know something of this man and why he was killed. And by whom.'

He said nothing at first, then drew a deep breath. 'I have never had dealings with Gurdin,' he said, 'but I admit I know the name. He has been the Cecils' man for some while, I believe. In fact, I think Sir Francis knew more than I did of his work, through his own collaboration with Lord Burghley, but Gurdin was never a part of our   service, merely dealing with small matters for Lord Burghley and his son.'

'Hardly small matters,' I said wryly, 'if they led to his death.'

'You cannot know that. In any case, it is no affair of yours or mine.'

'It is my affair if it can be proved who really killed Gurdin, so that Peter Lambert's name may be cleared.'

'In that,' he said, 'I cannot help you.'

'You are certain? Let us be honest with one another, Thomas. These two intelligence services, that of Essex and that of the Cecils, are at each other's throats. Is it too strange to speculate that an intelligencer of the Cecils might be . . . removed by one of Essex's men?'

'It is possible,' he admitted stiffly. 'If so, I know nothing of it.'

'But do you not run this intelligence service for Essex, under Anthony Bacon?'

'Aye, but they do not tell me everything.' He stared down at his hands, then looked up. His eyes were troubled. 'I concede that such a thing *might* be possible, but if so, I know nothing of it, not even a whisper. Might it not have been a papist agent who was responsible?'

'It might. There are several possibilities. And as no one seems to know much about this man Gurdin, there is no clear way to separate the wheat from the chaff. Still, you have made matters a little clearer.'

I smiled at him. I had no wish to be at odds with Thomas Phelippes, whom I regarded as a friend, and I believed he was telling me the truth. However, that did not mean that someone from Essex's faction might not have been the killer.

'Come,' I said. 'I promised you a couple of hours. What would you wish me to do? Hardly time enough to break a new code.'

He grinned, finally relaxing. 'Have you lost your touch? I can set you against the hour glass again. Nay, do you warm those reports of our own men over the candle to reveal their hidden ink, and we will see what they have to say. They will only be using our normal ciphers.'

I did as I was bid, holding one of the widely spaced letters above the warmth of the candle flame until the concealed message, written in lemon juice or milk or urine, began to appear in wavering brown letters. As Phelippes had said, it was in a code so familiar to me that I could read it as easily as the innocent letter within which it was hidden.

No further mention of Josiah Gurdin and his possible murderer was made until I was on the point of leaving, when Phelippes removed his spectacles and rubbed the bridge of his nose.

'Have a care, Kit. It will be best if you leave this matter of Josiah Gurdin alone. No good can come of meddling in the Cecils' affairs.'

Walking back to Southwark some while later, I reflected that I had made little progress. I was certain that Thomas Phelippes's hands were clean of the murder of Josiah Gurdin, but I was not sure that made the matter any clearer. There still remained the possibilities I had discussed with Francis Mylles.

Gurdin might have been killed by the Essex faction, but without Phelippes's knowledge.

He might have been killed by a papist agent.

He might have been killed because of some quarrel in his private life, unconnected with his intelligence work.

Or he might somehow have presented a risk to the Cecils, who had chosen to silence their own man. I believed that the Cecils had had some part in the killing of Marlowe, who had been, from time to time, their man.

All four possibilities seemed equally likely. Well, perhaps not quite. Could there truly have been something in Gurdin's personal affairs so serious that it merited murder? It might be possible to find out more about his life apart from his intelligence work. I was inclined to regard this as the least likely solution to the mystery.

As for a papist agent . . . Nick Berden's men might well have news about that. I must see him again in a few days. If the inquest had been adjourned only for two weeks, there was not a great deal of time to pursue anything they might have discovered.

That left what I considered the two most likely cases, that Gurdin had been killed by one of the two intelligence services, either the rival service, or his own.

It was another two days before I could find the time to visit Nick Berden again. He had sent me no word, so I assumed that his men had not been able to discover anything to the point. When I reached his premises in Poultry, it was only to discover that he was out, though expected back soon. I decided to wait.

'Will you please to take a seat in Master Berden's office, Dr Alvarez?' Goodwife Taylor, who was in charge of the women who hawked their baskets of eggs around Cheapside and the streets leading off it, wiped her hands nervously on her apron, although they were spotless. 'I could bring you a glass of ale. Or of wine, if you would prefer it. And the cook has been making sweet tarts today.'

Usually, I knew, Nick's clerk was in charge when he was absent, but today poor Goodwife Jesscot had been left to mind the business, and was somewhat at a loss.

'A cup of small ale would be a kindness,' I said, hoping that having something to do would allay her anxiety at being faced with an unexpected visitor. 'And I should be glad to taste one of the cook's sweet tarts. Just one, mind!'

I took a seat in Nick's office, noticing that the account books, which had presented such an untidy appearance before, were now neatly lined up on a shelf. I hoped the contents were as neat, and that the deficit was gradually growing smaller.

It was not long before Nick came in, apologising for keeping me waiting.

'You should have sent me word that you were coming, Kit, and I would have been here to meet you.'

'I was not sure when I should be able to come, but seized my time when I could. I wanted to discover whether your men have managed to learn anything of Josiah Gurdin and his possible killer.'

'A little.' He insisted on refilling my cup, and took a seat.

'Gurdin was, as you supposed, an intelligencer, working for Lord Burghley.'

'That, I too have discovered,' I said. 'I saw Francis Mylles on Sunday, and he confirmed it. He has had some dealings with the Cecils, and knew of the man Gurdin.'

'Mylles, eh? Not gone completely into country retirement, then?'

'Indeed not. It seems most of Sir Francis's men find it hard to give up the world of intelligence, whether for the world of poultry or for rural quiet. He told me he thought you might spend your time better than with chickens.'

Nick laughed. 'Aye, well, it provides an income. Or something of an income. And as I said to you before, I would be hard pressed to decide which intelligence service to work for. Let them fight it out amongst themselves, then I may reconsider. In the meantime, we may do a little intelligence work of our own, may we not?'

I nodded. 'So your men have discovered that Gurdin was an intelligencer working for Lord Burghley. Is that all?'

'Nay, give me time, Kit. It seems that of late Gurdin was used to infiltrate the Spanish embassy. As you may remember, Poley did so in the past, as well as the French embassy, but I think Poley is too well known and mistrusted to do such work now.'

'The Spanish embassy!' I said. 'Now that might have a bearing on his death.'

'Perhaps I put it wrongly. You know that Lord Burghley has always been in favour of peace negotiations with Spain, rather than remaining in a constant state of war.'

'Of course,' I said. 'It was the major point of policy on which he and Sir Francis disagreed. Sir Francis always said we could not trust any truce with Spain, we must be ever vigilant, watching over our shoulder for the next attack.' I paused. 'Though in his last months, I believe he was coming round to Lord Burghley's opinion. We do not have the resources, in men and coin, to be forever fighting the Spaniards. And he thought that King Philip was growing . . . not more kindly inclined towards England . . . but a little tired of constant war himself.'

'I am not sure he had the right of it,' Nick said, 'but how are we to know?'

'So when you say that Gurdin was infiltrating the Spanish embassy–?'

'A poor choice of words. I think he was acting as some sort of secret go-between, carrying messages between the Cecils and the Spaniards, as the first steps to approaching some sort of truce.'

'Interesting.' I thought for a moment. This cast a new light on Gurdin, and on the dangerous path he had been treading.

'Have you discovered anything about Gurdin's private life?'

'Blameless,' Nick said, 'as far as we can tell. A widower with no children. Devout. With a leaning to more austere Protestantism, though perhaps not quite a Puritan. Sober in his habits. Never been in any kind of trouble. Never in debt.'

'Then that seems decisive. It is very unlikely that he could have been murdered for some misdemeanour in his personal life. No stealing another man's wife, no failure to pay back large sums of money he owed.'

'Nothing like that.'

'One other possibility we discussed, that he might have been killed by a papist agent, because of something he had done against them in the past.'

'I think we may also rule that out,' Nick said. 'I may no longer work for Sir Francis, but I have not entirely clapped my hands over my ears. I suppose you might say that it becomes a kind of habit. I keep myself well informed of an movement of the so-called priests who slip into England with the blessing of the Bishop of Rome to murder our Queen and go straight to Heaven, with his thanks.'

He tapped his teeth with his fingernail.

'That scoundrel John Gerard is still at large. He has been in England since Sir Francis's time.'

I nodded. 'I know. Every time we had sight of him, he disappeared. They say he is as clever at taking on a new role as any player.'

'Aye, and the Catholic party in the country is just as adept at hiding him away. But I heard lately that he is well to the north, in Staffordshire. There's a nest of recusants there. And there has been no other word of papist agents in or about London. One may have slipped in, certainly, but I think we may assume that Gurdin's killer is not likely to have been one of them.'

He offered me more ale, but I shook my head.

'I am sorry,' he said, 'that we have not been able to learn anything of the visitor seen by the gatekeeper at Bart's but we will go on asking.'

'You have done a great deal,' I said. 'I always thought it most likely that the killer came from one of the intelligence services, probably that of Essex, and I think we may forget our other two possibilities. This news about the Spanish embassy and possible approaches to Spain . . . that seems important to me.'

'And to me.'

'Although Sir Francis was never, even in his last months, as wholly in favour of a truce as Lord Burghley, yet he never went so far as to advocate provoking Spain. If you remember, he was merely resigned to the Portuguese expedition to put Dom Antonio on the throne. He never approved of it.'

'I do remember.'

Memories of that terrible expedition conjured up images of Essex's behaviour at the time. 'On the other hand,' I said, 'the Earl of Essex is quite another matter. He sees himself as a great warrior, a great leader – which he is not – and nothing would please him more than inciting a war with Spain. He would not care how many men were killed, how many women left widows and children made orphans. He is supremely confident that *he* would survive, covered with glory. It is a very dangerous prospect, should he ever be able to persuade the Queen to his way of thinking, and away from Lord Burghley's slow caution.'

'I think we need have no fear on that score,' Nick said. 'Her Majesty has not survived these long years by listening to fools. She may let the Earl prance about Court with his cock o'the walk ways, to her amusement, but she is too shrewd in judgement to risk England, and herself, to such madcap schemes.'

'I am sure you have the right of it,' I said. 'I wonder whether she knows about Lord Burghley's overtures to Spain?'

'I cannot think Lord Burghley would have acted *against* her wishes,' Nick said slowly. 'She has always preferred to avoid war. But she might well choose to shut her eyes until something comes of it, one way or another. That way she may take the credit for peace if it occurs, or play the innocent if the overtures fail.'

'You are a cynic, Nick.'

'Nay, I am a realist.'

'Well,' I said, getting up, 'I must away. Thanks you for all you have done.'

'I wish it could be more. We are no nearer putting a name to the killer, though we will continue to search.'

'We are no further on that score, but we have narrowed the possibilities down to the killer being almost certainly an agent of one of the rival intelligence services, though I cannot believe it could have been one of the Cecils' men, unless through some quarrel or jealousy.'

I kept to myself my uncomfortable speculations about the murder of Marlowe.

'It could have been a hired killer.' Nick put the suggestion in a doubtful voice.

'Unlikely, do you not think? I almost forgot to tell you, yet it is important. I have seen Thomas Phelippes and he swears he knows nothing of Josiah Gurdin being killed by one of Essex's men, and I believe him.'

'I think you may trust Phelippes.'

'But he did also say that he is not told everything devised by Essex and the Bacon brothers. I met Anthony Bacon there. I did not like him.'

'Clever, vain, and a sodomite.'

'I do not suppose he will ever live that down, but it does not seem an impediment to him in his present occupation.'

'Rubbed you up the wrong way, did he?' Nick grinned. 'Like a cat's fur?'

'He could barely bring himself to notice me, except to sneer at Thomas Harriot's praise.'

'Ah, I daresay he is one of those who does not like to think that any man may be cleverer than he is.'

I laughed. 'He need have no fears on that score. I am no Cambridge graduate.'

'Nor, certainly, am I. But I survive. Even amongst my chickens.'

I left Nick and began the long walk back to Southwark, but when I reached Thames Street I changed my mind, and turned down to the nearest wherry at Cole Harbour Stairs. As it happened, it was one of the wherrymen I knew whose boat was pulled up there.

'Good e'en to you, Dr Alvarez,' he said, doffing his cap and grinning. 'Off home are you?'

'Aye, Ned,' I said, urging Rikki over the gunwale and following him, to take my seat in the stern. 'Business good today?'

'Not so ill.' He cast off, then, thrusting an oar against the side of the pier, he pushed us out into clear water before sitting down and taking up the second oar. 'And you had business late in the City?'

Wherrymen are almost as notorious gossips as stable lads and players.

'Aye,' I said idly. 'Tell me, Ned, what would your choice be, if, say, you were a counsellor to the Queen, or a Member of Parliament – would you choose to make a peace treaty with Spain, that we might have no more fighting? Or would you choose war?'

He rested his oars and leaned forward with a laugh.

'What would I choose, doctor? Why, war, every time, till we wipe those damned Spaniards off the face of the earth.'

There, I thought, is the voice of England speaking.

Chapter Seven

*L*ady Frances, it seemed, was not one to forget her generous impulses, for about a week later one of the nursing sisters came hurrying into the lying-in ward, where I had just delivered a very small and weak baby boy, born to one of the Winchester geese, though not one of Bessie Travis's women.

'Dr Alvarez,' she gasped, breathless with running up the stairs, and looking flustered, 'you have a visitor, waiting for you in Superintendent Ailmer's office.' Her eyes were wide with awe. 'It is the Countess of Essex!'

'Run back and say that I will be there shortly,' I said.

'But you must come at once!'

'I think not.' I held up my hands, which were bloodied. 'I must clean myself. And I must finish seeing to this little fellow. I am sure the Countess will understand.'

She looked doubtful, but hurried away.

I wrapped the baby in one of the small soft blankets we keep for newborns, and handed him to Goodwife Appledean. He was breathing, but very shallowly.

'You will need to keep a sharp eye on him,' I said. 'I am not sure how well he will feed when it comes to it. We may need to give him a little Coventry water and honey to start with, before he has the stomach for milk.'

I turned to the mother, who was lying pale and exhausted as two of the junior midwives eased the soiled sheet from beneath her, and wiped her face clean with a cool damp cloth. She seemed scarcely to notice them. I was

133

reluctant to leave either mother or child, but I hoped I could make my visit to Lady Frances as brief as possible.

Having washed my hands and removed the apron I had put on to protect my clothes, I donned my gown and ran my fingers through my hair to tidy it, before hastening down the stairs and along to the superintendent's office on the ground floor. I found Lady Frances seated with a cup of wine at her elbow, and Roger Ailmer looking nearly as flustered as the nursing sister.

'Lady Frances,' I said, bowing deeply, 'you have come to see St Thomas's for yourself?'

'Indeed I have, Kit.'

She smiled at me, and I saw Ailmer raise his eyebrows at this sign of familiarity. He should not have been surprised, for he knew that I had worked for the lady's father.

'I have told Her Ladyship,' he said, clearing his throat nervously, 'that she would not wish to visit the wards themselves, which are not fit for a lady.'

'Oh, but that is precisely why I am here!' She laughed and rose to her feet. 'I should like in particular to see the children and the new babies, Kit.'

She had turned toward me and behind her back Ailmer was making frantic negative motions with his head and hands, but I chose to ignore them.

'The children will be so excited to see you, my lady,' I said, 'but I am not sure about the lying-in ward. I have just delivered a poor little mite which is not like to live.'

A spasm of pain crossed her face, and I recalled that she herself had lost at least one baby, as had her mother.

'I am sure you will do your best,' she said.

'Aye,' I said. 'The next few hours are likely to decide it. If you will come this way, I will take you to the children's ward.'

'Excellent,' she said. 'My woman will wait here.'

I had failed to notice her waiting woman, discreetly withdrawn into a corner of the room, but she now looked mighty relieved not to be required to venture into the wards.

The visit to the children proved a great success. Being a mother, and – unlike many aristocratic mothers – taking a true interest in her children's lives, she had brought with her a pretty embroidered bag, which she took from the waiting woman and carried upstairs with us. It proved to contain a large box of sugar plums and other sweetmeats, and a lot of small toys: tiny cloth dolls for the girls, no longer than a handspan, and painted wooden knights for the boys. The first awed silence which greeted us when I introduced her to the children was soon overtaken by an outburst of excited chatter, even from those who were almost too weak to sit up.

'That was very kindly done,' I murmured, and I saw that there were tears in her eyes as she looked around at the children.

Although the ward was clean and comfortable, and the beds a world away from the dirty floors or straw palliasses these children would sleep on at home, there was no disguising the hollow cheeks and sunken eyes which betrayed the signs of ill nourishment in many of them. Several had rickets, and had lost teeth so soon after gaining them, and their hair was sparse and dry.

'What do you need?' she said. 'To help you here?'

'The hospital always needs funds. Many of the buildings are very old and require constant repair. Here in the children's ward, we are able to give them a good nourishing diet, much better than they would get at home, but a few treats like those sugar plums would never come amiss! And the toys will make them the envy of all their brothers and sisters, and their neighbours.'

I laughed. 'As soon as word gets about, I expect we shall have a sudden flood of children with imaginary illnesses.'

She smiled at me, but her eyes were full of pity. 'It is little enough, Jesu knows. I shall see what I can do, both for the hospital and for the children. Now, what of this famous

135

lying-in ward? For unmarried mothers? I had never heard of such a thing.'

'It was certainly needed,' I said dryly, 'here in Southwark amongst the Winchester geese. Men must take their pleasure, and women must pay the penalty.'

'This new birth . . . shall I be a trouble to you, if I visit the ward?'

I thought that by now the midwives would have cleared away the more unpleasant evidence of a new birth, and I was anxious to see the baby again, so I led her next door. Goodwife Appledean was still holding the newest baby, walking up and down, and looking worried. She shook her head at me, then, catching sight of the Countess, dropped a deep curtsey, while clutching the child to her chest.

'I will take him,' I said, relieving her of the small bundle, which hardly seemed to weigh more than the blanket itself. 'My lady, this is Goodwife Appledean, who is in charge of the midwives at St Thomas's.'

The midwife curtseyed again, seeming speechless, which was unlike her, and Lady Frances inclined her head and smiled.

'It is a great responsibility,' she said softly, 'bringing all this new life into an uncertain world.'

Mistress Appledean ventured a small smile in return. 'Dr Alvarez is a wonderful physician, My Lady. Many's the difficult birth when we'd have lost both mother and child without his skill.'

I found myself blushing at this praise, but turned my attention to the scrap of life in my arms. 'I think he needs some help to breathe better,' I said.

I unwrapped the child and laid him on his stomach, his head turned to the side, on one of the unoccupied beds. His breathing was still very shallow, and there was a bluish tinge about his lips. I moved his arms and legs in and out, up and down, then began to work my fingers and thumbs over his back, quite vigorously.

'Does that not hurt the child?' Lady Frances asked, peering over my shoulder anxiously.

'Perhaps, a little, but it is important that he should start filling his lungs. He is barely sipping at the air, and he has made no sound yet. A healthy baby will cry at once, and it sets the lungs to work. His mother is not very clever, and was not sure when he was due, but I'd judge he was at least two weeks early. And she is undernourished, so that affects the child.'

'I remember that both Elizabeth and Robert cried lustily at once.'

Even as she spoke, a tremor ran through the small body under my hands, and a faint wail broke from those bluish lips. Then the child coughed, and I could feel him take a deep breath at last.

'There,' I said, wrapping him again in the blanket and leaning him over my shoulder, continuing to rub his back, thought more gently. 'I think you will do, my lad.'

I handed the baby to Goodwife Appledean. 'Try him with the Coventry water and honey, perhaps in two or three hours from now, and we shall see how he fares. And the mother? How is she?'

'Sleeping, doctor.'

'Best let her rest then. She hardly had the strength to give birth.'

'Do these women keep their children?' Lady Frances asked, as we walked further down the room toward the window. 'If they have no husbands, perhaps no homes . . ?'

'They are not all whores,' I said frankly. 'Some are halfway decent women, abandoned by shiftless men. Or left like widows when the man they lived with died, but without the respect a widow receives. Not that uncommon in these parts, for the work the men do is often dangerous. Some do have homes, of a sort. Some are women from good families who have suffered rape. We had one young girl of that sort, a young servant raped by her master. I found her a place as a servant at Christ's Hospital, where her child could also be cared for.'

I stopped beside one of the wicker cradles we used for the new babies.

'This is one baby his mother could not keep. A whorehouse is no place for a child, though there are many growing up in such, here in Southwark. His mother was sad to give him up, but she knew he would have a better future elsewhere. In a few days I shall be taking him to Christ's Hospital, where he will find home, food, and love, and before long, learning. Did you know that they have a grammar school, which even the girls may attend?'

'Remarkable!' She smiled and shook her head. 'So much is happening in London which remains invisible to many of us. I wonder whether the Earl knows about all of this.' She made a wide gesture with her arm, taking in the women and babies, St Thomas's, and – I suppose – Christ's Hospital as well.

'I doubt it,' I said.

Three days later my afternoon was sufficiently unoccupied for me to leave soon after midday and take the baby I had shown to Lady Frances across the river to Christ's Hospital. By then the tiny newborn who had arrived on that same day had been persuaded to suck small amounts of honeyed Coventry water off a spoon. I had found that a horn spoon, being slightly soft and almost warm to the touch, served the purpose better than a cold, hard metal spoon. That morning he had accepted some of his mother's milk from the spoon, and the midwives would try him at the breast that evening. The mother too was looking a little stronger, after several days on the good sustaining beef broth cooked up in the hospital kitchens, and the morning porridge made more nourishing for our women with a dash of honey and a little cream stirred in.

The boy destined for Christ's Hospital had been named Adam by his mother, and had been kissed a tearful farewell by her, before she hung a lucky sixpence around his neck, punched with a hole and threaded on a ribbon. Such things are not safe on babies, for fear of strangling, so once she was gone I had removed it and tucked it into his blanket. I would give it to Mistress Wedderbury at Christ's to keep for him until he was older.

In winter we take the babies to Christ's well bundled in blankets, in a kind of basket, but the weather was still warm, although it was almost the end of summer, so I simply carried him, in a light woollen gown, with a knitted cap on his head, and wrapped in a blanket. It is too far to walk, for even in summer a new baby might catch a chill, so I boarded a wherry which would take me to Blackfriars Stairs. From there I could walk up from the river to Christ's, which is close by Newgate Prison, just inside the western part of the City wall.

We made the journey quickly, for the tide was on the turn, creating a period of almost slack water on the river as we headed up stream. I had often passed Burghley House before, standing on the north bank of the river just before Barnard's Castle, but I watched it with new interest as we rowed past, for this was one of the centres in the current battle between Essex and the Cecils, and it was here that Josiah Gurdin had served. Once landed at Blackfriars, I was soon on my way up Water Lane, then at the top of Warwick Lane, I emerged into the wide area in front of the orphanage, where Newgate Market is held, and I waited while a shepherd drove a flock of sheep past, on their way to Smithfield Market.

'Dr Alvarez!'

It was the chestnut seller, who had his pitch near the prison.

'I have not seen you these many weeks,' he said.

'Nay,' I said, smiling at him. 'I have not been this way.'

Shifting the baby to lie against my shoulder, I groped in my purse for a coin. 'Two papers of chestnuts for the prisoners today,' I said, giving it to him.

'This is too much, master. Some for yourself?'

'Nay, I have not a hand free to eat them! Make it up in extra for the prisoners.'

As the last of the sheep passed, I saw him shovelling up a good helping of hot nuts into a large screw of paper, and then thrusting it through the barred window where the Newgate prisoners begged for food from the passersby.

'From Dr Alvarez,' he said, 'an old friend to you poor wretches.'

I picked my way carefully across the street to Christ's, the sheep having left behind some scattered droppings, and nodded to the gatekeeper, who had known me now for a few years.

'Mistress Wedderbury be in the laundry, doctor,' he said, 'but I'll send her word you are here. Go you up to her rooms, and she will be there presently, to be sure.'

I climbed the familiar stairs to the rooms occupied by Mistress Wedderbury. A bedchamber, I supposed, must lead off the small parlour where she received visitors like myself, issued instructions for the care of the children (especially the youngest ones), and was often to be found with a small girl or boy on her lap, being comforted with gentle words and a sweetmeat or two. There were grander folk in charge of Christ's Hospital, but at the heart of it lay Mistress Wedderbury.

'Oh, Dr Alvarez!'

I was barely through the door of the parlour when a pretty girl rushed across to me from the table where she had been laying out a plate of small cakes and a jug of what looked like cold spiced ale, with slices of lemon floating in it.

'This cannot be Mellie White,' I said, shaking my head in disbelief and addressing Adam, who stared up at me with wondering blue eyes. 'She is far too much a young lady. Nay, it cannot possibly be the little girl I used to know.'

Mellie giggled. 'I do not work in the kitchens any longer, Dr Alvarez. Now that Moll is wed and gone with her new husband to his stationer's shop in Westminster,

Mistress Wedderbury has taken me on as her personal maidservant. I used to help sometimes before, but now I am to be always here. She told me you were to come today. Is this the new babe? Boy or girl?'

'Boy,' I said. 'Mellie, meet Adam. Adam, this is Mellie White.'

One of his hands had found its way out of the blanket and Mellie gave him her little finger, which he gripped at once.

'And how is Hannah?'

Her face lit up at once. 'Oh she grows so fast! And she is already in the petty school, starting to learn her letters. The master says she is going to be very clever.'

I smiled. 'And your own reading?'

'I can read anything now,' she boasted, then admitted with a grin, 'Well, *almost* anything. And I have learned figuring, too. Edwyn taught me, for he said it would be useful.'

Suddenly she grew very pink, and made a great business of taking the baby from me and settling him in the elaborately carved cradle Mistress Wedderbury always kept in her parlour. I could see that Mellie was full of some secret that she could not decide whether to tell or not. I sat down on one of the cushioned chairs and clasped my hands about my drawn-up knee.

'I am glad you are both doing so well,' I said, 'you and Hannah. I always thought that Christ's would give you a good home.'

Then I waited, for I saw that the secret was about to burst out.

Mellie came and stood before me, her hands clasped in front of her apron and her eyes shining.

'I am doing very well,' she whispered, and then she gave a joyful shout. 'I am to be wed!'

'Ah, that is wonderful to hear, Mellie,' I said. 'I wonder who it might be?'

141

'Do not tease, Dr Alvarez. You must know that it is Edwyn Somers, who is an assistant clerk in the steward's office here.'

Of course I had guessed, for I had heard of the young man before.

'You had not told me his name, Mellie. And when is the wedding to be?'

'Not yet.' She stepped forward eagerly. 'We do not want a winter wedding, and besides, Edwyn is to be promoted to full clerk next summer, so that is when we will wed.'

'And will you stay at Christ's?'

'Well, to be sure, he will do so, and I want Hannah to stay and get her schooling, which I never had. And since I don't want to part with her, Mistress Wedderbury says I may continue to be her maidservant, and they will find us rooms here. My room with Hannah is too small for a wedded couple.' She blushed at the words.

'That seems a very excellent arrangement,' I said.

'And later, when Hannah is older, Edwyn may take a post as some gentleman's secretary, or even a steward, and we might have a house of our own!'

I saw that she loved to repeat the young man's name.

'And perhaps brothers and sisters for Hannah?' I said.

She looked at me seriously. 'I thought I should hate Hannah, after what was done to me, but from the moment I saw her, I loved her. And if Edwyn and I should have children, I know it will be a blessing.'

I wanted to hug the child, but she was grown too old for that now, so I simply said, 'I hope I may be invited to the wedding.'

'It could not happen without you,' she said quietly, 'for without you, I should never have known happiness, and never met Edwyn.'

When I had concluded my business with Mistress Wedderbury, I realised there was still time enough to call upon Nick Berden. He had sent me no further word, but I was anxious to know whether his men had learned anything at all to the point. I had seen nothing more of Peter, who was yet without employment, but who had sent me a message to say that the inquest had again been postponed. It seemed that some notice had been taken of the evidence given by Bartholomew's gatekeeper, so the coroner must have felt uneasy at directing a jury's attention solely at Peter. Moreover, his father-in-law, the apothecary Master Winger, had returned to London and was to speak to the governors of St Bartholomew's on his behalf.

I found Nick at work, counting up the coins his egg sellers had earned on the streets that day and looking more cheerful than when I had found him gloomily surveying his accounts.

'You had the right of it, Kit,' he said, without preamble. 'The egg selling is a sound business, and I am increasing my stock of laying hens, but I shall still supply birds for the table as well.'

'Have you sent one of your men to "persuade" your defaulting customers to pay their debts?' I asked, pulling up a stool.

He shook his head, then grinned. 'Not yet, but I have allowed a whisper to get about that I might take such a measure. It is beginning to prove effective.'

He locked the coins in his strongbox, then sat down facing me.

'You come most aptly upon your time. I should have sent you a letter this evening, had you not forestalled me.'

'You have discovered something about the murder?'

'It was Tom Lewen. Do you recall Tom Lewen? You patched him up once.'

'I remember. A thin slip of a man.'

'Aye. He goes unnoticed, for he's so small and insignificant, but he has a keen eye and a sharp mind. He overheard some tavern talk and followed it up.'

'And?' I said.

'He thought it unlikely at first, so I did not send you word, lest it proved a parcel of moonshine, but now it seems that it is true.'

'Why did it seem unlikely?'

'I suppose,' he said thoughtfully, 'that nothing is unlikely in the confused world we live in. You will recall, after we decided other possible reasons for his murder were out of the question, that – since Josiah Gurdin was an agent of the Cecils – it was most probable he was killed by one of Essex's men.'

'Certainly,' I said, 'that seems most likely.'

'Well, Tom Lewen heard a fellow boasting that he had earned a good fee for disposing of one of his master's "unreliable" servants. He was scattering some of the coin around in drinks for all, as proof of his riches.'

'And did Tom discover who was his master?'

'Not at first. But the talk of disposing of someone seemed it might have a bearing on Gurdin's death, so he followed the man when he went home last night, in his cups and singing.'

I was puzzled. 'Do you mean he went to Essex House? On the Strand? Or did he go to report to Anthony Bacon at Grey's Inn?'

'Not at all. He went to Burghley House.'

I drew in a sharp breath. 'I see. Of course. One of "his master's servants". *Both* of them servants of Lord Burghley?'

'So it seems. Or of Sir Robert Cecil, which comes to the same thing.'

'This seems . . . This is a nasty piece of work, Nick.'

'It is. But there is more.'

I waited, feeling somewhat sick. The Cecils' man had been killed by one of the Cecils' men. Because he was 'unreliable'. What did that mean?

'Tom may not look much of a fellow to us, but he has a way with women, at any rate with kitchen maids. I suppose it is that look of a starving mongrel he wears. They take pity on him. Today he took up one of his usual poses, a threadbare pedlar, down on his luck, hasn't had a solid meal for days. He went round to the kitchens at Burghley House, and even managed to sell one of the kitchen maids a bunch of ribbons for twice what they were worth! He could make a good living as a pedlar if he chose, but he reckons that it's too tedious.'

'So, the kitchen maids fed him?' I prompted.

'Aye. He sat down to a good dinner of the leftovers from the family table. Roast beef and gravy, frumenty with leeks and more gravy, and a plum tart.' He grinned. 'A better dinner than I had, you may be sure.'

'And the kitchen maids talked?'

'It took him some time, he says, to work them around to it, but they were ready enough to talk. Josiah Gurdin was a quiet man, it seems, kept somewhat to himself, but he was well liked, even so.'

'Not unreliable?'

'Not at all, so it seems. A well trusted servant of long standing. Then a few weeks ago there began to be whispers that he was selling the Cecils' secrets. Either to Essex or even to the Spanish. He had been seen entering the Spanish embassy.'

'But that was on the Cecils' business!'

Nick shrugged. 'I do not suppose the kitchen servants knew that. At any rate, the rumours within the household began to grow, that Gurdin had turned traitor. And somehow the women had heard that two men had been sent to give him a beating when he was well away from the house. As a warning. It was not meant to kill him.'

'And that was when he was found by the Watch at Smithfield,' I said. 'Although from what Peter told me, it was a bad beating. He lost a lot of blood. If the Watch had not found him and brought him to St Bartholomew's, he would likely have died before morning.'

'Perhaps they exceeded their orders. At any rate, word came back that he was in Bart's, and had told the people there that he was from Lord Burghley's household. The other servants thought that was an end to the matter, until Gurdin was recovered enough to come home, but one of the maids told Tom Lewen that she had seen one of those men who had administered the beating going out in the evening, a day or two after Gurdin was known to be in the hospital. Not one of the household servants, one of what she called "those folk who run about on the master's business, and never do a hand's turn of other folks' real work". I think we may take it that she meant one of the intelligencers.'

'Did she see where he went?'

He nodded. 'A girl with a long nose for other folks' business, Tom reckons. She followed him almost all the way to St Bartholomew's, but had to turn back before she was missed. It seems likely he is our man.'

I drew a deep breath. 'If we can discover his name, he can be arrested by the coroner's officers to answer for himself. He *may* not be the killer, but if he was one of those who gave Gurdin the beating, he can still be called to give evidence.'

'Tom did get the man's name. And he is one of Burghley's intelligencers, for I have heard of him before. Esau Miller, he's called.'

'Esau?'

'Aye.' Nick gave a wry grin. 'Perhaps his parents were godly Puritans.'

'Now, if we can find him,' I said, pleased that Tom Lewen had learned so much, 'and also the other man who took part in the beating, even if he was not the killer . . .'

'We know who he is, and also that he was the one who spread the rumours that Gurdin was a traitor, which I'm minded to think he was not.'

'Who is he, then?' I said. 'This other man?'

Nick gave me a penetrating look.

'His name is Robert Poley.'

I must have stared at Nick for several minutes, while all that he had told me went whirling about in my head, until the pieces of Gurdin's story settled down again in a new pattern

'Poley,' I said slowly. 'So Poley spread false rumours of Gurdin's treachery. But why?'

'We are assuming they were false.'

'Very well, *assuming* they were false. We know that the visits to the Spanish embassy were concerned with the Cecils' tentative approach to securing a peace treaty. Poley did not know this? He might not. After all, when we worked for Sir Francis, we did not know the missions of other agents, except by chance. It was safer that way. Thomas Phelippes and Francis Mylles might have known, but you and I would not. Yet why would Poley accuse him of treachery?'

'Perhaps he did know that Gurdin was trusted as a go-between with the Spanish embassy. Perhaps it was nothing more than jealousy,' Nick said. 'It might be that Gurdin, because of his long service to the Cecils, was entrusted with the more important work, and Poley wanted him out of the way.'

'But he did not murder Gurdin,' I pointed out. 'That seems to have been this other man. Though the two of them joined in beating Gurdin. I wonder whether they were truly ordered to do it, or whether that was another falsehood put about.'

'It might have been,' Nick said. 'Whatever Poley's part in the affair, he appears to have been a small player. Why Miller killed Gurdin, we cannot know. Was it of his own intent? Or was he ordered to do it?'

'You mean,' I said reluctantly, 'ordered by the Cecils?'

'If they believed Poley's assertions that Gurdin was a traitor?' Nick sounded uncertain.

'They knew *why* he had gone to the Spanish embassy.'

'But the other accusation, that he was selling their secrets to Essex?' Nick shrugged. 'These men are ruthless, Kit, let us never forget that.'

'It leaves a very nasty taste in the mouth,' I said.

'It does. Ah, here is Tom now,' he said, as Tom sidled in. 'Did you contrive to follow the man Miller, Tom?'

'Aye.' Tom took off his cap and scratched his head. 'Good e'en, Dr Alvarez.'

'And to you, Tom.'

'Well?' Nick said.

'He be in a tavern next the Fleet,' Tom said. 'The Cat and Ha'penny. Fool of a name. Seems well settled there, him and that Poley fellow.'

Nick and I exchanged a glance.

'Both of them,' I said.

'Indeed.' Nick stood up briskly. 'Tom, I want you to go straightaway, as fast as you may, to the Guildhall. Find the coroner's officers and bring them to the Cat and Ha'penny. Tell them we think we have found the killer in the case of the recent poisoning at St Bartholomew's. They will know about the adjourned inquest. Quick as you can. Dr Alvarez and I will go straight there, and follow Miller if he leaves.'

'Right,' Tom said, pulling on his cap again and slipping away, silent as ever.

Nick and I hurried out and turned right toward Cheapside, then stopped. A cart had overturned, spilling a load of metal vessels – cooking pots, kettles, ale cups – every kind of product of the metal-worker's craft. A huge crowd had gathered, some to steal, some to prevent the stealing. The whole of Cheapside was blocked.

'Quicker by river,' I said.

'Aye.'

We turned and ran down to the waterside, and luckily found a two-man wherry at Three Crane Stairs.

'Take us to the Fleet,' Nick said, 'and if you make it fast, you shall have an extra sixpence each.'

The tide was now rising, so it helped us on our way, slowing the downward flow of the river. It was by far our best choice, for if we should need to chase after Miller, or even tackle him, we would not have wasted energy and breath running across a crowded City.

The mouth of the Fleet came into view.

'Drop you here, maister?' one of the wherrymen asked, the older man, indicating Blackfriars Stairs, where I had landed earlier, which lay just before the Fleet.

'Nay,' Nick said, 'take us up the Fleet to that tavern, the Cat and Ha'penny.'

The younger man, probably the son, made a face. 'You don't want to be going there, maister. 'Tis no place for a gentleman.'

'Never fear,' Nick said, 'we have no plans to drink there.'

The men turn the boat to the right and headed up the Fleet river. As usual, it carried an unsavoury cargo at which I did not look too closely, though I could not avoid sight of the dead pig, bloated and swollen, which bumped against the side of the boat close beside me. The Fleet was not as bad as Houndsditch, which held stagnant water, in which the careless citizens of London dumped their stinking rubbish, including the dead animals for which it was named. The Fleet, at least, was flowing water, and carried its rubbish down to the Thames. Indeed, when the tide came in twice a day, as it was doing now, it scoured out the lower reaches, so the stench here was not unbearable, though higher up, if the weather was hot and the water level low, it could be very unpleasant.

The Cat and Ha'penny, it seemed, was some little way up the river, so that the wherrymen were obliged to manoeuvre their boat under the narrow Bridewell Bridge, while we all ducked our heads. The underneath of the bridge was thick with green slime, so I realised that at times the river must rise almost to the top of the arch. I do not usually suffer from a fear of enclosed spaces, but I was seized with an involuntary shudder at the thought of the boat becoming wedged as the tide forced us up against those slimy stones. When we reached the other side of the arch, I drew in a long breath of relief.

'That be the tavern, maister,' the younger one of the wherrymen said. 'And a jetty this side of it.'

The rotting platform of rough planks hardly merited the name of jetty, but there was nowhere else to land. Nick and I stood up, and he gave the wherrymen their pay. He scrambled awkwardly on to the jetty, which shook perilously under his weight, then stepped across to the muddy bank, where he slipped and went down on one knee, miring his hose. I hesitated. It looked to me as though that unstable structure might as soon tip me into the Fleet as on to the bank, and I had no wish to join the dead pig and his unsavoury companions in that disgusting soup.

'Us cannot wait all day, maister,' the older man said rudely. 'Get you ashore.'

I cast about to see whether there was a bush or a tree I might grab to stop myself sliding backwards. A little further along, just at the far end of the jetty, a bush of broom hung down, half over the planks, half over the bank.

'Another stroke or two with your oars will put me ashore there,' I said, pointing. 'It is hardly safe, but less risky then here.'

Grumbling, they eased the boat a little further up the Fleet. Nick had climbed to the top of the slippery bank and was watching our manoeuvres. As I was deciding how best to make my way up to join him, I glanced along toward the tavern, which was every bit as filthy and unpleasant as the boatman had implied. Between the place where I hoped to climb out and the tavern itself, two men were standing on the edge of the bank, arguing.

They were too far away for me to hear their voices, with their backs turned to me, but I could tell from the way they moved that trouble was brewing there. I glanced back over my shoulder to alert Nick, but his eyes were still on me, presumably wondering why I had not followed him, though perhaps he saw me reach out to grab a branch of the broom bush to steady myself as I set one foot on the rotten planks of the jetty.

The two men must have made up their quarrel, for one man threw his arm about the other's shoulders, friendliwise. Something stirred in my mind, some memory. Then there was a sudden sharp cry, and the other man seemed to turn slowly under that embracing arm, then tip over, like a top at the end of its spin, and fall without a further cry, into the Fleet.

I let go of the bush and stepped back into the boat.

'Quick!' I said to the wherrymen. 'That man is in the river. Catch him before the current carried him away.'

They knew their trade and moved swiftly, swinging the boat out to block the flow of the river. While one wherryman held it steady, the other reached over the side and caught the floating man by the back of his doublet, dragging him aboard over the gunwale.

It was a man I had never seen before, but I could not ask his name, for his neck was slashed from ear to ear, and his blood was pouring over my shoes.

That memory suddenly sharpened in my mind and I looked up to where the other man still stood on the bank. As he began turning to walk away, a servant came out of the tavern carrying a flaming torch to thrust into the sconce beside the door, lighting up the dimming evening.

It lit up also, for one brief moment, the face of the man standing there.

It was Robert Poley.

Where I stood in the boat, on the open waters of the Fleet, I must have been clearly visible to him. For a moment, his eyes met mine. Then he melted back into the shadows beyond the tavern, made all the darker by the light of the torch. And vanished.

The two wherrymen, frozen into brief horror by the unsavoury catch they had hauled aboard, now became loud in their protests.

'We'm not having that thing in our boat!' the elder one shouted.

'Aye,' said the other, 'heave it overboard and let the Thames take 'un.'

They both seized the body and would have tossed it back into the Fleet, despite my protests, if a sudden crowd had not appeared above us on the bank, led by Nick Berden.

'There, sir,' he said, pointing down at the boat. 'My friend has just ordered the boatmen to save the man who fell into the river.'

On the edge of the group I made out the slight figure of Tom Lewen. These must be the coroner's officers, so he had made good time fetching them. Fortunately the Guildhall was nearer this side of the City than the other.

'Best make up your minds to it,' I said quietly to the wherrymen. 'You needs must say what you saw, and how we fished this man from the river, already dead.'

The older man gave a mirthless, gap-toothed grin. 'Not much chance he'd come out of that alive, not with that pretty bit of knife work.'

With glum resignation, they rowed the boat back to the jetty, which shook and groaned dangerously as the wherrymen, with help from two men on shore, managed to heave the body on to the planks, where it wept water and blood together. The bleeding had almost stopped, but my shoes would never recover.

I grabbed hold of the bush again, and with some difficult managed to climb on to the jetty without stepping on our sorry catch. I saw now that Tom had brought not only half a dozen of the coroner's officers but also a gentleman, whom I took to be the coroner himself.

After the body had been carried up the bank and laid on the scrubby grass near to the torch for the benefit of the light, the gentleman leaned over, peering at it closely.

'He cannot have been in the river long,' he said, 'for I can see he was still bleeding when you dragged him into the boat.'

'We saw him fall,' I said, 'these men and I.'

I indicated the wherrymen, who glowered at me. I felt some sympathy for them, despite their rudeness, for no one likes to be caught up, innocently, in murder.

'Either he fell,' I amended, 'or he was pushed.'

By now, customers of the tavern had come crowding out, gaping at this unexpected spectacle which had come to enliven their evening.

'Did you see aught else, Kit?' Nick had joined the gentleman, who turned to him.

'You know this man, Master Berden?' he said.

I was not surprised to find that Nick was known to one of the City officials.

'This is Dr Alvarez, sir, of St Thomas's hospital. We both arrived here in that wherry, but I had already come ashore. Kit, this is one of the London coroners, Sheriff Robert Taylor.'

I made my bow, conscious of my dishevelled state. I knew one of the coroners, Sir Rowland Heyward, former Mayor of London and Governor of the Muscovy Company, but this man was unknown to me.

'Dr Alvarez.' He returned my bow. 'And did you see anyone else with this man?'

I looked around. Besides the coroner's officers and the wherrymen, we now had a considerable audience, many of them decidedly disreputable, no doubt regular clients of the Cat and Ha'penny.

'Aye,' I said cautiously. 'But were it not best to discuss this somewhere less open to view?'

'You have the right of it,' he said. 'We will return to my office in the Guildhall. You!' He pointed to the wherrymen. 'Leave your boat here and come with us. I want to know just what you saw.'

'But, maister!' the older one objected, 'if we leaves our boat here, 'twill be stolen in half an hour.'

Sheriff Taylor considered, then nodded. 'Two of my men will row it down to Three Cranes Stairs, and you may collect it there, after you have told all you know.'

They grumbled, but had no choice but to join our gloomy procession back over the small Bridewell Bridge and through the postern gate in the wall, then on to the Guildhall, where we were shown into a panelled room behind the great Hall. A servant, unbidden, carried in a tray with glasses and a flask of wine, but it was not offered to us. Two of the coroner's officers had carried the body with us to the Guildhall, on a litter improvised from a broken door taken from one of the tavern's outbuildings, to the wrath of the tavern keeper. Fortunately, they did not accompany us into the sheriff's room.

The watermen told what they had seen, which they claimed was nothing, except the sight of the body floating down toward us. Once they had given their names and where they might be reached for the inquest, they were allowed to go, leaving only Nick, Tom, and me with the sheriff.

'Now, Dr Alvarez,' he said, pouring wine for us, then sitting back and regarding me shrewdly, not altogether friendly. 'Tell me what you saw.'

I cleared my throat.

'Goodman Lewen came to fetch you to the tavern because he had followed two men there, one of whom he believed to be the man who gave poison to one Josiah Gurdin, lying in the hospital of St Bartholomew. This was a man who had been boasting publicly of the deed. A man called Esau Miller. I have had no chance to speak to Goodman Lewen since we pulled the body from the Fleet, but I believe it may be Miller.'

I turned to Tom, who was doing his best to disappear into the shadows of a corner.

'Is that who it is, Tom? The man in the river?'

'Aye, doctor. That is Esau Miller.'

'Suddenly and conveniently dead,' Nick said.

'Aye.' I smiled grimly. 'So that now he cannot stand trial for the murder of Josiah Gurdin.'

The sheriff laid his hands together, palm to palm, and rested his chin on his finger tips. 'And you say that you saw another man, doctor? His killer, do you believe?'

'Aye,' I said. ''Twas the other man Tom Lewen had followed to the tavern. I saw the two men standing on the bank as I was about to climb out of the wherry. They were talking together, arguing, it seemed. Then it was as though they had made up their differences, for the other man threw his arm about Miller's shoulders, like a friend. A moment later there was a cry, and Miller fell into the river.'

I thought back to what I had seen. 'I believe there was a glimmer of metal in the other man's hand, but I cannot swear to it. It was growing dark, and the tavern servant was only just coming outside with his torch.'

'There was no other man there when we arrived,' the sheriff said, 'which cannot have been many minutes later.'

'It was not,' I agreed, 'but the other man slipped away very swiftly, although he must have seen us pull Miller out of the water.'

'And can either you or Lewen here put a name to this other man?'

'I can,' I said. 'He is in the employ of Lord Burghley, and used to work for Sir Francis Walsingham. His name is Robert Poley.'

I watched the changing expressions which flashed over Sheriff Taylor's face. At the mention of Lord Burghley, he looked alarmed. And I could swear that he recognised the name of Robert Poley, although he managed to conceal how it affected him.

Nick Berden, Tom Lewen, and I all gave as full an account as possible of the events of that evening, and a clerk, summoned by the sheriff, wrote it all down. At last, to our great relief, we were allowed to leave. Tom slipped away so quietly that I never saw him go, while Nick and I walked a little way together. I bade him farewell before I turned down toward the river to take a wherry home, intending to avoid the surly fellows we had engaged earlier. It seemed like a month since I had brought little Adam to

Christ's Hospital, instead of the few hours I had spent north of the river. In two days' time, we must give evidence at the inquest on Esau Miller.

The inquest duly took place. It settled some matters, but left others as baffling as before. A number of new witnesses had been found, besides Tom Lewen, who had heard Miller boasting about the killing of Josiah Gurdin. In his cups, it seemed, he had sometimes given his victim a name. To my great relief, the coroner ruled that there was no longer any suspicion attached to the apothecary Peter Lambert, who should be restored to his position at St Bartholomew's forthwith.

However, the true reasons for the killing were now sealed for ever behind the silent lips of Esau Miller, over whose body the present inquest was being held. Clearly the coroner had not ventured to call either Lord Burghley or Sir Robert Cecil to give evidence at the inquest. Instead, one of Sir Robert's secretaries attended on their behalf. I do not think I have ever seen a face so bland, with no marks of emotion or life on it. To my eyes, it looked like a sculptor's model of smooth, flesh-tinted wax. The man assured the coroner and jury that nothing was known of these killings in the Burghley household. He agreed that both Josiah Gurdin and Esau Miller had been members of that household, but confessed himself to be entirely baffled, assuming that there must have been a private quarrel amongst the men – perhaps over gambling debts? He left the suggestion hanging in the air.

I repeated my evidence, and it seemed the coroner believed me, for he directed the jury to consider the guilt of Robert Poley in their deliberations. They did not deliberate long, but found Poley guilty in his absence.

For the coroner's men had scoured London, every street, alleyway, tavern and inn.

But of Robert Poley there was no trace.

Chapter Eight

I had not seen Sara Lopez for some time, but around the middle of September she sent me a note, inviting me to sup with her that evening, as Ruy was much occupied with business, and inviting me to bring Simon. I sent a reply by Matthew, accepting, and we set off in the late afternoon, after the playhouse closed, taking Rikki with us. As we mounted the steps to Mountjoy's Inn, Ruy was just bidding farewell to a man I knew from our Marrano community, a quiet, somewhat insignificant man called Gomez d'Avila.

'Good day to you, Senhor d'Avila,' I said, as we passed on the steps.

He seemed disconcerted. 'Ah,' he said, 'ah, Dr Alvarez! Good day to you, good day!' He scuttled away down the street.

He seemed an unlikely ally for Ruy in whatever schemes he was currently developing, but Gomez was a follower of Dom Antonio, so perhaps he had come merely on some affair of the Dom's.

Ruy stood holding the door ajar for us, and welcomed us into the house with great joviality.

'Come to sup with my wife? I am afraid I am much occupied with affairs and must go out again almost immediately.' He tapped the side of his nose and winked, which I thought was an ominous sign.

There was a barely suppressed excitement about him. It was as if he throbbed like the air during a thunderstorm, just before lightning strikes. He was an old man now, but he sprang into the house like a youth of twenty, and the very hairs of his beard seemed to crackle with energy.

Sara welcomed us with her usual sweet courtesy, and sent for wine and sweetmeats to entertain us until supper was ready. The three of us and Sara's eldest daughter, Anne, took a simple but excellent supper in Sara's small parlour, Anthony having returned to Winchester with the start of the school term and the younger children taking their supper with their governess. Before we left, however, Sara drew me aside while Anne was showing Simon round the garden, and I saw that she was worried.

'Kit, Ruy says that we may need to travel abroad again, to Constantinople, where his cousin Alvaro Mendes is advisor to the Sultan on English affairs. You remember, perhaps, that we lodged with him when we travelled there before. I do not want to go!'

She drew in her breath in a ragged gasp, and I noticed that her hands were shaking. All her earlier calm welcome had been overcome by some deep fear.

'Anne will not leave, for she will be married by then,' she said, 'and will stay in London with her new husband. Ambrose works for my father, of course, and will someday take over his business, for he is growing old and frail. Poor Father, he needs me here. And Anthony is doing so well in his studies at Winchester. I do not want to remove him from the school where the Queen herself has sent him, and I do not want to go!'

I realised that despite her care to conceal it, Sara was very frightened about something. Ruy excited and Sara afraid. I did not like the omens. Yet what could I do, what could anyone do, when Ruy was once again swept away by one of his great schemes? I said what I could to reassure her, that perhaps it would come to nothing, that perhaps she need not go.

Was Ruy planning some great adventure with the Ottomans now? Or was he a party to some scheme of the Cecils? Although he was still physician to both the Cecils and to Essex, his political allegiance seemed to lie with the

Cecils. Was he somehow involved in those secret negotiations with Spain, that Nick Berden had discovered? When most men of a like age are happiest in slippered and pantalooned ease, Ruy was running like a young colt out of control.

He had been behaving recklessly in other ways in recent weeks, for he had been spreading rumours that the Earl of Essex was afflicted with syphilis. Essex was his patient, and to reveal such a thing about a patient was unpardonable. Why had he done something so disgraceful and so rash? If he heard these rumours, Essex's fury would be Olympian. For syphilis is not merely a shameful illness, caught from diseased prostitutes. In its later stages it affects the brain, making a man wildly irrational, apt to outbursts of terrible anger, and leading in the end to madness.

It was whispered that King Henry had caught syphilis from the whores of France when he went to treat with the French king at the Field of the Cloth of Gold, and that this was why, in his later years, he had become so cruel, subject to dreadful bouts of violence. If Essex did indeed have syphilis, it meant the end to any hope of his becoming the Queen's chief advisor instead of Robert Cecil. Essex was already a rash and violent-tempered man, but I believed that was innate in his nature, painfully revealed in his beating of little Lady Elizabeth. Once Essex heard what Ruy was whispering about him, his vengeance would be implacable. Perhaps that was why Ruy was planning an escape to Constantinople. But why, then, had he seemed so excited? Or might the defaming of Essex be some plan of the Cecils, intended to undermine his standing with the Queen and his ill-deserved popularity with the people of London?

'We encountered Gomez d'Avila speaking to Ruy when we arrived,' I said tentatively.

She shivered. 'Aye. He is in and out of here. I never know when I shall come across one or other of them, in the house or lurking about the garden like a sneak thief. D'Avila, Ferreira, Tinoco. All of them slippery,

159

untrustworthy men. I wish Ruy would have no more to do with them, or with Dom Antonio. Let him stick to his profession and leave these perilous affairs of state to those who understand them, like Lord Burghley.'

'He is certainly working for Lord Burghley?' I asked hesitantly, thinking of Josiah Gurdin and the secret approaches to the Spanish. And how it had led to his murder.

'That I do not know for sure, Kit, nor wish to know. He tells me nothing, or almost nothing, and I would prefer to shut my eyes. Yet I fear for myself and my children, if he ventures into deeper waters. Even the great men of England can be as treacherous as the little men who slip through the shadows.'

She hesitated, then burst into speech again, as though she could not contain herself.

'There is one thing I *do* know. Ruy was working on some projection devised by Sir Francis not long before he died. It had to do with Spain, of that I am certain, and also Dom Antonio, though in what way, I do *not* know. There was a whisper of some great ruby. When Sir Francis died, the plan died with him, though I believe it has been taken up again, for Ruy speaks of a scheme which will bring great benefits to Lord Burghley.'

She paused, and shook her head. 'Yet I think Ruy is directing the whole venture himself, using that man Tinoco and others. You know how he is, Kit. He believes he can conduct these great affairs himself, but he is as simple as a child in the hands of men like the Earl of Essex and Lord Burghley. I am not sure . . . but I think he plans to present his scheme, all completed, to Lord Burghley, in the hopes of great advancement.'

I nodded. This was the Ruy Lopez who had been a great mover in the disastrous Portuguese expedition, believing he could put Dom Antonio on the throne and rise to greatness as his first minister. And he would not be the first to try to buy advancement with the Cecils through some bold – and perhaps illegal – gesture. Had not Poley done the same, with the secret papers stolen from Sir Francis's office?

'This half-knowing, Kit, and the thought of Spain . . . what it may mean . . . it haunts my sleep with fearful nightmares.'

I comforted her as best I might, although at the back of my mind there continued to linger the thought of Josiah Gurdin's fate. However, I was determined to put Ruy and his affairs out of my mind. The threats against Strangers had died down for the moment, but the hostility that had been abroad in London early in the year, before the murder of Marlowe, remained like a festering sore in my mind. It might burst forth again at any moment, and this time be directed more strongly towards Marranos. The attack of the apprentices came back in my dreams, so that I would wake sweating in the dark. Like the Lopez family, I might need to make my escape from the country.

As though Sara's fears had brought it about, it seemed there was a sudden flood of intelligence work for Thomas Phelippes, and he requested my help less than a week after our supper at Mountjoy's Inn. Anthony Bacon, he informed me, had arranged matters with St Thomas's, on Essex's authority. I would continue my work at the hospital in the mornings, but would spend the afternoons at the office in the Customs House. Although I was reluctant to have my hours at the hospital cut short, there would be some advantages in gaining an insight into the activities of Essex's secret service, so I gave my agreement.

I hardly had any choice in the matter.

So it was that I began to spend the afternoons at the Customs House, sorting, deciphering and transcribing documents from a pile which never seemed to grow smaller, for as quickly as I worked, more reports and intercepted letters were brought to Phelippes's office. For the most part I worked on my own, since by the time I had finished my morning duties at the hospital and crossed the river, Phelippes would have departed by wherry for Essex

House or – more often – Grey's Inn. Arthur Gregory was usually in his small office next door, and I sometimes needed his assistance to lift a seal from a letter, or to reseal it, or to apply the official seal to an agent's passport. He was immensely skilled at his work, but mostly showed little curiosity about the documents he handled.

About a week after I started work at the Customs House I opened a report from one of the agents based in Paris, whose main occupation was spying upon the activities of Mendoza, the Spanish ambassador who had been forced to leave London after the exposure of his part in the plots to put the Scottish queen on the throne. Now he sat in Paris, like a fat, vengeful spider, directing his own network of spies to find any means possible to destroy our Queen. He was responsible for slipping many Catholic priests into England disguised as innocent travellers, relying on them to spy at the same time as they strove to convert the Protestant English, and he was in constant touch with his master, King Philip of Spain.

The report I began to decipher that day started with the usual minor dealings of Mendoza, and an account of the current mood in the French Court, but then came a paragraph, addressed urgently to Essex himself, which turned me cold. Although I was alone in the room, I glanced fearfully over my shoulder. Then I blotted the transcription I had been making and stowed it, together with the original report, in the breast of my doublet. My heart was pounding and my hands were slippery with sweat. The hidden papers rustled with my every breath, but I must behave as though nothing had happened. I was thinking furiously. Paper. I must find some paper as near as possible to that on which the report had been written. There were assorted papers kept in a court cupboard, so that when forgeries were made, the paper could be matched. I found one close enough to pass muster, and tucked that, too, inside my doublet. Then I sat down and continued at my work, hoping that none who saw me would detect any agitation in my manner.

'Sara,' I said, 'I must speak with you. At once. Alone.'

She gave me a swift, startled look, but quickly dismissed her housekeeper and beckoned me to a chair. I wondered whether her long marriage to Ruy Lopez had trained her to expect the unexpected and to be ready for danger.

'I want you to look at this.'

I laid on the table two sheets of paper, the coded report from the agent in Paris and my transcription of it, which I had completed, crouched in a secluded corner of an inn, after leaving the Customs House.

'I don't understand,' she said, peering in bewilderment at the meaningless jumble of letters in the Paris report.

'Don't concern yourself with that. This is my transcription here, on the other sheet.'

She read it quickly. When she reached the fatal paragraph, she began to tremble and pressed the back of her hand to her mouth.

'Where did you get this, Kit? What does it mean?'

'It means,' I said grimly, 'that Ruy is in danger, your family is in danger. Our whole community is in danger.'

I left the rest hanging in the air. My own life was in danger. Ever since I had read the report, my breathing had felt constricted, although I had driven myself on, knowing that my only hope was swift action.

I read the paragraph aloud slowly, to ensure that she understood:

I now know for certain that those matters My Lord ordered me to investigate are true. Lopez is in the pay of the Spanish king and treats with him of matters concerning the throne of Portugal and the son of the Pretender. This Machiavellian Jew and his nest of intelligencers are all of them infected with the poison of treason and must be rooted out. The poison is spread so wide that Her Majesty and the kingdom may not be assured of safety until the entire

163

Portingall nation in England be destroyed. I beg you to warn My Lord that he must act with all haste. You may know of the Jew doctor's perfidy by a great ruby that the Spanish king himself hath bestowed upon him.

Sara's face grew so white on hearing the words read aloud that I poured her wine from a silver-mounted crystal flask and stood over her until she had drunk it all. Then I poured a glass for myself and the rim clattered against my teeth. I could not control the shaking in my hands.

I had been in danger before – danger from the Inquisition, danger of being exposed as a girl, danger of death many times over during the Portuguese expedition, but this time I knew that if I chose the wrong course, I would be putting my own head in a noose. And both paths seemed to lead to the same end.

'Who has written this?' she whispered.

'One of the agents working for Phelippes and Anthony Bacon in Paris. It is not signed. That is the common practice, but I recognise the hand.'

'And who is "My Lord" that is spoken of?'

'The Earl of Essex, who employs them. It may mean nothing more than a desire to discredit Ruy because he and his . . . agents act for Lord Burghley and Sir Robert Cecil, but if the Essex faction can produce evidence to satisfy the Privy Council and the Queen, then his life is certainly in danger.'

Sara sat twisting her hands together and raised a stricken face to me.

'What is it?' I asked urgently. '*Has* Ruy been treating with King Philip? Could they have evidence?'

'The ruby,' she said.

I looked at her in horror.

'That ruby you mentioned before, given by the Spanish king?'

She nodded. 'It was all a part of that plan of Sir Francis Walsingham's. You remember, surely, Kit. The man Andrada, who was sent to spy on the Spanish court.'

'It was he who brought back this ruby?'

'A large one. From the king. It was intended as a pledge of good faith.'

I thought her choice of words unfortunate.

'Where is it now?'

'I don't know. Ruy does not tell me such things. He will have it safely hidden away. He intended to use it for Anne's dowry.'

A large ruby. All red stones are valued by my people as fortunate, bringing blessings, even those which are not costly. But a large *ruby*! It existed, and it carried a burden of terrible guilt and danger with it, whatever had been the original projection Walsingham had devised – a genuine approach to the king to treat of peace, or else some complex plot to foil Spanish aggression. Never before had I felt the loss of that clever, devious man so much. Nor longed so much for the wise counsel of Hector Nuñez.

'We must warn Ruy,' I said briskly, pretending more confidence than I felt, for the thought of that perilous ruby made me physically sick. 'He must go to Sir Robert Cecil and explain everything. He told Lord Burghley, did he not, about the original plan, when Andrada returned? If he told him at the same time about this ruby he was given, all is clear and open, and the accusation of treason can be countered by the Cecils themselves.'

Sara looked terrified, her eyes darting about the room.

'Sara? What ails you? Ruy did tell Lord Burghley about the ruby, did he not?'

'I am not sure, Kit, but I'm greatly afraid he may not have done. Else why would he have hidden it away? You know him of old, Kit. He always believes that he can manage affairs himself.'

I felt my heart squeeze together coldly in my chest and then begin to pound furiously. Ruy, in his arrogance and greed, had endangered the lives of all of us. Though I worked with Phelippes, I would be suspected of infiltrating Essex's network to spy upon them. I laid my hand upon the document I had stolen, which seemed to sear my very flesh. For a moment I closed my eyes, feeling dizzy. Babington and the others, they had been convicted of treason. Would that be my fate? Hung. Drawn. And quartered. I could not speak for terror.

At last I managed to say, 'Sara, is Ruy at home? Send for him to speak with us.'

Ruy came at last, frowning and impatient at being interrupted in whatever business he had been about, business I thought it better not to know. I gave him the transcription of the report. His frown deepened as he read it, then he paced about the room for a while, before throwing the paper down on the table.

'I have no fear that this will harm me,' he said brusquely. 'Tittle-tattle from Mendoza's little coterie of discontents and troublemakers in Paris. Essex is a fool, but he is not so great a fool as to try to damage me, the Queen's most valued physician. I have Her Majesty's ear and trust. Essex dare not touch me.'

How typical that was of Ruy. He feared only for his own skin and took no account of the trap he had laid for others.

'I do not share your confidence, Ruy,' I said, feeling a slow anger beginning to burn in me and drive out my weakness. 'Essex is rash, and rarely looks ahead to consider the consequences of his actions. He is bent on defeating the Cecils, and by destroying you he will damage them. Besides, you may be the Queen's favourite physician, but you hardly rank beside the first nobleman in England and the Queen's especial darling. You must tell the Cecils about the ruby.'

He looked angered at this frank speaking from one he had always considered his inferior, but he gave me a condescending pat on the shoulder and turned to leave.

'Don't concern yourself with it, Kit. It is nothing but a vain puff of wind, soon vanished away.'

With that he strode out of the room, leaving Sara and me staring at each other.

166

'Oh, Kit, what shall we do?' she implored.

'Bring me ink,' I said, selecting a fresh quill from my pouch. 'I will do what I can.'

While she watched, I wrote out a new version of my transcription, omitting the damning paragraph and using the ink in my own portable inkhorn. As I worked, I tried to close my mind to the implications of my actions, which would place me in unimaginable danger. Then I transcribed this new document back into the original code of the report, using Sara's ink, another quill, and the paper I had removed from Phelippes's office, carefully copying the handwriting of the Paris agent. The forged report now contained the general information about Mendoza and the French Court, but said nothing of Ruy.

'I will place these amongst Phelippes's papers tomorrow,' I said, 'and hope to stave off trouble for Ruy, at least for a time. But you must understand, Sara, that the agent may report again, or ask why his warning has not been heeded. It may be necessary for you all to escape abroad. The passports you were granted to travel to the Continent before, are they still valid?'

She nodded. She seemed stunned into helplessness.

As for myself, if the agent reported again, I knew my forgery would be discovered. Treason. It could only end in death.

The next day I took the forged report to Arthur Gregory for sealing, which he did with his usual skill, never querying my request. Back in Phelippes's office, I waited until the wax had set hard and cold, then broke it open, as if I had just received the report for deciphering. I added this forged report and its transcription to the pile of documents I was preparing for Phelippes, and continued with my work for the rest of the day, flinching at every sound of voices and footsteps in the corridor outside. To my infinite relief, Phelippes did not return before it was time for me to go. I left the neat stack of paper on his writing table, and fled thankfully back to Southwark.

I slept badly and rose at last in the dark, lit a candle and huddled, shivering, in my cloak, looking out over the pewter sheen of the river towards the City, where an occasional window showed a glimmer of light. I longed to talk to Simon, to share the burden of my knowledge, yet I must not.

What should I do? If Phelippes discovered that I had forged the report, I thought little of my chances. I would be branded at once as a conspirator with Ruy, and if he was charged with treason, then, by my actions in forging the document, I would be charged too, and face the most fearful of deaths. The reality of it danced before my eyes, blotting out the sight of the river, and suddenly I was retching in my terror. Yet what could I have done? I was certain Ruy's confidence was nothing but more of his accursed arrogance.

It was Sara and the children I cared about. Ambrose, the eldest, a young man now, making his way amongst the merchants of London. Anthony, proving himself a fine scholar at Winchester. Anne soon to be married to the merchant Francisco Pinto de Brito. The younger children – Cecilia and Tabitha. I had known the whole family ever since I had come to London. And Sara, who had comforted a frightened motherless child, a girl disguised as a boy in a strange land with an unknown language, penniless, bereft. I could not let them hurt Sara. It was for their sake that I had made the forgery, but doing so put me in far greater danger than I would have faced merely as a member of the Portuguese community. I put my head in my hands and wept.

There was one other person I ought to warn. Now that Dr Nuñez was dead, only one man remained of the former leaders of our community in London: Dunstan Añes, international merchant, Purveyor of Groceries and Spices to Her Majesty the Queen, and father to Sara. I had seen little of him since the planning of the Portuguese expedition, in which – like my father and Dr Nuñez – he had invested and lost heavily. Since I had come to live south of the river and

168

did not attend our people's services, I no longer had occasion to meet him.

He was an old man now, but if the agent's report from Paris reflected the intentions of Essex to attack the whole Marrano community, Dunstan Añes must be told of it. Like Ruy, he was well placed at Court and trusted by the Queen, but an accusation of treason is like a poison for which there is no antidote. If it is once credited, however weak the evidence, however moved by malice the accuser, the supposed traitor will forever be suspected. Since the time of the Queen's father, many had been executed for treason whom later evidence had shown to be innocent, but we lived in brutal and ruthless times.

The usual course with suspected treason was to stamp upon it first, then ask questions later. I shuddered to remember my own small part in the entrapment of Anthony Babington – pushed and prodded by Robert Poley into acts he would probably never have committed otherwise – and the forged evidence against him and the Scottish queen so cleverly prepared by Thomas Phelippes. Such tricks could be used to destroy others. Could be used even against someone of as little importance as I was. They could certainly be used against Ruy Lopez.

It was two days before I was able to visit Dunstan Añes. To avoid any suspicion, it was essential that I should continue the usual pattern of my days, working in the hospital until the late morning, spending two or three hours in the Customs House, then calling upon any private patients in the City and Westminster who required my services. Dunstan Añes was much occupied at the time down river at Greenwich, where some formal banquet was being prepared, but in the early evening of the third day, I found him at his house in Crutched Friars. I was distressed by how much he had aged. He leaned heavily on a stick, and his face, which used to be rubicund with good health and good eating, had sunk in with the loss of teeth and the withering of elderly skin.

With a few words of explanation, I gave him the original Paris report and my transcription. As he read it he grew pale, and his hands, knotted with swollen knuckles, began to tremble.

'I have substituted a coded report and transcription which omit the part about Ruy and the Marrano community,' I explained. 'So far, it seems to have been accepted as authentic. At least, no one has mentioned any problem in my presence.'

I hesitated. 'But there may be other reports. Or even without the information this agent says he possesses, it may be that Essex will falsify charges.' I paused again, not sure how to put into words a certain uneasy feeling which had assailed me these last few days, but which might be no more than my own pricking conscience at having forged the document.

'Perhaps my imagination is playing tricks on me,' I said, 'but I have thought that some of those who work for Phelippes have looked at me . . . a little askance of late. As though they knew something that I did not, or they were suspicious of me.'

'If that is so,' he passed his hand wearily over his face, 'it might be wise for you to go into hiding. There is the house in St Katharine Creechurch . . .'

'Nay,' I interrupted him. 'I think I will be safer if I continue to work as I have done before. If I hide, that will only arouse more suspicions.' I thought with a shudder of the house where Ruy stowed his slippery double agents and, for all I knew, criminals and assassins. Southwark, for all its petty thieves and whores, seemed a paradise by comparison.

As Dunstan Añes showed me out, he fetched up a deep sigh.

'I wish my son-in-law had never become entangled in the affairs of Dom Antonio, with his claim to the Portuguese throne. To supply Sir Francis Walsingham with information from our mercantile agents in other countries was one thing; to play at king-maker is quite another.

Whatever we may do to try to protect him, Ruy will burn his hand in the fire one day, and what will become of my Sara and the children then?'

My anxiety began to subside a little as Phelippes continued to treat me as a respected colleague on the rare occasions when we met and I decided that the suspicious looks I thought I had noticed were merely a phantasm of my guilty conscience. I heard nothing about the forged report, and there was no talk of the matters it had mentioned, though I continued to walk on hot coals. There had been no further despatches from Paris and I learned that the agent who had sent the report had been transferred to Dieppe to investigate the present activities of the Catholic seminary for English priests there, which bred so many who had slipped into England to foment treason and religious dissent.

For the moment, I hoped I was safe.

After a fortnight of this arrangement for me to work with Phelippes, the flow of despatches dried up, as it often did, and I returned to spending the whole day at St Thomas's. That I should have been the one to discover the accusation against Ruy seemed like a curious turn of Fortune's Wheel. But was it for good or ill?

Almost exactly a month after Simon and I had met Gomez d'Avila on the steps of Mountjoy's Inn, Phelippes sent word one early evening that he would be glad of my services again, not merely for deciphering but also for my knowledge of Portuguese. On reading this summons, I felt a sudden chill, remembering that conversation with Sara about Andrada and the ruby. I read the message through again. It was quite clear. No mention of Spain or overtures for peace. What did it mean? However, Portuguese suggested Dom Antonio, and that suggested Ruy Lopez. I folded the note and slipped it into the purse at my belt.

'Tell Master Phelippes that I will be there shortly,' I said to the boy who had brought the note, and gave him a farthing for his trouble.

I took my time walking over the Bridge and paused in the centre to watch the ships heading down river and out to sea. There was a Dutch caravel under full sail. Perhaps it was setting off for Amsterdam, a city where I could be free of Essex and the Cecils and all their works. I remembered my time there with Nick Berden, when I had found Rikki, or he had found me. He was sitting on my feet, looking up at me and wondering why I had stopped here. Like Sara, I did not want to leave England, which felt to me like my home now, even though I might be designated a Stranger.

However, I could not linger midway across the river for ever. My reluctant feet took me over the Bridge and even as I touched the north shore I hesitated, wanting to turn back to Southwark. The Customs House loomed above the docks as it had always done, but never had I felt so unwilling to enter it, as though that brief note from Phelippes had contained a warning. As I stepped from the bright day into the gloomy hallway, I shivered. Then told myself not to be a fool.

When I reached Phelippes's office on the first floor, he fixed me with a look not altogether friendly, which I could not interpret.

'You are, I believe, a friend of Dr Roderigo Lopez,' he said, without so much as a 'Good e'en'.

I looked at him in astonishment, unable to understand his curt tone. 'I know Dr Lopez,' I said, frowning in puzzlement. 'You know that. All members of the Portuguese community here in London are known to each other. There are so few of us. But a friend? I would not say so. I am a friend of his wife, Sara Lopez, daughter of Dunstan Añez, the Queen's Purveyor of Groceries and Spices. You also know that very well, Thomas. She is English born herself. She was very kind to me when I arrived in England as a child, having just lost my mother.'

'Hmm,' he said, and walked to the window to look out over the docks.

Suddenly, he whirled round. 'There is a matter of the gravest danger which has been revealed to My Lord Essex.'

At these words, my heart gave a jump, and I felt sick. Had further word come from Paris?

But Phelippes continued. 'This morning we have arrested a man called Ferreira da Gama, lodging at a house in St Katharine Creechurch which belongs to Dr Lopez. Certain documents have come to hand. Some in cipher, some in Portuguese and Spanish. My Spanish is good, but my Portuguese less so. I need your assistance, but if it proves that you are in any way implicated in this matter, My Lord Essex is not inclined to show you any mercy.'

My lungs could not draw breath. I could barely speak, but at last I managed to say, 'I swear to you, Thomas, that I am not implicated. I have no idea what this may be, that you have discovered. Or the Earl has discovered.'

I hoped to God it was true. Could it possibly be connected to the death of Josiah Gurdin, and my enquiries into it? That, certainly, had something to do with Spain, but I could not see how Ruy Lopez was implicated. Or Ferreira da Gama. Unless it was the 'business' about which Ruy was so elated that evening when Simon and I had supped with Sara. The scheme he hoped to present to the Cecils. The spectre of Andrada and the ruby hovered at the edge of my mind.

Phelippes frowned at me, tugging at his lower lip with his long, ink-stained fingers. Finally, he seemed to make up his mind.

'Very well. I shall arrange for a cot to be set up here in the office for you. The matter is of such gravity that the Earl has decreed that we cannot risk your leaving the building. You will stay within the walls of the Customs House until he gives you leave to go outside.'

'But . . .' I said, angry and afraid.

He held up his hand.

'You must understand the Earl's concern, Kit. You have friends amongst the Marrano community who are under suspicion. You admit yourself that you are a close friend of Sara Lopez, who is the wife of one of those apparently most involved. Even if the Earl could be certain of your loyalty, you might reveal something of this matter inadvertently. He has decreed that you will remain within these walls.'

His voice softened at last. 'I am sorry, Kit. This is not my decision. The Earl and Master Bacon have decided how we are to proceed, and I can do nothing but carry out their orders. We will settle the matter of your absence with St Thomas's.'

'You should never have taken a position under such men,' I whispered, but he pretended not to hear me.

'And what of Rikki?' I said, gesturing at my dog, who always made himself at home here.

'That is a difficulty,' he admitted. 'Either we must send him away, or . . . make arrangements . . .'

Rikki would need to go outside, and if I were not permitted . . .?

Arthur came through from his office, carrying one of his small tables. His face was bleak, but he attempted to smile at me reassuringly.

'They will put a cot for you in my office, Kit. I am making room for it. And do not concern yourself about Rikki. I will walk him for you. Unless you would wish me to take him home with me?'

I felt a small glow of warmth amidst this sudden terror. I reminded myself that both Arthur Gregory and Thomas Phelippes had been my friends since Sir Francis's time. They might be forced to carry out Essex's orders, but they would do their best for me.

'Thank you, Arthur. If you would walk him for me, and see that food is brought. But I should like to keep him with me.'

It would be some comfort to have Rikki. Arthur was as friendly as ever. Even Thomas, after that first, cold greeting, seemed to have relaxed.

And yet–

The fine office, with its linen-fold panelling and moulded plaster ceiling, its elegant furniture and its views over the Thames, bore little resemblance to the dank stone chambers of the Tower.

But just as certainly as any malefactor in the Tower, I was a prisoner.

A formidable stack of papers confronted me the next morning. I was seated alone at a desk in Phelippes's office, while he consulted downstairs with armed men of Essex's who had just arrived from Eton. Ferreira da Gama had been handed over, nominally, to his own *soi-disant* monarch, Dom Antonio, King of Nowhere, the pauper ruler of a paper kingdom, living off the charity of Queen Elizabeth and the hand-outs from his impoverished Marrano subjects. Ferreira was imprisoned in the former monastery at Eton. This had been allocated as a residence to the Dom after our return from the abortive expedition to Portugal, where he lived with a threadbare court, almost as much a prisoner as I now found myself.

Ferreira might be guarded by Portuguese gaolers, but there was no ambiguity about who was controlling this puppet-show. Essex had persuaded the Queen to put him in sole charge of the whole gamut of Portuguese affairs. He had issued instructions that every Portingall (for so he contemptuously designated us) who attempted to enter England through any of the Channel ports was to be arrested immediately and brought to be questioned by Anthony Bacon, Thomas Phelippes, and their inquisitors.

Every letter travelling by the public mails 'directed to Portingall merchants and others of that Nation' was to be intercepted and brought to this office for examination. Familiar as I was with the scale of Marrano mercantile enterprise, I could see that I should be working day and night.

'But this is nothing but harmless commerce,' I said to Phelippes later that day, pointing to a fresh pile of documents he had dropped on my desk that morning.

'I'll spend my time translating orders for goods, shipping manifests, bills of lading, and invoices, most of them as innocent as Dunstan Añes's orders for two barrels of East Indian peppercorns or his shipment to Flanders of three dozen bales of Lancashire woollen cloth.'

He shrugged. 'It must be done. Winnow the chaff to find the grain.'

Time crawled past. For several days I had been working my way slowly through this tedious assignment, being in no hurry to expedite any scheme of Essex's. I had no idea whether Ferreira da Gama was guilty of any crime, or whether Ruy Lopez had strayed into unlawful territory with his habitual scheming. From my observation of Essex on our Portuguese voyage, I had a poor opinion of his intelligence and his political acumen, but I did not doubt the depth of his hatred of Ruy or the strength of his determination to destroy the Cecils, father and son.

I wondered whether Essex had heard that Ruy had been spreading rumours that he had contracted syphilis. Was it true? Given the Earl's wanton behaviour, he might well have done, and that would put both his wife and his children at risk, for the children of a syphilitic father are often barren. And poor Lady Frances, who could easily become infected. Of course, it might not be true, but no more than an act of malice by Ruy, either for some personal reason of his own . . . or perhaps acting for the Cecils, to undermine Essex. That, I supposed, was quite likely.

The Queen maintained her strange, coy relationship with the Earl, which in my eyes seemed absurd, almost sickening. He was young enough to be her son, or even her grandson, and he had not one tenth of her intelligence. I suppose some women thought him handsome, but his physical beauty had always been marred for me by his arrogance, his bluster, and his violent temper. It was said that the Queen favoured neither the one side nor the other in the contest between Essex and Sir Robert Cecil, but watched them with amusement, touching the scales on which they were balanced with the tip of her finger, whenever one seemed like to gain the ascendancy.

However, at present I had no choice, had I wished to ally myself with one faction or the other. Which I did not. Like Nick Berden, I felt it was better to withdraw and await the outcome. However, I had now been arrested to serve Essex's purpose as surely as Ferreira had been, and I had better make the best of it.

I took up another letter in my ink-stained hands and wriggled my cramped shoulders. The letter was written in Portuguese and not coded, but used the language of merchants in a somewhat ambiguous manner. This might, indeed, be one of the letters Phelippes was looking for. I felt suddenly afraid. What if I were to find something which clearly condemned Ruy Lopez? Only a short time ago I had concealed that letter which might have brought danger to Sara. I could not, this time, hide the letter in my doublet and carry it away to be doctored elsewhere.

The present letter had been sent by one Francisco de Torres and was directed to Domingo Fernandes. I knew most of the Marrano merchants, but I did not recognise these names. It contained many conventional phrases, indicating that the merchants with whom Francisco was dealing were pleased with the merchandise supplied by Domingo. They found the wares 'special good, rare, well-coloured, and in great request'. This all sounded too vague for a normal letter from a business-like merchant.

There was mention of 'cloth, scarlet threads, pearls, a diamond, and sundry kinds of merchandise so sorted' and asked that 'the jewels be sent'. There was certainly something not altogether genuine here, for jewels were normally not exported *from* but imported *into* England, coming from such lands as the Spanish and Portuguese colonies, where they were mined. Unless the letter referred to the export of finished jewels from an English goldsmith's hands? Which it might.

On the other hand, these terms for precious merchandise might stand for a different kind of merchandise altogether. 'Pearls', as I knew from my work in the past for Walsingham, could stand for 'peace'. Might

177

this be its cipher meaning? Was this document partially in cipher, masquerading as an innocent letter about commercial goods, but in truth connected to some gesture towards peace with Spain, such as Lord Burghley had been advocating for many years? Such as Gurdin had been implicated in? Had it some connection with the Cecils? In which case the 'jewels' might refer to a serious offer or guarantee from the peace party in England. Phelippes, however, would understand that as well as I, there was no need for me to point it out to him. My own private allegiance, if I could be said to have one, was rather to the Cecils than to Essex, though I knew they could be equally ruthless.

If this letter somehow referred to a scheme of the Cecils, then it was easy to understand that the Earl would pursue it as eagerly as a hunting alaunt would pursue a stag, scenting blood. Perhaps he hoped to cause serious damage to them, harm them in the Queen's eyes, and raise himself up by trampling Sir Robert Cecil's face in the mud under the heel of his bejewelled shoe.

Then another phrase in the letter caught my eye. I had translated it into English without giving it proper attention, thinking at first this was a routine merchant's letter, until I noticed the emphasis on jewels lower down. Now, however, the phrase leapt out from the page: 'the musk and amber was highly esteemed'.

Musk and amber. 'Senhor Musk and Amber'. Antonio Perez. I had heard Ruy call Perez this more than once, based on the man's curious habits of dosing himself with these two precious commodities. Antonio Perez, condemned murderer, fugitive from justice and the Spanish court, house guest (of course!) of the Earl of Essex and amateur physician extraordinary. It was common knowledge that representatives of the Spanish government had made requests to the English government to hand over Perez to face punishment in Spain, where he had been tried and found guilty of murder after he had fled to England. Why Essex should shelter him, I had no idea, except that he might prove useful, being now a declared enemy of Spain, should the Earl wish to press his desire for a war against Spain all the more forcefully.

If 'pearls' was code for 'peace', then 'musk and amber' might be code for Antonio Perez. It was no great leap of the imagination to suppose that this letter was connected to some business of the Cecils and their approach toward peace with Spain. Part of the negotiation might be a demand from Spain that Perez be handed over to them to face trial and punishment for murder. Aye, it made sense. And somehow Essex's men, or Anthony Bacon's men, had managed to intercept this letter. If it did implicate the Cecils, it could be a powerful weapon in Essex's hands.

I swallowed nervously and glanced around the empty room. This letter might be more explosive than a cannon packed full of gunpowder. But I would not call Phelippes's attention to it. He might not know Ruy's nickname for Perez. I laid the original letter and my English translation on top of my completed work on Phelippes's desk and took up the next document, a simple shipping manifest for a cargo of Baltic timber. My hands were shaking so much that I blotted the first line of my translation and must needs begin again.

Chapter Nine

During this time that I was confined to the Customs House and to my work translating and deciphering, Essex was not only hunting down Marranos and pawing through their correspondence. He was also manoeuvring to have his protégé Francis Bacon, brother of Anthony, appointed to the high office of Attorney General. The Cecils were promoting Sir Edward Coke, a slightly younger man, but much more experienced. Securing the position for its nominee would increase the power and influence of the winning faction.

The Queen, with her usual wise tactic of delaying, refused to decide in favour of either man at present, and before I had been confined to the Customs House I heard the jests, going the rounds of Southwark, about the fight between 'the Cook and the Bacon'. Intriguing at this high level of government did not prevent Essex, however, from continuing to urge on all his staff of agents and others to find – or perhaps manufacture – some evidence to provide him with any intelligence coup, however small, to undermine the Cecils.

On the fourth day of November, when I had been trapped in Phelippes's office for two and a half weeks, another Marrano fell into Essex's net. Gomez d'Avila, last seen by me back in September on the steps of Mountjoy's Inn, was arrested as he landed in Dover from Calais. He appeared far from reluctant to talk to Essex's men, for he eagerly handed over to them another letter from Francisco

Torres to Domingo Fernandes, revealing that it was from Tinoco. I found myself sweating with fear when Phelippes told me. The net was tightening about Ruy Lopez, and Sara had seen all of these men – d'Avila, Tinoco, and Ferreira – in Ruy's company and making free of her home.

Tinoco! The very agent I knew Ruy was running on the Continent as part of that projection Sara had said would bring great benefit to Lord Burghley, and which had begun during Sir Francis's lifetime, when it had involved Andrada. I had heard nothing of Andrada of late, although I knew he was being hunted, believed to be a traitor to England. The pieces began to fall into place. This hunting down of Marranos was manifestly all part of Essex's war against the Cecils, and it reeked of double-dealing and treachery every step of the way. I wondered whether Gomez d'Avila had been a double agent and Essex's man from the start.

'Torres,' said Phelippes to me, rubbing his hands together gleefully, 'is now revealed as Tinoco.' He picked up the letter and waved it at me. 'I think we may take it as certain that Fernandes is Ferreira. How simple-minded these fellows are!' he added with contempt.

I did not answer. The links to Lopez must soon emerge. All these men – Tinoco, Ferreira, and d'Avila – were connected to Ruy. I did not need Sara's unhappy words, for I had seen them myself, talking in his garden, coming and going from Mountjoy's Inn. But what did Essex hope to gain from knowledge of Ruy's projection, whatever it was? Merely to demonstrate that he could outsmart Lord Burghley's own network? Or to destroy any delicate peace overtures the Cecils might be making? For Essex continued to be eager for war, always dreaming of himself as a great warrior, whereas surely both Queen and Parliament knew that his military adventures had all proved farcical and disastrous in the past. It was said that, if he could not lead a campaign against Spain, he longed to be put in command of the English army in Ireland.

'Aye,' Phelippes went on, grown a little less cautious in front of me now by his return to our former friendship and his delight in securing another Marrano agent, 'Tinoco has proved useful to us in the past. Though I think he does not tell us all he knows.'

For a moment I did not take his meaning. Then I understood. Tinoco himself was *also* a double agent, working for both Essex and the Cecils. I had gathered from Sara that he might also be working for the Spanish, thus he could even be a triple agent. His treachery must surely endanger Ruy. During all my time imprisoned in Phelippes's office I had been frightened and angry. Now I felt physically sick. I walked to the window and threw open the casement. The November wind swept in, scattering Phelippes's papers.

'What are you doing, Kit!' he cried, stooping to gather them up.

'I needed air,' I said abruptly. 'I am sick at heart from this confinement. When will Essex allow me to go home?'

'Not long, not long. We must keep our eyes upon Ferreira once he knows d'Avila has been taken, to see which way he jumps.'

It was not long before Phelippes was able to confirm that Ferreira had indeed jumped. In a state of panic, I suppose (for he was not a professional intelligencer), Ferreira began writing letters. One of these was addressed to Ruy, and Essex's men followed it to Mountjoy's Inn. Ruy, however, was no fool. He took the letter straight to Dom Antonio. Nothing secretive about Ruy Lopez, gentlemen, he is as open and honest as a daisy in the sunlight!

Frustrated in their attempt to ensnare Ruy, Anthony Bacon's men in Eton tried another approach. Ferreira's gaoler, who had been carrying his letters, was questioned, and handed over a letter Ferreira had written to his contact in the French embassy. Proof of treachery? Phelippes was over the moon, Anthony Bacon informed Essex, and on the eleventh day of November Ferreira was interrogated – and, no doubt, tortured – until he agreed to write a full declaration of the plot in which he had been involved.

This document was brought to the Customs House and I had a sight of it. Phelippes was but partially pleased with the contents.

'So,' he said, 'there is here set out the offer to put forward Dom Antonio's son, Dom Emanuel, as claimant to the Portuguese throne in his father's stead. Ferreira has offered his service to the Spanish, and he says that Dr Lopez has contrived all this. A certain fifty thousand crowns, that we have heard of elsewhere, Ferreira claims is to be paid to Dom Antonio.'

'But . . . ' I said, recalling something which had slipped my mind in all the recent plots and counter plots.

'What is it, Kit?' he asked irritably.

'Did not My Lord Essex himself at one time employ Dr Lopez to make such an approach to Spain? Soon after Sir Francis's death, when he hoped to take over the intelligence service, without rivalry from the Cecils?'

Phelippes looked even more irritated.

'Aye, but that is an old story. Lopez told my lord nothing of *this* latest arrangement.'

'Surely Walsingham always instructed his projectors to proceed with the utmost secrecy, until the trap might be sprung,' I said. 'Could it not be that this is such a projection, and My Lord Essex has . . . has stumbled upon it before all was in place?'

I did not believe what I said. I was certain Ruy was working for the Cecils in this, but thought I must do my best for him.

Phelippes pointed a warning finger at me.

'My Lord Essex will not like to hear you say so. I warn you, Kit, keep your tongue behind your teeth. Do not even mention it to Anthony Bacon and I will forget that I heard you say it. My Lord Essex is searching for a chain that links King Philip, Ferreira, Lopez, and the Cecils, and you would do well to remember it.'

I was astonished into silence. That Phelippes should be so frank with me once more, as in the past, was testimony to the fact that he now thought that I was a totally trustworthy servant of Essex, but the knowledge of what he had said placed me in danger, for I could now be a threat to the Earl himself. This was open acknowledgement that Essex was trying to find, or indeed manufacture, evidence that Lord Burghley, the Queen's most trusted adviser, was a traitor.

A few days later, Phelippes imparted more disturbing news.

'My Lord Essex,' he said, 'does not intend as yet to reveal the extent of our discoveries to the Queen.'

For the first time I thought he looked deeply worried, and with good reason. To keep such dangerous knowledge to himself was tantamount to treason, but Essex clearly thought himself above the law. Instead, ignoring the careful advice of Anthony Bacon and Thomas Phelippes, he went to the Queen and dramatically denounced Ruy Lopez for making contact with the Spanish, without revealing the rest of his own activities.

I was amused – or as amused as I could be in such a perilous situation – to learn that the Queen had responded exactly as I had, pointing out that Ruy Lopez had been doing exactly what Sir Francis – and later Essex – had ordered him to do. The Queen trusted the man who had been her personal physician for two decades, and who had cared for her with skill and tenderness. Essex was too arrogant, too puffed up with his own importance, to understand such a bond.

We were told that the Queen had decided that all of Ferreira's papers which had been seized from St Katharine Creechurch were to be examined again on her behalf. As they were in Portuguese, this must be done by a man who spoke Portuguese, but under the watchful eye of Anthony Bacon and his men. With a fine sense of irony, she appointed Ruy Lopez to translate them. I had already translated all these same documents in the office, but

Phelippes decided that he and I should ride out to Eton and sit as witnesses to this second translation process.

'You will keep your ears open and your eyes alert,' he said, 'and indicate to me at once if Lopez deviates from the Portuguese text.'

Never had the dank, misty weather of a November morning seemed so delightful to me as we mounted our horses outside the Customs House and headed west on the road to Windsor and Eton. It was just before dawn, with hardly anyone about in the streets of the City. I filled my lungs with the sooty, sodden air and felt I was tasting manna, after more than a month's incarceration in the Customs House. Phelippes was grim and silent, not appreciating the humour of having Essex's prey appointed by the Queen as assistant gamekeeper in this pantomime of a hunt. I did not care. I was free to move about again, and matters could not now be so dangerous for Sara and the children if the Queen herself had favoured Ruy, despite Essex's accusations. She must have realised that the whole sorry business was yet another skirmish in the war between Essex and the Cecils.

In the former monastery where Dom Antonio was lodged, we were shown into a large room, where tension was palpable in the air. It was already somewhat crowded with Essex's people – armed men, clerks, Anthony Bacon, several gentlemen I did not know, and, going in ahead of us, Ruy Lopez, white-bearded and venerable in a sumptuous physician's gown of black silk and velvet. He looked calm and at ease, shaking Anthony Bacon by the hand and enquiring solicitously about his health, which was ever poor. Bacon seemed somewhat disconcerted at this, but asked him to be seated at a table which had been set ready, with paper and ink and the collection of documents removed from St Katharine Creechurch.

Ruy worked steadily through them, first reading out a sentence at a time in English, then writing it down. I had brought copies of my own translations and followed him sentence by sentence. Apart from the usual differences when two people translate the same piece of prose (the order of the sentence, the occasional choice of a different word) our versions were remarkably similar. As each document was completed I nodded to Phelippes that the translation was correct. Ruy must have seen me there, but he gave no acknowledgement of my presence.

When he reached the dangerous letter from 'Torres' to 'Fernandes', he proceeded to translate it with perfect composure, not indicating by any flicker of the eyes or twitch of the cheek that the contents might in any way be dangerous for him. Even the phrase 'musk and amber' was delivered with no indication that it meant more than it said. The man, I thought, is a consummate actor. He should be gracing the playhouse with Simon. I wished Simon could be there to appreciate the performance.

Thanks to the intervention of the Queen and her support of Ruy, it seemed that all Essex's plots had achieved nothing. After our expedition to Eton, the pursuit of Marrano agents slackened and the paperwork dwindled away. Essex had been outmanoeuvred for the moment, but it was clear that the rivalry between the two factions would continue until one triumphed and the other was destroyed. Small fish like myself could still fall victim to their enmity and I was not so foolish as to suppose that this was an end to any danger I might be in through my nationality and my links with the Lopez family.

However, at last Rikki and I were allowed to go home. I found my room in a sad state, for when I had gone out that evening, I had expected to return the same day. Food that I had left there had been eaten by rats and mice, which had left their droppings everywhere, even in my bed. My medicines and instruments were dusty, and something had been nibbling at the fur lining of my good cloak. I spent that first day restoring my room to the clean and tidy state which I felt appropriate for a physician's lodgings, then in the evening took myself off to the Lion where the players from the Rose usually came after the performance was finished. It was too cold to sit outside, so I found myself a bench by the fire with my mug of ale and a dish of boiled beef and onions, luxury indeed after the poor fare, always cold, that one of the junior clerks had fetched for me while I was confined to the Customs House.

'Well,' said Simon, half an hour later, when he came in with a crowd of players, shouting out their thirst to the innkeeper. 'So you have returned to us at last.' He was flushed and angry.

'I have been kept a prisoner by Phelippes, on the Earl of Essex's orders,' I said. 'Forced to decipher and translate secret papers. He would not allow me to go out of the building, nor to send word to my friends.'

Simon raised his eyebrows as he studied me over the rim of his tankard. It was clear he did not believe me.

'It is true!' Shamefully I felt tears springing to my eyes. I suppose it seemed an unlikely story, but I had not thought Simon would disbelieve me. I had expected to be welcomed warmly, not glared at. I was exhausted. All the fear and misery of my confinement overwhelmed me, as I turned my head away to hide the tears, but I was suddenly too tired and too disheartened to argue further.

'Could you not have sent word?' he snapped, accepting a second tankard of ale from Will and glowering at me.

'Nay! I tell you, I was treated like a prisoner at the Earl of Essex's orders. Phelippes needed me to translate papers from the Portuguese, but his masters, Essex and Anthony Bacon, half expected me to be involved in some treasonable plot that Essex thought he had nosed out. I was only released today.'

'What was I to think?' He was still angry, but he lowered his voice as Will sat down on the bench beside me. 'You disappeared for more than a month. No word. No one knew what had become of you. I went to Sara, but she could tell me nothing, except that she was worried about Ruy. I feared you might have fallen in the Thames.'

187

I gave a weak smile. 'Not as serious as that. But I hate Essex. And his cat's paw, Anthony Bacon.' My voice rose, and I could not control it. I was glad of the rowdy noise from the players.

'These men are dangerous, Simon.' Will intervened in a quiet voice. 'There's little Kit could have done, without risking suspicion. One false step . . . Think of Marlowe.'

That sobered Simon. He drained his tankard and then said grudgingly, 'I'm sorry, Kit. But we were all worried what had become of you.'

'I hate those men and all their schemes,' I said bitterly. 'If I had never met Robert Poley . . . Never been drawn into intelligence work . . .'

'And that was my fault,' he said, looking down into his empty tankard.

'Finished already?' said Will. He was clearly puzzled here, by something he did not understand. 'I think you need another. I'm in the chinks today. Burbage has finally paid me.' He looked aside and beckoned to a serving girl.

'Nay, we were but children then,' I said to Simon. 'Others were using us for their own ends. What could we do? But, oh, Simon,' I lowered my voice to a whisper, 'sometimes I dream of starting a new life somewhere where I am not known. To rub the slate clean and write myself anew.'

'I'll go with you, then,' he said, attempting a lighter tone. 'Be sure to tell me next time and we will start a new adventure together.'

Phelippes had said he still wanted me to come to him one day a week, so I returned to my work at St Thomas's hospital, going over the river to the Customs House only on Wednesdays. Often he had no work for me, but asked me to continue coming. On the second of these Wednesdays I was setting off home again when Arthur Gregory came out of his tiny office and laid his hand on my sleeve. He looked sick with worry.

188

'Kit,' his voice was pleading, 'I know you take some private patients. I'm not a rich man, but . . .'

'What is amiss, Arthur?' I was alarmed by his appearance.

''Tis my little lad. He's only four years old, and he is so sick, burning up with fever. We sat up with him all night, my wife and I, but I do not know what to do. We had the barber-surgeon to him yesterday, to bleed him, but he was worse in the night. Could you . . . ?'

'Of course. Where do you live?'

'Not far from here, near Sir Francis's old house in Seething Lane.'

We set off at once. I had brought my satchel of medicines with me, as I was intending to visit another patient on my way home, and I was glad of it when I saw the boy. He was a beautiful child, with the golden curls of some angel from a stained glass window, very like a younger version of my patient Tommy Atgate, but lacking that imp's mischief. Without the wasting effects of the fever he would have had the plump rounded limbs of a perfect child's body. Gregory's wife was very young, and beside herself with worry. She had called in the barber-surgeon again while her husband had been out, and the poor lad was bled as white as a veal calf, with angry red blotches of rash standing out against the milky skin. He was screaming with pain and fever.

'It isn't the plague, is it?' the girl sobbed, clutching the child to her thin bosom. 'Oh, please, doctor, let it not be the plague!'

'Lay him down on his bed,' I said, 'so I may examine him. And nay, it is not the plague. What is his name?'

'William.' She laid the boy down and then fell to the floor at my feet and kissed the hem of my robe. Embarrassed, I told her to fetch a basin of boiling water and some clean cloths. Very gently I peeled off the child's clothes, which were sodden with sweat and urine.

'It is the measles,' I said, 'not the plague, but it is a bad case, and you should not have had him bled.'

I added soothing herbs to the water, *calendula officinalis* and *ocimum basilicum*, then, when they had infused, I strained the cooled water, soaked a cloth in it, and bathed him all over. He screamed the louder when I started, but soon relaxed as the cool infusion comforted his skin.

'He still has a high fever,' I said, 'but now that the rash has broken through, it will begin to go down. Find me a soft towel to dry him. And do you have a piece of red cloth? A petticoat or a tablecloth?'

The girl looked mystified, but fetched me a towel and a red underskirt.

'Fasten the red cloth over the window,' I told Arthur as I dried the child gently, 'so the only light comes in through it.'

He did as he was told and soon we were bathed in a soft rosy glow. I told the girl to dress the child in a loose shift and change his damp bedding for dry, while I measured out more of the herbs for the cooling baths. Then I asked for more boiling water, and made two further infusions: one of *hyssopus officinale*, *plantago lanceolata*, and *althea officinalis*, the other of *euphrasia officinalis* and *prunella vulgaris*.

I poured the first infusion, strained, into a jug and stirred in syrup of raspberries to make it more palatable for a child.

'You must give the child a small cup of this, four times a day,' I said.

The second infusion I strained three times, the last time through a fine silk handkerchief which I kept for the purpose.

'This is an eye-bath,' I said, 'and you must be most particular that it is perfectly free from any particles. Use a clean cloth for each eye, for the eye is most delicate and must be treated with the greatest care.'

I showed the girl how to bathe each eye, then threw the used cloths on the fire.

'If you will bring me a spoonful of honey, I will mix it with this powdered *tanacetum parthenium* to ease his fever. You must bath him every two hours or so, unless he is deep asleep, in which case leave him. Sleep is the best physician. I will come again tomorrow.'

I raised the child on my arm, so that he was sitting up.

'Now, William,' I said, 'this is a delicious honey which will make you feel better, then you shall have a cup of this special pink raspberry drink. I am sure you are very thirsty, aren't you?'

The little boy took the spoonful of medicine happily enough, for the honey concealed the bitterness of the feverfew, then drank down the infusion eagerly. Once I had settled him, Arthur walked with me to the door.

'Will he recover?' He was still anxious, but I could see that he had laid aside the worst of his fears.

'Aye. Certainly. Measles can be dangerous, but I think he is strong enough to survive. He looks a fine healthy boy.'

He gave a wan smile.

'I never thought to have a son. My first wife died childless. And to lose him . . .'

'I know. Keep the cloth over the window.'

'But why?'

'The eyes can be harmed by measles. You must shade them from the light until he is better.'

'What is your fee, Kit?'

I touched him lightly on the shoulder.

'Forget the fee. I treat him for comradeship's sake.'

After my release from duty at the Customs House, I wanted to see Sara, but thought it would be unwise, in case Essex's men were watching my movements. It was best that they should not connect me too closely with the Lopez household. Instead, Simon took word to her that I had reappeared.

He clattered up the stairs to my room on his return, demanding ale and throwing himself down on my bed, his arm around Rikki.

'I am as full of news as a peacock stuffed for a Court banquet,' he said, when he had drained his cup and held it out for me to refill.

'Well?' I said. 'Do not tease!'

'First, it seems that Dr Lopez has at length begun to show the common sense of a common man, instead of wreathing himself in impenetrable mystification, like some Turkish magician.'

'That,' I said dryly, 'can but be a change for the better.'

'According to Sara, he has gone to Lord Burghley and Sir Robert Cecil, and then to the Queen herself, and laid everything before them. He has explained that Sir Francis Walsingham's projection, in which he was to play a significant part, was no more nor less than a prelude to peace negotiations with Spain. Something which both Lord Burghley and Her Majesty had been considering for some time, since the endless state of war between our countries has proved a drain both on our men and the public purse.'

'It is true,' I said, 'that toward the end of his life Sir Francis had begun to favour Lord Burghley's desire for peace, if it could be had on the right terms for England. I think he would never have trusted King Philip altogether, but, like Burghley, he knew that the constant fear of invasion was proving a blight on the country as well as a burden to the Queen. He must have hoped that, with his advancing years, the Spanish king himself would abandon his desire to invade England, seize the crown, and convert us all to popery. King Philip is growing frail, if reports can be relied upon. But what could Sir Francis have offered to persuade him? Or now the Cecils? That has puzzled me ever since we first learned that Josiah Gurdin was sent by the Cecils to the Spanish embassy.'

'Ah, well, that is where Ruy Lopez comes into the plot,' Simon said. 'I beg your pardon. Not plot. "The projection." That sounds less devious, does it not?'

'Certainly Ruy had intercepted and passed messages for Sir Francis,' I said, 'over a number of years, but, as far as I know, he was never actively engaged in any of Sir Francis's or Phelippes's projections. Until this affair Sara hinted at, which Sir Francis was planning shortly before his death. Why this one?'

I said nothing of the fragments of intelligence which had come to light in Phelippes's office, for they had not revealed why Ruy had first become implicated.

'It was the Portuguese connection,' Simon said. 'That is what Sara believes. Dom Antonio, we all know, proved but a broken reed in that Portuguese affair four years ago. Arrogant, overweening, and misguided, he has become more of a liability than an asset to England.'

'Very true.'

'It seems, however, that Ruy Lopez has been wooing Antonio's son, young Dom Emanuel, seeking to substitute him for his unreliable and aggressive father.'

'Ah.' I remembered what Phelippes had told me.

'Indeed. I do not know – Sara herself does not know – whether the scheme to make use of Dom Emanuel originated with Ruy or with Sir Francis. It may be that Ruy went to Sir Francis with the idea of substituting a submissive Dom Emanuel as a puppet-king of Portugal, who would be acceptable to Spain. Or it may be that the idea came first to Sir Francis, and he drew in Ruy as a man who had worked with him and who was also well acquainted with the exiled Portuguese royal family.'

'In any case,' I said, 'Ruy would agree readily to such a scheme. He would hope to be rewarded both in coin and in better standing here in England, and he might still have some hopes of the gains he had once expected to make in Portugal under Dom Antonio, which ended so disastrously with the failure of the expedition.'

'However it came about in the first place,' Simon said, 'with Walsingham gone, Lopez must have found himself in a difficult situation. Without Sir Francis as his leader, he seems to have thought he could carry through the projection himself. At least, that is what Sara assumes. It seems he did not confide in her fully until this all came out with his confession to Lord Burghley. There was something about a ruby, which I did not quite understand. Oh, and he handed over some stolen correspondence of Antonio Perez. Who is he?'

'A Spaniard,' I said. 'A convicted murderer, who fled to England, and is living as a guest of the Earl of Essex.'

Simon's lips formed a silent whistle. 'A Spaniard! A guest of Essex! I thought he hated all Spaniards?'

'Not this one. Since Perez is wanted by the Spanish government, he too hates Spain. I expect Essex thinks he might be useful.'

I jumped up and strode across to the window. The shutters were open and I leaned out, watching the busy river traffic. Below me in the street, half a dozen young lads were kicking a ball about in the dust.

'I am afraid that all this has the ring of truth about it,' I said, 'and bears out the half story Sara told me before. Ruy Lopez is a clever man, but he is not as clever as he thinks he is. How arrogant! To suppose that *he* could negotiate directly with the king of Spain, on behalf of England, without the authority of one of our great men like Sir Francis or Lord Burghley or even Sir Robert Cecil. Dear Heaven, even the authority of the Earl of Essex, fool that he is! Little wonder Ruy fell under suspicion. He is fortunate indeed that his neck is not already in a noose. And to choose as his instruments such disreputable fellows as Ferreira and Gomez d'Avila. And the treacherous Tinoco. Poor Sara, to be tied to such a man!'

Rikki had jumped off the bed when I got up, hoping for a walk. I bent down and fondled his ears.

'As you say, disreputable fellows, certainly,' Simon said. 'Lopez asked that Ferreira should be released from prison, but Lord Burghley and Her Majesty refused. He claimed the man would be useful in pursuing the peace negotiations, but they said Ferreira was already too compromised. He did manage to secure the release of Gomez d'Avila.'

'That sneaking, treacherous little rat!' I spat it out. I had never liked the man, and his recent behaviour made him quite loathsome. 'Do not tell me. Lord Burghley welcomed him with open arms as a fellow conspirator.'

Simon laughed. 'Nay. Sara says the moment d'Avila was released he disappeared. No one knows what has become of him, not even Ruy.'

'I would not give a fig for d'Avila's life, once his treachery is known to Dom Antonio's supporters.'

The breeze through the open window carried in the sound of the clock at St Mary Overy ringing for one o'the clock.

Simon jumped up. 'I must go. I am on near the start of the first act today. That is everything I have learned, Kit.'

'Aye, I thank you for such a bundle of news. I am glad that Ruy has been open with Lord Burghley at last. We must wait and see what will become of this famous projection. I do not believe Lord Burghley will follow it up. Even if it was planned by Sir Francis, months and years have passed since his death. Matters with Spain will have changed. Besides, Lord Burghley would not trust a plan which has been compromised by Ruy Lopez with his shady fellow conspirators, and which has been sullied by all the investigations into that suspicious correspondence. The Cecils will make their own plans. Indeed, it seems they were already busy about some projection of their own, which involved Josiah Gurdin.'

'I am sure you have the right of it,' Simon said as he opened the door. 'Shall you dine at the Lion tonight?'

'Perhaps.'

Ruy was safe for the time, it seemed, back in the Cecil embrace, and Essex, after all his arrests and interrogations, was no further on the way to levering the Cecils from power. Essex had lost this round of the contest – outwitted, outflanked and outmanoeuvred. No wonder he made such a poor military commander. His response to this defeat was what might have been expected. When next I visited the Customs House, I heard the whole tale. I found Essex's chief intelligencer in a black mood, the worst I had ever seen.

'How has the Earl taken the latest course of events?' I asked. 'Dr Lopez's confiding of Sir Francis's projection to Lord Burghley?'

'My lord of Essex?' Phelippes said, his mouth pursed.

I could not tell whether it was with disgust or with amusement.

'It seems, having been outwitted by the Cecils, my lord was not pleased. He disappeared for three days, in a childish fit of the sulks. No one knew what had become of him, not even his wife.'

The Lady Frances, I thought privately, might not have been sorry for this disappearance.

'He reappeared,' Phelippes said, 'or so I am told by friends at Court – he reappeared, strutting about the Court to the covert amusement of all the courtiers and palace servants. Perhaps their amusement was not so covert, after all, for then – behold! – he vanished again, this time for *four* days, until the Queen herself was concerned enough to talk of sending forth a search party.'

'I can imagine him,' I said, 'like a spoilt child, thinking: *Now they will be sorry they were not kinder to me.*'

Phelippes shook his head, as if reproving me for such disrespect towards the man who financed the makeshift intelligence service to which he was unfortunately attached, but he did not utter any rebuke.

'Who would serve such a man, Kit?' he said, incautiously. 'Sir Francis Walsingham, now there was a man! Intelligent, subtle, working always for the good of country and Queen, not a power-hungry, rash, stupid puppy like this Robert Devereux of Essex.'

I raised my eyebrows, but said nothing, remembering when Phelippes had once been less than kind about Walsingham. At that time, soon after Walsingham's death, he had hoped to be carried to the heights on the Earl's coat-tails, flattered at being taken up by the Queen's noble favourite. Perhaps now he was finally beginning to acknowledge his mistake, that he might have chosen the wrong faction to support.

Winter was coming on apace, with the first veil of snow thrown over the town and the first beggars found frozen to death in the streets. Arthur Gregory's son, however, had made a good recovery. The last of the rash had faded and he was gradually regaining his strength.

One evening early in December, I called in at Arthur's house to see the child, who rushed to cling to my legs like a limpet until I picked him up and tossed him in the air.

'So, William!' I said, 'you are strong enough now to hobble me like a wayward horse.'

He giggled and burrowed his head into the angle of my shoulder. He was an affectionate child. I found myself wishing that I might have such a son to hold warm and sleepy in my arms, when he was tired of play and the night drew in. I pushed such thoughts down into the depths of my mind, for how could I ever hope for a child? At least I had the affection of this little boy. Ever since my physicking of the measles, Arthur and I had become closer friends, and I had twice taken supper with his small family.

Christmas revels were preparing at Court, where Lord Strange's men were summoned to appear again.

'We are to present an old-fashioned thing,' Simon said, 'though new written. Dick and Cuthbert and Will have put their heads together over it. A sort of masque. It seems masques are all the fashion this year at Court. Good and evil fairies contesting for possession of England's soul, with the forces for good, of course, triumphant – everyone longs for a happy ending at Christmas.'

Neither of us mentioned it, but I knew that he was remembering, as I was, how Marlowe's play of Faustus had been rejected as too dark for the Christmas Revels a year ago. Was it truly only last Christmas?

What overtones this year's masque might contain, of the recent battle between Essex and the Cecils, I did not ask. Were the Cecils the good fairies in the masque of England's future? Only the passage of years would decide.

Not long before Christmas I decided it would be safe to pay a visit to Sara, whom I had not seen for so many weeks, while Ruy stood in peril. Even so, I made my way to Mountjoy's Inn by a devious route, though I did not think I was followed. Riotous noises floated over the garden wall from Gray's Inn, where the students were preparing their own Christmas revels.

'Is all well with you now, Sara?' I asked.

She sent Anthony, who was home from Winchester for the Christmas holiday, off on some errand before she answered.

'Ruy seems content,' she said, 'though I think he is unsure what Essex may yet force Ferreira to confess or invent. The man is like to say anything which he hopes may keep his own neck out of the noose. And that blaggard Tinoco is still lurking somewhere, as full of poison and danger as the venomous toad.'

'But the Cecils are standing by Ruy, are they not? They believed what he told them of Sir Francis's final projection, an overture to peace with Spain, which must accord with their own plans? And the Queen still holds him in high regard?'

'Aye. But the favour of the great endures only as long as it serves their turn.'

'That is true, Sara. Alas, I fear that is very true.'

When Anthony came back, full of eager talk about his time at school, we turned to more cheerful subjects. He showed me the Greek texts he was now reading, and we fell into an eager discussion of the plays written in that lovely language. He possessed a lively wit, and I could understand why the Queen had sent him to Winchester at her expense.

'One day,' I said to Sara, as she bade me farewell at the door, 'Anthony will make a fine diplomat, an ambassador for England.'

Her smile was a little bleak.

'If we survive so long.'

I made my way from Mountjoy's Inn back to St Thomas's without any particular care to conceal myself. It was growing dusk and there were few people about in the chilly streets, all of them hurrying about their own affairs and showing no interest in mine. On reaching the hospital, I went to Ailmer's office, where I found him preparing to go home. I had a proposal to make to him. Usually we made little of Christmas in the hospital, save for a particularly good meal on Christmas Day, but I was restless after my absence at the Customs House, and felt the need to mark my own release with some kind of celebration. Overhearing the sounds of revelry amongst the students of Grey's Inn had given me an idea.

Once before I had introduced a small Christmas Revels to St Bartholomew's, when Burbage's company had entertained the patients. Why should they not come to St Thomas's? I put the suggestion to Superintendent Ailmer, who allowed himself to be convinced that it could do no harm, and might even benefit the patients. I undertook to persuade Lord Strange's Men to give a performance of their Court masque at the hospital on the morning of Christmas Eve, for those patients who were well enough to attend, especially the children. Ailmer would instruct the cooks to make some extra Christmas delicacies with part of the money Lady Frances had sent to him while I was away at the Customs House. The cooks were also to prepare a Great Cake for Twelfth Night, with its special tokens baked inside. I made my rounds of my patients that evening and checked that all would be in place for the Christmas festivities in a few days' time, before I left to return to my lodgings.

Snow had begun to fall again, and I pulled my cap down and turned up the collar of my cloak to shield my neck from the icy wind. Rikki ran ahead, without looking back, anxious to reach the Atkins house. Through the spinning flakes, I made out a shape I thought I knew, a man walking before me down the road. In a few quick strides I had overtaken him and seized him by the elbow.

'Senhor d'Avila,' I said, 'so here you are, in Southwark.'

He leapt sideways like a frightened deer, but I kept a firm grip of him.

'Who? Oh, Christoval Alvarez. Good evening to you.'

Underneath his polite greeting there was something like fear.

'Everyone has been wondering,' I said, 'what had become of you.'

'Nothing has become of me. Here I am, as you see, in Southwark.'

'A long way from your usual lodgings in Crutched Friars.'

He did not answer.

'And how do you account for your great friendliness to Essex's inquisitors? And the doubts you cast on Ruy Lopez's integrity?'

He must have wondered how I knew all this, but he resorted to bluster. It was a tactic I was familiar with in the man I suspected was his patron and employer, Essex.

'And who dares say I did not speak the truth!' he cried. 'Why, Dom Antonio is so disgusted with his treatment by Lopez and the Cecils that he has departed for France.'

This was news to me, but I did not let it show on my face.

'It might have been better for all of us, had the Dom never come to England,' I said bitterly.

'And as for the loyalty of Ruy Lopez,' he said shrilly, 'I am not alone in my opinion. My lord Essex has written to the Queen, denouncing him as a traitor. Do not think this affair has reached its end. Lopez will answer for it.'

He jerked his arm from my grip and gave me a curious look before he slid away into the thickening snow. It was compounded partly of fear, and partly of a kind of shifty triumph.

Chapter Ten

In the bleak days of January 1594, I suddenly fell ill. As a rule, my health was robust. I moved amongst my sick patients apparently secure from contagion or infection. It is often the way, that those who work regularly with the sick seem to develop some defence against sickness, even when their own mode of life may lack comfort and good food. I have known our sisters in the hospital, often from less fortunate homes, work a lifetime amongst the sick without taking harm from it. And so with the Searchers in time of plague, who go from house to house investigating suspected cases and reporting them, so that the house may be marked with the sign, 'Lord have mercy upon us', and the inhabitants confined, until all are dead or recovered. These Searchers, usually frail old women, often prove immune to the attacks of the devil's worse instrument, the plague. While those who live soft, in warm houses, with excellent food and abundant clothing – these are no proof against it, unless they take themselves off and hide away in their country estates.

However, this time I did fall ill, putting it down to my airless confinement in the Customs House during those earlier months, when I had been denied my usual vigorous exercise of body and had been exposed to much distress of mind. For ten days I burned with fever, and could take nothing but small ale, vomiting even that for the first two days. I lay on my bed, alternately sweating and shivering, unable to sit up without finding the room spinning about me like a child's top. Simon visited me every day, taking Rikki out and bringing me simple food once I could stomach it, but I ordered him to keep to the far side of the room. I could see how distressed he was.

'Shall I fetch one of your fellow physicians from St Thomas's?' he said.

'I would rather dose myself.'

'But you are too weak to lift your head from that pillow. Please, Kit, it would be best.'

'Nay!'

I would have shouted, had I had strength enough. I knew what would happen if another physician examined me. My secret would be revealed in five minutes. I could not run the risk, not unless I was dying, and it had not yet come to that.

When Sara heard of my condition, she took to sending me fruit and other delicacies every day. The Lopez family lived well and ate well, even in winter and even now after all the troubles of the past months. Sara dared not come herself, lest she was being watched, but sent the old housekeeper. As my fever eased I was glad of the dates and dried apricots and raisins of the sun, and sometimes a glowing orange, for I could face little other food, save for plain bread and a simple broth which Simon learned to prepare over his fire.

At last I was able to sit for a little while each day in a chair, wrapped in a blanket, but I was still exhausted, sleeping for most of the day as well as the night, and with constant pain gnawing at all my joints. I felt as though a weight of years had descended on me.

Then one day the basket of treats did not arrive from Sara, nor the next day. I worried what this might mean, wondering whether Essex had begun his assault again upon Ruy.

'Simon,' I said, when he came to visit me later in the morning, 'would you call at Mountjoy's Inn, and assure me that nothing is amiss?'

He returned some three hours later and I read at once in his face that he had found serious trouble.

'There is naught amiss with Sara herself,' he said, 'although she has been gravely worried by what is afoot again between the Cecils and Essex. But soon after I arrived, Ruy rode up on a sweating horse, flung himself into the house, and began running from room to room, gathering up every scrap of paper he could find and throwing it on the fire. I never saw such a panic. The man was like to run mad! There was paper flying up the chimney and floating down into the garden half-burnt, and out he goes, gathering it up, tearing his robe on a gooseberry bush, and rushing in again to feed the fire. Some of the paper fell out upon the carpet and set it afire, but he stamped it out with his own feet. He was a man possessed.'

I started up from my chair, then fell back as my weakened body would not obey me.

'Give me your shoulder,' I said. 'I must go to Sara.'

'Nay, that you must *not* do.' He pushed me gently back as I tried again to rise. 'Sara herself has told me that you must stay away from Mountjoy's Inn.'

I groaned and covered my face with my hands. 'What if Essex succeeds after all, and destroys Ruy? What will become of Sara? She is my oldest friend.'

He knelt down beside my chair and took down my hands, holding them firmly in his.

'That is exactly why you must do as Sara says. She may need a friend – a friend who is above *any* suspicion of being implicated in whatever Ruy has been plotting. You can help her best by keeping away now. Besides, you have no strength. You must recover if you are to help her.'

I knew he was right, but I raged at my weakness and inability to act. I dared not think what might happen next. I knew soon enough. On Tuesday the twenty-ninth day of January, a date I am not likely to forget, Simon came as usual with a basket of bread and cold meats and a flagon of ale. He stood just inside the door and regarded me soberly, as if he were assessing whether I was strong enough to hear his news. I felt my heart begin to skip to an irregular beat and drew a long breath to steady myself.

'What is it?' I asked. 'What have you heard?'

'It is Ruy again.' He set the basket down on the table and busied himself unpacking the contents.

'Simon,' I said through clenched teeth, 'do not dangle me in suspense. It is much worse to be kept guessing than told the truth. What has happened?'

'The Earl of Essex has denounced Dr Lopez to the Queen again, claiming that he has been plotting against her life. That he planned to poison her. This time Lopez has been sent to the Tower.'

For a moment I felt my feverish dizziness return, then I shook my head to clear it. Few who were sent to the Tower returned. Some were executed out of hand, some tortured and their bodies destroyed, some kept confined until they withered and died.

'But the Cecils will surely defend him!' I burst out. 'Ruy is Burghley's man. This is yet more of Essex's war upon the Cecils. This is some plot he has contrived to use Ruy Lopez as a stalking horse in his aim to destroy Lord Burghley and his son.'

Simon's face revealed that he did not fully understand me, and indeed I had never yet dared to share the full scope of my dangerous knowledge with him. However, he knew enough from the gossip on the streets, and he knew what Sara had told him, weeks past, of that last fateful projection of Walsingham's to treat for peace with Spain, the projection in which Ruy had been implicated.

'There must be some new evidence,' he pointed out, 'else why would he be sent to the Tower now?'

'Nay, there may be *no* evidence. Such an accusation, of treason against the Queen's own person, made by one of such a high rank as the Earl of Essex, must be treated with seriousness. The Queen, I suppose, must take *some* action. But I have known Ruy Lopez half my life. He is greedy for riches and power, but he is devoted to the Queen. Truly and sincerely devoted. He would never do such a thing. Poison! Whyfor should he? The Queen is his greatest patron! It is she who raised him up from a simple physician at St Bartholomew's, like my father, to the highest position in England. She values his skill as a doctor, and she has trusted her health and life to him for twenty years. She has shown great kindness to his family, and sent his young son to school at Winchester, at her own cost. He owes everything to her.'

'There is a rumour that he is in league with the Spanish. It is being said . . .' and now he looked wretchedly uncomfortable, 'that all Portingalls are treacherous and treasonous.'

'Dear God!' I shouted. 'Can you not understand that we *hate* the Spanish? Do you understand what they have done to us? As a nation? As individuals?'

It was unjust of me to take out my anger on Simon. He knew well enough how I felt about Spain, and was doing no more than repeat the gossip on the streets, to forewarn me of what to expect, once I ventured abroad once more.

I stood up suddenly, then staggered as my weakness came over me again, and was forced to clutch hold of Simon's arm. I decided to tell Simon a little more of what I knew.

'Listen,' I said. 'Listen carefully. You know that Ruy was being used by Walsingham shortly before his death, but in recent months Ruy has been working secretly for Lord Burghley and Sir Robert Cecil, making further overtures to the Spanish for peace. *Not* because he is in the pay of the Spaniards, but to bring safety to England and avert the danger of another invasion. Lord Burghley has always spoken for peace rather than war. Sir Francis, who saw with his own eyes the horrors of the St Bartholomew's Day massacre of Protestants, believed for most of his life that England should arm herself for war, to withstand a Spanish invasion.'

I frowned, trying to muster my thoughts in an aching head.

'I know most of this already, Kit,' Simon said quietly, but I was trying to clarify my own thoughts, and ignored him.

'You know that was Sir Francis's policy almost to the last. But in the end, with his own life slipping away, he must have foreseen this struggle between Essex and the Cecils. I am sure now that must lie behind what happened. It would be inevitable that Essex would claim leadership of the war party, which could end in nothing but disaster for England. Sir Francis trusted to the wisdom of Lord Burghley and his son, who must head the peace party. I was not privy to the reasons for his change of policy at the time, but looking back, with what I know now, I can see how it came about. This must have been Walsingham's final intention, to make the first tentative overtures for peace with Spain, rather than leave the country to the dangerous leadership of Essex.'

I coughed. My throat was dry, so I took a sip of ale.

'It is the policy that the Queen and the Cecils themselves support, though the negotiations are so subtle and risky that they must be kept secret. Could that be why Gurdin was killed? Had he let something slip? And Marlowe – what of Marlowe? You *know* Marlowe always had a loose tongue. Had he become too risky a tool for their purposes? Like a poker grow too hot in the fire?'

Simon sat with his head in his hands.

'Poor Kit Marlowe,' he said. 'So much brilliance, and yet . . .'

'And yet betrayed by his arrogance and violent temper,' I said. 'There have been a deal of arrogant men in this – Marlowe, Essex, Lopez. That is where the Cecils will triumph in the end. Reserved, cool, calculating. Sir Robert Cecil may not be the most lovable of men, but he has the best pair of hands to guide England.'

'And would not hesitate to sacrifice his own men, if policy called for it.'

'Like Gurdin,' I said. 'And perhaps Marlowe. These delicate probes put forth in the hope of securing peace must remain secret. Hatred of Spain is so mighty amongst the common people that nothing must be generally known of these negotiations unless they succeed. Then a peace treaty favourable to England can be proclaimed as a great triumph for our government. In the meantime it must be kept secret. Above all it must be kept secret from such a man as Essex, who sees himself as a great military leader against the forces of Spain – which the Portuguese expedition showed clearly that he is not. Should he take command, he would lead us into disaster.'

I paused, short of breath, and wiped my forehead with a handkerchief.

'Somehow the affair of Gurdin's murder must have been linked with this, since he was used to carry proposals to the Spanish embassy, or to negotiate there. He was murdered to silence him, but I do not suppose we shall ever know why. Did he turn traitor, and inform the Earl? Or was he killed because someone wanted to destroy the negotiations? Was Esau Miller in the pay of Essex? Or did the Cecils *want* Gurdin silenced?'

'And what part did Robert Poley play?' Simon said, slowly. 'Which faction was he working for? Or had he some reason of his own to silence Esau Miller?'

I shook my head, which was throbbing like a drum.

'How can we know? What we can know is that Essex would bleat out the secret negotiations to the world and destroy everything. No one, certainly not the Cecils, would trust him. He must have invented this accusation against Ruy Lopez out of spite. Or because he now knows Ruy works for the Cecils and hopes to harm them through defaming Ruy. Jesu! Ruy is not a man who would work for the Spanish to murder the Queen. Dear God, Simon, he is in the Queen's closest confidence and acting in this on *her private wishes*.'

Nothing has ever shaken me from that belief, through all that happened afterwards. Though I did not care over much for Ruy Lopez, I have never believed the accusations made against him. From all that I could learn, then and later, Ruy kept silent about the Spanish negotiations. If that was the way of it, he did so under torture. Which argues that he was a braver man than I had supposed. It was Essex who had secured Ruy's arrest. Therefore, I was sure the Cecils would come to his aid and all would be well for the Lopez family. But the news of Ruy's imprisonment in the Tower must have undermined my health more than I realised, and I relapsed into illness the next day.

Despite Simon's urging, I continued to resist his suggestion of fetching another physician, but I became very ill again. I was subject to terrible headaches, aggravated by the fever, and I could barely keep any food down, so that I grew very thin. Also, I was tormented by nightmares. The thought of Ruy in the Tower brought back memories of the Inquisition's prison in Coimbra. The very stench of it seemed to fill my nostrils. I could hear them torturing and raping my mother, while I cowered, a helpless child, in the filthy straw of our cell. Night after night I woke myself up screaming, till Goodman Atkins threatened to put me out of my room for terrifying the other lodgers, so that I hardly dared to allow myself to sleep.

There was a sickness abroad in the State as well. Cut off from the privy secrets of Phelippes's office, I knew only the gossip that everyone heard on the streets, which was brought to me by Simon, and soon by Guy and Will, who took to visiting me.

'For until the playhouses reopen in the spring,' Will said, 'can we do better than come to entertain a sick friend?'

I emerged at last from my room, pale and weak, on the last but one day of February, taking a gentle walk with Rikki along Bankside. Gratefully I filled my lungs with the outdoor air – even London air – which was free of the closed and stale atmosphere of my sickroom. There was no hint yet of spring in that air, but it did not catch in the lungs like the bitter air of midwinter. About the foot of the rowan tree opposite the Atkinses' front door, a few tentative snowdrops had pushed their way up through ground which was still in the rigid grip of frost. Soon, I hoped, I would be able to return to my work at St Thomas's, for I had been fretting for my mothers and children. Simon had called on Superintendent Ailmer a few times, with reports of my slow recovery, and brought back kind messages that the other physicians were lending their aid with my wards. Still, I felt a certain jealous anxiety that all might not be done as I would wish it.

'Kit! I am on my way to see you.'

It was Guy coming toward me from the direction of the Rose. He grinned and shook my hand, while Rikki jumped up eagerly to greet him. 'This is good news indeed, to see you once more on your feet.'

'Atop somewhat shaky legs,' I said ruefully. 'I think I have walked far enough. I must turn back. I thought I should manage as far as the Rose, but I am not halfway there.'

He took Rikki's lead from me and seized my elbow in his other hand.

'Just up here there is a decent alehouse. You will be the better for a cup of hot spiced ale and some food. When did you last eat?'

'Simon has been bringing me food every day, but I had no appetite this morning. However, I think perhaps my brief foray into the world outside has awakened it.'

Guy steered me into the alehouse, up a short alley off Bankside. It was no more than one room in a small house – the alewife no doubt lived here with her family – but it was clean and tidy, with a good fire blazing on the hearth, where a pot of spiced ale was already simmering. The alewife herself, a plump and comely young woman, came through from the kitchen with a tray of new made pies. The heartening aroma of mutton and gravy sharpened that first hint of appetite into genuine hunger, so that I nodded eagerly when Guy urged a pie on me, to accompany the large beaker of steaming ale.

'That is better,' I said, after consuming both pie and ale with unaccustomed enthusiasm. 'I feel almost a normal human creature again.'

I noticed that Rikki was regarding me reproachfully. He must have been missing the good meals of hospital scraps he usually enjoyed in companionship with Tom's dog Swifty. I broke off a piece of the bread the alewife had supplied and mopped up the last of the gravy.

'You must make do with this,' I said, holding it out to Rikki.

'You are not the only one to have grown thin,' Guy observed. 'Have you kept Rikki on short rations, too?'

'I think Tom spoils him,' I said. 'I haven't such an abundance of food to give him at home.'

I sat back, cradling my second beaker of spiced ale in both hands. 'And so what is the news on the street, Guy? You always have an ear for London's gossip.'

He looked at me soberly and I had a sudden premonition.

'There is bad news, is there not?' I said. 'That was why you were coming to see me. Is it Ruy Lopez?'

Reluctantly, Guy nodded.

'Tomorrow,' he said slowly, 'Dr Roderigo Lopez is to be tried at the Guildhall for treason and planning the murder of the Queen.'

I gave a gasp, then covered my mouth with my hand. Two workmen, stonemasons by their looks, had joined us in the ale house and were sitting not far off. I had no wish to draw attention to myself. I leaned forward.

'The Cecils have permitted it to go this far?' I murmured. 'But they know that this is all false, some trumped up foolery of Essex's.'

'I have heard that the Cecils are not disputing the charge,' Guy said. 'It seems that they too hold Lopez to be guilty. Or else it is policy not to oppose Essex in this. That agent who was missing – Tinoco, is he called? – returned to

England while you were ill and was arrested at once. He was interrogated and alleged that Ruy Lopez was plotting regicide, in collusion with the King of Spain. Not only regicide. He is charged with planning to foment revolution and the overthrow of the State.'

'Mighty convenient for Essex,' I said sourly, 'that someone has been "persuaded" to make such a confession, or allegation. And hardly surprising when it should prove to be Tinoco.'

Guy raised an interrogative eyebrow.

'Tinoco is a double agent,' I said, 'a man in the service of Essex as well as Burghley, as the convenience of time or the size of remuneration should prove most rewarding. For all I know, he may serve other masters as well. Perhaps King Philip? Or the French king? The man is no more trustworthy than an adder. What has become of the Cecils, for whom Lopez had been working? Both charges, of course, ring as false as counterfeit coinage.'

But I began to suspect the answer.

I traced patterns in some spilt ale on the tabletop as I felt my way toward an explanation. I had never discussed this with Guy before, but I felt compelled to speak out for Ruy Lopez, for it seemed that no one else would do so.

'This all started,' I said quietly, 'with Sir Francis Walsingham's last projection before he died. It was then only in the early stages, and he was making use of Ruy Lopez because of his close connection with the exiled Portuguese royal family. As far as I understand it, the plan was to abandon any support for Dom Antonio's claim to the throne. He has long since shown himself unworthy of support and an inveterate enemy of Spain. His son Dom Emanuel is more biddable, and more likely to be accepted by Spain as a puppet king. Thomas Phelippes believes Dom Emanuel even signed some document of submission to the king of Spain. The Spanish could then be spared the trouble and expense of occupying Portugal as an enemy country, while still controlling its affairs through Dom Emanuel. They would also continue to have the use of the country's

212

valuable Atlantic ports for their ships travelling to their colonies in the New World.'

'Aye,' Guy said. 'Simon has told me a little of this. Was not some great ruby passed to Lopez as a pledge of good intentions from Spain?'

'Sara Lopez said something about a ruby. Probably it was intended to be presented to the Queen, but then Sir Francis died, the negotiations stalled, and Ruy kept the ruby for himself. Simon thinks that he may have intended to use it as part of his daughter Anne's dowry.'

'Dishonest.'

'Perhaps. Aye. Almost certainly. Although it is just possible it *was* indeed intended for him as a reward for his efforts. I do not know the rights of it. Ruy seems to have had the arrogant notion that he could carry on treating with Spain, in his own name, on behalf of England, but without the knowledge of Burghley or any other great man.'

I sighed. How could such a clever man have behaved so foolishly?

'Then when several of Ruy's untrustworthy agents were arrested and a great deal of ambiguous and dangerous correspondence was intercepted, Ruy finally confessed all to the Cecils, who appear to have believed him. It has always been Lord Burghley's belief that England should seek peace with Spain, not war.'

I realised that I was spelling out again what I had discussed not long before with Simon, but I had always trusted Guy's judgement. Besides, matters were far worse now, if Ruy had come to trial.

'Then why,' Guy said, 'have the Cecils turned against him now?'

I shook my head. 'When all the earlier evidence was discovered, as you know, Thomas Phelippes summoned me to decipher the documents, so I had a notion of what was happening – as much as anyone did. Although Phelippes works for Essex, through Anthony Bacon, he is not altogether happy in his service. I am sure he values Lord Burghley far more highly. But I have not seen Phelippes for weeks. The politics of Court factions may have changed a great deal in those weeks. Alliances and antipathies constantly shift between men scrambling up the ladder to power and prestige. That was something I learned during my service with Walsingham. The politics of the Court are as shifting and treacherous as Goodwin Sands.'

A memory of last summer flashed through my mind.

'Shortly after Marlowe's death, I came upon Phelippes conferring with Lord Burghley and his son. It took me by surprise, since he is employed in service to Essex. I wonder whether he thinks of changing his allegiance.'

'That still does not explain–'

'Nay, it does not. But I wonder . . . If Essex has managed to put together enough evidence to bring Ruy to court – however unreliable the source, or the means used to obtain it – perhaps the Cecils feel there is real danger in this stage of Essex's campaign against them. If Essex can persuade the court that Ruy is guilty of treason and is involved in some plot to murder the Queen, the Cecils might want to break themselves free of any association with him. Ruy must always have seemed a risky collaborator, and they can have had no particular loyalty to him. Perhaps, like Pontius Pilate, they have chosen to wash their hands of the connection.'

'I suppose,' Guy said, 'Ruy Lopez is much at fault himself. He should not have been so secretive.'

'You have the right of it,' I said. 'And he should never have attempted to act on his own, without the authority to do so. I have always felt that Ruy is his own worst enemy.'

That evening I made my weak-kneed way to our usual inn, the Lion, and found Will there, scribbling away at a bundle of inky paper, which he set to one side.

'So, you have come back like a ghost to walk amongst the living again,' he said, beckoning to the inn wife to bring more ale, and then fixing me with that gaze of

214

his, sharp as a gimlet boring through oak. 'I suppose you have heard that your fellow countryman is being tried on the morrow, at a court of Oyer and Terminer?'

I nodded. 'Guy told me.' I was not very desirous of talking, but Will might have new information. He was always one to keep his ears pricked.

'I cannot understand why the Cecils have let their man come to this,' I said, 'unless it is to save their own necks from the rope or the axe.'

Will tapped the side of his nose. 'Deep policy, Kit. I have heard that they set William Waad to investigate the case. 'Tis said that he has investigated it with such vigour that the three prisoners, Lopez, Ferreira, and Tinoco, can barely stand or even write their names to their confessions.'

I shuddered.

'William Waad?'

I could not keep the horror out of my voice.

'William Waad,' I repeated. 'An unscrupulous forger. A relentless torturer. A man who could twist the truth until black shone like virginal white, and white was dyed inky black.'

Will poured ale for me, but did not speak.

I stirred restlessly on my stool, and Rikki, sensing my disquiet, whined and laid his chin on my knee.

'At one time Waad worked for Lord Burghley,' I said, 'then later for Sir Francis Walsingham, and in that role he was deep-dyed in the plot to incriminate the Scottish queen through the Babington affair. It was my early days in Sir Francis's service and merely to find myself in the same room as Waad terrified me. What must it be for those who fall, helpless, into his hands? In those days I used to see him from time to time in the house in Seething Lane, but since Walsingham's death I am thankful never to have crossed his path.'

'So he is more than a mere torturer?' Will said.

'I am not sure there is anything "mere" about the act of torture,' I said, surprised at Will's choice of words. He was usually precise. 'Waad is almost as clever as

Phelippes, but Phelippes has a conscience. He may be ruthless in his pursuit of traitors, but in all else he is a decent, honest, even a kind man. Waad is a rabid Puritan. He loathes Catholics and French and Spaniards and Portuguese with an equally intense and violent hatred. Indeed, I think he despises the more gentle nature of our English Church. As a whole, most Englishmen under our Queen have not that streak of fanaticism you find in the "godly" Puritans. If the Cecils have agreed that Ruy should be handed over to Waad, it means they have abandoned him for some policy of their own. Not because they wanted to aid Essex, but because they fear somehow for their own safety through their association with Ruy.'

Will nodded. 'I suspect you have the right of it, Kit. Let all men keep their heads down and avoid drawing the attention of England's great ones.'

'Some of us have little choice in such matters. I had no choice when Phelippes summoned me to work for him on this case. If Waad has now taken the investigation into his hands,' I said, with weary resignation, 'then no matter how innocent Ruy Lopez may be, Waad will have manufactured evidence to prove him guilty.'

'There is also strong feeling growing against Lopez in the streets,' Will said, 'while you have been on your sickbed. Made all the worse because he is a Jew. It is a repetition of what occurred last year, before the death of Kit Marlowe, though I think there have been no placards this year, inciting hatred against Strangers and Jews.'

He looked at me keenly to see how I would respond to this. I put my head in my hands and gave a bitter laugh.

'Do we not grieve as you do?' I said. 'Do we not bleed? What am I? Christian or Jew? We have no choice in the blood which flows in our veins, but we have a choice in how we shape our lives. Ruy Lopez was born of Jewish blood, but he is a baptised Christian. As I am. As you are, Will. As you are.'

We were not to be long in hearing the outcome of Waad's 'investigation'. We had decided to go the following day to the Guildhall, where the trial of Oyer and Terminer was to be held. Simon, Will, Guy, and I set out across the Bridge when the first sliver of cold light seeped across the sullen grey waters of the river. The tide was on the turn, sucking and swirling about the starlings, the stone platforms which supported the piers of the Bridge.

No one had any doubt of the outcome – there is but one outcome to such trials, trials of Oyer and Terminer. The accused would be found guilty. What followed the guilty verdict would either be death by hanging, or a pardon from the Queen. Surely Her Majesty would pardon her personal physician, trusted for so long? Essex and the Cecils had also placed their lives and health in his hands for many years, trusting him implicitly. Now those same men, Essex and the Cecils, turned birds of prey, would have the satisfaction of destroying Ruy's own mind and health, and demonstrating their zeal – however baseless – in protecting the safety of Queen and country.

This trial would be a piece of theatre, all show and no substance. And as when a new piece for the playhouse was to be performed, tantalising whispers had already been noised abroad about the plot of the play. What Waad had extracted from his helpless victims, or forced them to sign, was a murky tangle of poisoning and insurrection. Gloriana, our matchless Queen, was to be done to death by foul poison at the hands of her wicked, treacherous physician. And this same man was on the point of leading a violent revolution to overthrow the State. How anyone – even of the weakest brain and the most credulous nature – could believe that an old man of seventy, with no military experience and no armed following, could lead a revolution, is beyond all understanding.

There *was* no plan of regicide. There *was* no plot of rebellion. Every one of the players in this farce knew that to be true. Yet London was restless and spoiling for trouble, still nursing the grievances of the previous year, when that

217

clumsy series of placards had pointed the finger of suspicion at Christopher Marlowe. If that affair had carried the whiff of a witch-hunt, the present case made no attempt to hide its true nature. And when the mob is roused to the excitement of a witch-hunt, its prey rarely escapes. The noble accusers would be able to bask in the spurious acclaim for averting an imaginary disaster, but must Ruy sacrifice his life as well?

'I do not think you should attend this trial, Kit,' Guy said, as we reached the City and turned west toward the Guildhall. 'You look as weak as a newborn lamb and as pale as milk. It will cause you nothing but distress. The trial will proceed with commendable speed and a verdict of "Guilty" brought in without hesitation. We all know that at such trials, in such a court, the verdict is always the same. A man brought before the Court of Oyer and Terminer is a dead man. All that will be wanted afterwards will be the Queen's signature on the death warrant.'

'Of course I must attend,' I said grimly. 'It is Sara Lopez who is my friend, but I have been a guest at Ruy's table many times, ever since I was a child. I lived in his house when first we came to London, and again after the Portuguese expedition, when I found myself homeless. You remember that I even minded his household when he took his family to Venice and Constantinople. He will see few friendly faces in the Guildhall today. Let him see mine.'

The others did not press me further, for which I was thankful. It is a long walk from Southwark to the Guildhall and I had not fully recovered my strength. I had none to spare for argument. There was a cutting February wind screaming upriver from the east, whose icy fingers seemed to claw through every gap in my clothing. At least we had our backs turned to it. Even so, I found myself aching and short of breath when we finally shouldered our way into the Great Hall of the Guildhall.

How different this was, from my last visit here, when we had come to the sheriff's office to set down what we had seen of the killing of Esau Miller, murderer of Josiah

Gurdin. And that other killer, Robert Poley – where was he now?

The place was crowded. It seemed as though half London was there, from the courtiers in their silks and velvets, to a cluster of street traders in their rough kersey, and every rank in between – wealthy merchants, shopkeepers, lawyers and physicians in their gowns, a few sailors in salt-stained slops, sharp-faced street urchins, a scattering of Winchester geese, even some respectable merchants' wives. And now a refugee Portuguese physician from St Thomas's in company with a handful of players. More than a handful, indeed, for we were soon joined by the three Burbages, who pushed through the crowd to us, and Christopher Haigh, looking like a minor hanger-on of the Court in his best doublet and hose.

The noise was overpowering. A sense of febrile excitement seemed to have seized the audience at this spectacle, the talk was punctuated by shouts and laughter. I wondered whether it had always been thus, at the great trials which had been held here in the past. Thomas Cranmer had stood here, archbishop beloved by both our present Queen and her young brother, who refused to buy his life at the cost of his conscience when the Queen's sister Mary had sat briefly on the throne, preferring death to denial of his faith. And I knew that some of those accused along with Queen Anne Boleyn had stood trial here. What were Queen Elizabeth's feelings about that, the calumny against her mother? Was she remembering that other false trial, acted out here when she was no more than a babe? And here had also stood that hapless girl, Lady Jane Grey – another innocent, a pawn in the hands of unscrupulous wielders of power. So many trials this place had witnessed, so many innocent victims of the struggle for power. Yet all power must turn to dust and ashes in the end.

I shuddered. We lived in terrible times, when a false step, or even unblemished innocence, could lead to the hangman's noose or the executioner's axe. How could this crowd seem so . . . so eager, so pleased? Did they *believe* the false accusations? Or did they look upon this trial as nothing more than entertainment to pass the time?

Suddenly silence fell upon the crowd, as suddenly as a snuffer clapped down over a candle flame. People shifted, drew back, leaving an open pathway up the centre of the Great Hall to the raised dais at the far end. More than ever this seemed a play enacted for the benefit of a London crowd, for on that stage were assembled all the players but one, all the players but the victim. I counted them. Twenty-one. All men of power and standing, in their finest robes, with their gold chains about their necks, seated in judgement. A jury of England's greatest.

I recognised a few of them. Keeper of the Great Seal, Sir John Puckering. The Vice Chamberlain, Thomas Heneage. The torturer, William Waad (what was he doing in this company?). Sir Cuthbert Buckle, Lord Mayor of London, a City vintner, looking uncomfortable. Lord Howard, High Admiral of England and formerly patron of the players' company the Admiral's Men. Others I did not recognise.

But there, on one side of the stage, Lord Burghley and Sir Robert Cecil, both soberly dressed, as for a funeral. On the other side, eying them and glittering with pearls and cloth of gold, the Earl of Essex.

In the centre, his chair raised above the others, the Solicitor General, Sir Edward Coke. Prosecutor.

Slowly, along the path cleared for him by the drawing back of the crowd, came Ruy Lopez. He could barely walk, shuffling his feet forward, limping, bowed over and somehow twisted, as though his back gave him grievous pain. His hair and beard had grown quite white, and were unkempt and matted. I felt a spurt of anger. Could they not have allowed him so much as a comb? His clothes, too, were creased and stained, as though he had not changed them during the weeks he had been imprisoned in the Tower. His eyes were sunken and his nose as pinched as a sharpened quill. His beard hid most of his face, but what could be seen of it was emaciated. His right arm dangled

220

awkwardly, as if the shoulder joint was dislocated. The rack, of course.

Even if – vain hope – he were to be pardoned, he could never use his great skills as a physician to heal the sick ever again.

Chapter Eleven

*T*he crowd hushed, the prisoner brought to stand before the implacable jury, Sir Edward Coke read out the arraignment.

> *'He did conspire, imagine and fantasise the death and destruction of the Queen's Majesty, and to stir Rebellion and War within the Realm, and to overthrow that State of the whole common weal of this Realm.'*

Like a player rendering a well known and practised speech, the Prosecutor spoke the standard words of the accusation of treason with no visible show of emotion. How many times during the present reign had these words been spoken? All those past conspirators were summoned up, like fearful ghosts, like the spirits in Marlowe's play of Faustus – all those servants of Spain and France and Rome, clustering, invisible but palpable, in the shadowy corners of the Great Hall, where the thin February sun, filtering through the high windows, could not reach.

The ranks of jurors on the stage sat blank-faced, except for Essex. A faint smirk lingered about his lips. But in the audience, here on the floor, there was a concerted intake of breath as the accusation was read out. Rumours had spread about the city, but here the words were spoken at last and what before was no more than air was made manifest, a solid accusation. So *this* was the evil plotted by the notorious Jew.

The Prosecutor continued his indictment. There was no mention of Walsingham's final projection. No mention of tentative moves toward peace with Spain. No mention of Lopez's recent work for the Cecils. Indeed, no mention of the Cecils at all. One must not forget, of course, that Coke was the Cecils' man and Lord Burghley's candidate for the prestigious office of Attorney General, in rivalry to Essex's candidate, Anthony Bacon. It was surely significant that Coke, as Solicitor General, held the conduct of this trial in his hands. The more rigorously he carried it through, the stronger his claim on the higher office.

Coke enumerated the details of the ambiguous correspondence in which Lopez had been involved, taking care to represent it as treasonous. He listed the meetings with those infamous fellows, Manuel d'Andrada and Ferreira da Gama. The ruby sent by King Philip was cited as proof of the bribe Lopez had accepted, to betray England to a Spanish invasion.

I had experience enough in the world of conspiracies and intelligence work to understand what was afoot here. Coke was taking acknowledged facts and twisting their significance. The overtures for peace were being transformed into a plot for war and rebellion. The ruby, which was probably a token of good intent, meant for the Queen, was transformed into a traitorous bribe. So much was being left out. Not only the involvement of the Cecils, but the part Dom Emanuel was to play as a king of Portugal acceptable to both England and Spain, in the place of his untrustworthy and degenerate father, Dom Antonio. The fact that even the Queen favoured a peaceful settlement on acceptable terms for England was, of course, never mentioned.

My head had begun to throb again, and I found my attention was wandering from Coke's irritating and rasping voice. I knew I could now almost predict everything he was likely to say. The fatigue which had been with me ever since my illness was beginning to overcome me. I hoped I would be able to remain on my feet.

Curiously, nothing was said of that other conspiracy, in which I believed Ruy Lopez to be really implicated – the plan either to assassinate Antonio Perez, or hand him over to Spain, the 'musk and amber' plot, which I had detected in the letter purporting to be concerned only with the import and export of merchandise. But no. To raise that matter would have also brought into the daylight the dubious parts both Lord Burghley and the Earl of Essex had played in that abortive affair. It would have been necessary to mention that Ruy Lopez had passed Antonio Perez's stolen correspondence to Lord Burghley himself, when he had confessed all to the Cecils and laid all before them. Better by far to keep silent on that. As the Cecils' man, Coke would suppress all mention of a connection between Ruy Lopez and the Cecils.

Coke's voice ground on, starting to hum in my ears like a swarm of bees. The jurors mostly remained impassive. One or two nodded wisely. The Lord Mayor, I thought, looked puzzled. Perhaps he had not been put fully into the picture beforehand and was detecting the *lacunae* in the Prosecutor's argument.

Would this tirade never come to an end?

I knew that the prisoner would be allowed to make a short speech, but he might not question the Prosecutor nor ask him to produce any evidence for the accusations he had made. What evidence, after all could have been produced? But Coke had nothing to fear on that account. All that Ruy Lopez could do was to defend himself.

When at last the prisoner was permitted his few moments to speak, he declared himself: *Not Guilty*. Despite his weakened and broken state of health, he spoke resolutely.

He did not deny his meetings with Andrada and Ferreira, nor the existence of the great ruby, but said that it was all intended to cozen the King of Spain into making a peace favourable to England. Surprisingly, he said nothing to refute the charge that he intended to foment a rebellion. Perhaps it seemed simply so absurd an accusation that he

224

dismissed it out of hand. I thought he should have made some protest, but what good would it have done? Perhaps he did not realise that the accusation of inciting revolution was designed to taint him with the same evil as all those past Catholic conspiracies. In the public mind he would be linked with Throgmorton and Babington and all the others who had threatened England in recent years.

Coke had cited, as finally damning, both Tinoco's manufactured evidence against Ruy, and Ruy's own signed confession, which had been seen by the jurors.

'Aye,' Ruy said, and now his voice shook. 'I signed that false "confession", prepared by William Waad. I signed it after suffering the torments of the rack and the thumbscrew.'

He held up his right arm, supported by his left, for it seemed he could not raise it unsupported. Even from my position, some distance from him, I could see his mangled right hand.

'I signed it,' he said grimly, 'to spare this weak and aging body of mine further encounters with those implements of torture. There is no truth in it. I never sought to harm Her Majesty, who is dearer to me than my own life.'

This brought a jeer from the crowd, who began to jostle forth toward the prisoner and had to be restrained by the sergeants of the court.

'I lied,' Ruy protested desperately. 'I lied to save myself from further racking. That confession is false.'

Sir Robert Cecil spoke for the first time. Leaning forward. 'By our Souls' witness,' he said, 'the vile Jew is lying.'

Ruy had made his defence. I could see that his little strength had almost failed him, for he staggered and would have sunk to the ground, save that one of the sergeants took him by the elbow and hauled him to his feet. The jury did not withdraw, as I had seen them do in the course of a coroner's inquest. They merely leaned their heads together, murmuring quietly. Why should they take the trouble even to make this pretence? The Prosecutor rose to his feet.

'The verdict of this court is that the prisoner is guilty as charged.'

The crowd – the audience – broke out into vile cheering and laughter. Freed of any sense of decorum, they milled about like the crowds leaving the playhouse after a successful performance. In the ensuing chaos, I lost sight of Ruy, who must have been bundled away and carried off, back to the Tower.

'A travesty,' I said angrily.

'Aye.' Will looked thoughtful. 'Such a trial is no credit to us as a nation.'

'Come,' Guy said, 'let us fight our way free of this stinking crowd. The man may be a slippery fellow, and perhaps not altogether trustworthy, but this performance has left a vile smell in my nose. I need air.'

With one accord we turned and thrust our way out into the sharp February air.

Guilty. So would Ruy hang?

And this was no foregone outcome. Ruy had protected the Queen during the trial, never revealing that she knew of his projections and that he was acting in her interests. She sent word to him that not a hair on his head should perish. She knew, none better, that he was innocent. But although she would not sign the death warrant, his case continued desperate. He was still held a prisoner in the Tower, an old man past seventy, who was said to be growing weaker by the day and like to die, frustrating those who panted for a gruesome public execution. After the passing of the guilty verdict, his property was attaindered to the Crown. On the orders of Essex, still claiming the right to control all affairs involving those of the Portuguese nation, Thomas Phelippes locked up Ruy's merchandise in the Customs House and would not release it, while Ruy's creditors came howling round the family, who lingered on in a corner of Mountjoy's Inn, penniless.

Some time after the trial, while Ruy remained in the Tower, I went to see Sara. By now I was sure that the spies of Essex and the Cecils had no further interest in my movements, so I went openly to Mountjoy's Inn. I was shocked at Sara's ravaged looks. She seemed suddenly old, her skin greyish and slack about cheeks and chin, her eyes red with weeping and sleeplessness. I put my arms around her and she laid her head on my shoulder. She did not weep. I think by then she had wept herself to a desert dryness.

'I do not know what is to become of us, Kit,' she said. 'I have given up any hope that the Queen will overrule the court and pardon Ruy. It is full six weeks since the trial, and she has given him assurances that he must be patient and wait, but I no longer believe her.'

'Yet she has refused to sign the death warrant,' I said. 'Without it, they cannot proceed to an execution. Have you been able to see him?'

'Once,' she said. 'I was allowed just once to go to him with the children. To say our farewells to him, so Sir Michael Blount said, the governor of the Tower.'

I looked around the room. Apart from a little furniture it was stripped of all its ornaments – china and glass, tapestries and painted cloths, silver and pewter. Sara wore a plain gown, and no jewels. She caught my eye.

'Aye, they have taken everything, except a handful of possessions I could prove were mine. I have been selling my few remaining jewels in order that the children and I may eat, and pay our rent to Mistress Allington.'

Her mouth twisted as she spoke the name, as if she had bitten on aloes. I wondered about Mistress Allington. Was she glad that her faithless lover had been brought to this? Or did she care for him still?

'I wish I could help you with money,' I said, 'but while I was ill I earned no salary from the hospital, and I have nothing but a few shillings left. Now that I have returned, I am earning again, and so—'

227

She laid her fingers against my lips to silence me.

'Nay, Kit. Do not think of it. You have so little yourself. Somehow we will survive. My father may be able to help us, though his position as Purveyor to the Queen may be threatened because of the disgrace, and he has never fully recovered his fortune since the Portuguese expedition.'

'Did I see Anthony when I arrived?' I asked.

'He is sent home from Winchester. The Queen has withdrawn his scholarship.'

She turned aside and sank down wearily on a hard chair. Even her embroidered cushions had been carried off.

Oh, Ruy, I thought angrily, how many people have you brought crashing to the ground with all your folly and your scheming!

In despite of everything I said, Sara would take no help from me.

Once I had fully recovered from my long illness and shortly after the trial, I had returned to the hospital and to work amongst my patients. The children seemed glad to see me, and the women in the Whittington ward, but on the part of a few of my colleagues and one or two of the older patients I noticed a reserve, and avoidance of my eyes. I suppose, as a fellow Portingall, I was tainted in their minds with the scandal of Ruy Lopez. Once or twice I heard a mutter of 'Jew' behind hands and in corners, though never amongst the midwives or the nursing sisters in the children's ward.

When I reported on my return to Superintendent Ailmer, I found Mistress Maynard in his office.

'We are relieved to have you back amongst us, Dr Alvarez,' Ailmer said. 'The other physicians have done what they might in your wards, but none have any particular skills with women and children.'

'Aye, you have been sadly missed.' Mistress Maynard scrutinised my face with some concern. 'Are you sure you are quite recovered?'

'Quite.' I smiled at her. 'Nothing that steady work and a good hospital dinner at midday cannot cure.'

They both laughed at that. The food in the hospital refectory was substantial and sustaining, but it would have been scorned by any gourmet. Nevertheless, I was glad to return to the routine duties of my work at St Thomas's. There is much to be said for work which occupies both mind and hands, leaving little time to brood. In the following weeks we had a fine crop of Southwark newborns, a few of whom I conveyed to the sanctuary of Christ's Hospital. It was always a joy to visit my former charges there, and to listen to Mellie's plans for her wedding.

It was shortly after my return to St Thomas's that I learned of the death of Dunstan Añes, exhausted by shame at his son-in-law's fate and by worry about the future of his daughter and grandchildren. I remembered his words to me last year: 'What will become of my Sara and the children?'

In the middle of April, the rumour in the streets told of another poisoning. Ferdinando, Lord Strange, was writhing in agony, vomiting blood and suffering the most extreme curative measures taken by his doctors. I had heard that Master Winger had returned to St Bartholomew's. Had he remained with Lord Strange, might he have fathomed what ailed him? He must have been glad that he was no longer employed within that household, after the accusations against his son-in-law. Peter himself was restored to his former position at the hospital, and his wife had given birth to a healthy daughter.

Lord Strange had a distant claim to the throne, and his family was of the old faith. His cousin, Sir William Stanley, had proved a traitor to England, serving as an officer in the army of the Spanish king in the Low Countries. Some months since, a group of Catholic conspirators had attempted to persuade Lord Strange to become their figurehead for an uprising against the Queen. He had refused and they had been arrested and executed.

Two conflicting stories were now sailing on the wind. One asserted that Lord Strange had been poisoned because of his claim to the throne. The other, with equal vigour, and perhaps more probability, claiming that surviving members of the conspiracy had silenced him, lest he reveal their guilt to the authorities. Whichever had the right of it, young Ferdinando died in excruciating pain on the sixteenth day of April, and whispers of poison ran everywhere in London.

No one knew what Lord Strange's death might mean to Simon's company of players, for he was their patron, and by law every such company must have a noble patron. The players were deemed to be servitors of his household, even if they never crossed his threshold or saw him. Otherwise, without a patron, they were branded vagabonds and could suffer the full force of the law. Despite this uncertainty, the company continued to perform under the designation of 'Lord Strange's Men', until it could be determined what to do with them.

At this time, *The Jew of Malta* was enjoying another successful run at the Rose, and on the streets anti-alien feelings were brewing again, as they had done exactly a year ago, when Marlowe was murdered. Only this time the hatred was directed against Jews and Portingalls instead of Dutchmen and French – placards were posted again on walls, in Tower Ward and Crutched Friars, the main parts of London where Marranos lived. But this time the authorities made no move to put a stop to it. One evening I returned from the hospital to find a paper pinned to the door of the building where I lodged. It was a piece of crude and filthy verse declaring all Jews to be the devil's servants, murderers of Christ, and treasonous plotters against the Queen. I ripped it up in anger and tossed the fragments to the wind, but I began to be afraid again.

In the great Marrano mercantile houses of London, plans were being laid, business arrangements quietly proposed, baggage packed. Wives and children, a few at a time and discreetly, began to take ship for Amsterdam. It was not so easy for the poorer folk, those who dealt in rags and old clothes out at Shoreditch, to make plans to leave.

Still, the Queen had not released a death warrant for Ruy and the others condemned at the same time, though it was whispered that one had been signed in the days of panic following the poisoning of Lord Strange. Signed, but not released. Essex and others must have persuaded Her Majesty to sign in the aftermath of that poisoning of her cousin, but afterwards her conviction of Ruy's innocence meant that she refused to release it. Some said that the warrant would be effected at the beginning of the new law term on the fourth day of June. I had not visited Phelippes's office since before my illness, but now, towards the end of May, he sent for me to translate some Portuguese documents for him. They proved to be nothing secret or dangerous, and before I left I called to see Arthur Gregory.

'And how is your son?' I asked.

His face lit up with pride.

'He is learning his letters, Dr Alvarez, and not quite five years old! As strong and healthy a boy as any in England, through your skill and kindness.'

We fell to discussing the political gossip and he touched on the Lopez case.

'He will be executed, that is certain,' he said, soberly. 'But for the moment all the parties are tossing the matter from hand to hand like a game of hot chestnuts. Nobody wants to be left holding it, and have his fingers burnt. My Lord Essex, My Lord Burghley, Sir Michael Blount, Sir John Puckering, Keeper of the Great Seal, they're all in the game, but ducking the blame for it, in case Her Majesty turns on them, for she ever favoured her physician.'

'Indeed she did.'

'I have heard that something may happen while she is out of town,' he said, 'staying with the Cecils at Theobalds.'

That made logical sense. While the Queen was away, might not those who wished Ruy's destruction take some final and fatal step?

Arthur was proved right. The verdict in the court of Oyer and Terminer required the Queen's signature on the death warrant, but there was another way to go about the business, which did not require the royal warrant. On Saturday the seventh day of June, with Her Majesty safely out of London, in Osterley on the way to Theobalds, the three prisoners, Lopez, Tinoco, and Ferreira, were conveyed from the Tower by river to Westminster, where the Court of the Queen's Bench was to sit under the Chief Justice, Sir John Popham. It was quite legal to subject them to a second trial, and the Court of the Queen's Bench had the power to pass the death sentence without the need for the monarch's signature. It was summary justice, but had the pleasing effect of removing blame for Ruy's death from both the Essex and Cecil factions, and from the Queen herself.

The trial was swift, brutal, and predetermined. In the Court of Queen's Bench the defendants should have been given more leave to speak than in the Court of Oyer and Terminer, but their attempts at defence were ruthlessly silenced, lest they reveal something that might harm the great men who had used them and then brought them there. Ruy was heard to protest that he had never plotted to hurt the Queen, but he was derided and cut short.

With pitiless speed the three men were ferried across the river the same day, to be handed over by due legal process to the Sheriff of London at the Marshalsea. I stood there with Simon and Will and other friends from the playhouse, outside the prison and not far from the Rose – two buildings which had played a considerable part in my life – and watched Ruy Lopez dragged from the wherry in chains, a man whose life, through none of my wish, had become entangled with mine.

It casts a clear and unquestionable light on the twisted nature of justice in the fate of Ruy Lopez that the three hurdles for the prisoners were already prepared and waiting in the street. This time, not only was the verdict decided before the trial, but the means of execution had been set in motion without need for any delay. The men, who could not walk for weakness and had to be dragged by the armpits, were tied down on the hurdles, a few inches above the dusty street, face upwards, so that they looked up through the encircling heads of the gathered crowds towards the soft azure sky of early June. The hurdles were harnessed to cart horses, which would drag them over the Bridge and through the streets of London, out past Mountjoy's Inn, where Sara and her children cowered, until they reached the place of execution at Tyburn Fields.

I felt sick.

He is an old man, such an old man. Sara's husband and the Queen's own doctor, whom she loved. I wished you damned in Hell once, Ruy, after the Portuguese expedition, but no longer. Not this. Never this. You look so small and pitiful now, your velvet gown stained and torn, your hair, once white as a swan's breast, matted and filthy. The sickness rises in my throat. I am back in the streets of Coimbra, stripped and flogged, with the rusty stench of my own blood filling my nostrils. Dear God, that it should come to this.

The crowd watched eagerly, and many were preparing to follow the procession all the way, so they could witness the satisfying spectacle of the horrible execution of the Jew doctor who had plotted to poison their beloved Queen. A rabble of apprentices in their blue tunics began throwing stones and clods of mud and rotten vegetables at the helpless men on the hurdles. Ruy turned his face aside and caught sight of me. I leaned forward, not caring who heard me, appalled by the spectacle of that frail old man about to be dragged to his death.

'God go with you, Ruy!' I cried. 'I will look after Sara and the children.'

At that, one of the apprentices, who had just prised a heavy stone out of the mud and was hefting it in his hand, turned and flung it, not at the prisoners but at me. It caught me on the side of the head, the sharp edge cutting deep into my right temple. Simon took hold of my arm and dragged

233

me back into the crowd. Behind me I heard the rasping sound as the hurdles began to be dragged along the street towards the Bridge. The onlookers gave a cheer. Glancing over my shoulder, I caught sight of Ruy Lopez's feet. The sole of one shoe was worn into a hole, and the sight of those pathetic up-turned toes dragged away to humiliation and gruesome death caused my tears to well up, clouding my last sight of the great Marrano physician, merchant, and intelligencer, who had risen higher than any of us, only to be brought to defilement and a traitor's death.

Simon steered me away from the crowd, in case anyone else had taken note of what I had called out to Ruy, and we began walking south along the Kentish road. We must have walked for two hours or more, stopping at last in a village where a local ale wife had tied a bush above her door as a sign for travellers. There we ate a simple meal of pease pottage, bread, and hard cheese, and walked back towards Southwark as the lingering summer twilight dwindled and the young leaves on the trees faded from green to silvery yellow. By then Dr Roderigo Lopez was dead, his body dismembered, and his head and limbs nailed up above the Bridge gatehouse.

As they put the noose round his neck for the first act of that extended and cruel ritual, he had cried out, 'I love the Queen as well as I love Our Lord!'

They laughed him to scorn for a lying Jew.

Chapter Twelve

*A*fter Ruy's death, I visited Sara as often as I could, but the disaster had made her withdrawn and reclusive, and I felt my visits were not always welcome. All Ruy's possessions were still impounded by the government and she was only able to stay on at Mountjoy's Inn because the next quarter's rent had been paid in advance. By moving into just a few rooms of the house, she was able to persuade Mistress Allington to extend the tenancy a further six months for no additional rent.

'I hope by then some of our belongings will be returned to us,' she told me. 'The Queen has sent some messages of hope, but how far I can credit them, I do not know.'

I could see how humiliated she was by Ruy's downfall. The distress at his death, and the manner of his death, had left her pale and drawn. The children were very quiet. As well, I had an uneasy feeling that my own involvement with the intelligencers had left me somehow tainted in her eyes, though I tried not to show that I suspected it. I was saddened by this estrangement from my oldest friend, and indeed my only woman friend, with whom I could be at ease, almost slipping back into being the girl Caterina again. However, the awkwardness between us meant that I was reluctant to call often at Mountjoy's Inn.

Free for the moment, at least, of Essex, Bacon, and Phelippes, and all their works, I was able to spend more of my time with my patients and still have leisure to join Simon and the other players in the evenings.

'The matter of our patron is settled at last,' said Simon one day, when I met him at the Lion after the performance. 'We are no longer Lord Strange's Men, but My Lord Hunsdon's, the Lord Chamberlain's Men.'

So Lord Hunsden had his wish at last, to have his own company of players, and those the finest in London. It was evident how pleased Simon was, after all the uncertainty following the death of Lord Strange. To belong to a company whose patron was a high official at Court was to be raised above the rank of a mere journeyman player, even one with a lordly patron.

Shortly afterwards, Lord Hunsdon wrote to Sir Cuthbert Buckle, the current Lord Mayor of London, requesting permission for his new company, under the direction of Cuthbert Burbage, son of James, to perform during the winter months at the Cross Keys Inn in Gracechurch Street. Permission was granted, and so Simon, Will, and the others had a winter playhouse (of sorts) to look forward to, not so convenient for the players who lived south of the river, but, lying as it did in the very heart of the city, it was marvellous convenient for most London playgoers. They had used the Cross Keys before, and been satisfied with it as a winter playhouse. James Burbage had not abandoned his role as director of the company, but after a bout of ill health he handed over more and more of the business to his elder son. His younger son, Richard, was above all in love with acting, not directing, so the division of responsibility between Master Burbage's two sons appeared to satisfy them all.

At long last the repairs to the Burbages' Theatre in Shoreditch had been completed, despite repeated contentions with the owner of the land on which it was built. The Lord Chamberlain's Men, as they now were, would return there next spring, although there would remain a group of players at the Rose, under the direction of Philip Henslowe and Edward Alleyn. After the shifting about in the players' companies caused by the plague and their exile from London, when they had toured the English countryside, they had gradually rebuilt themselves over the last year. The Lord Admiral's Men had reformed and would take over the Rose. Many of my friends amongst the players regretted the move back to the Theatre, after enjoying the comfortable quarters and new devices at the Rose.

'Master Burbage is loath to spend his coin on adding such clever but costly devices to the Theatre,' Simon said. 'He fears that the time will come when the ground lease will not be renewed. Now that there is so much building of new houses out at Shoreditch, the landlord can make a far greater profit from rows of close packed houses than from a playhouse on the same ground, taking up so much room.'

'But what shall you do then?' I asked. 'If the Lord Admiral's Men are in possession of the Rose, where shall the Lord Chamberlain's Men go?'

He shrugged. 'I think Cuthbert is searching for a suitable place to build a new playhouse. Shoreditch is unlikely, I suspect. There is much to be said for Southwark, away from the direct control of the City Council. And ground rent will be cheaper.'

I nodded. 'And it is more and more the place for entertainment, just as Westminster is the place for government. We have the whorehouses, the bear and bull baiting and cock fighting, the Paris Garden for courting couples and families, the ale houses with intimate private rooms a little way down river, and now the Rose for more refined pursuits.'

He laughed. 'Truly. Every need provided for.'

All this shifting about from one part of London to another proved unsettling for the players. Will seemed ever to be moving from one lodging to another, though that was sometimes due to his need to escape from amorous landladies.

'I cannot decide whether I should take lodgings north of the river,' said Simon, after the Lord Chamberlain's Men

237

had been told of their winter playhouse at the Cross Keys. 'What say you, Kit?'

'I say you must decide for yourself,' I answered, trying to hide my dismay that he might be moving away into the City.

'Well, perhaps I will wait till the spring, when we begin to play in Shoreditch. ''Tis not so long a walk from here to the Cross Keys in Gracechurch Street during the winter. Will has a new play for us to con for next month, a comedy. I shall be too much occupied to hunt for new lodgings.'

'And besides,' I added cunningly, 'if you are right that Cuthbert is looking for a plot of land on this side of the river, you were best to stay here. If you leave your room at the Atkins house, you may never find something so convenient again.'

'Aye,' he said, with an innocent smile. 'That is probably true. Perhaps I shall stay here, at least until we see which way the wind blows.'

It was the day following this conversation that I received a note from Francis Mylles, inviting me to sup with him that evening at an inn in Cheapside. He was to be in London for a few days on some business to do with his work as clerk of the Privy Seal.

'So,' he said, once we were seated and had given our order to the serving man, 'I have not seen you since your visit to us last year, but I was glad to receive your letter about the outcome of the affair of the man murdered at St Bartholomew's.'

'Not very satisfactory,' I said. 'The coroner ruled that Esau Miller, who was heard to boast of it while in his cups, was guilty of the murder, but Miller was dead by then.'

'And Miller himself was also one of Lord Burghley's men?'

I nodded. 'With Miller dead, there could be no investigation into whether he acted on his own, for some reason unknown, or whether he acted on orders from the Cecils.'

'That is what you believe?' Mylles said.

I shrugged. 'Who can say for sure? But there seems to be a pattern here, which repeats. All the pieces fit in the pattern. Men who work for the Cecils slip out of favour for some reason or other. The next thing that happens is sudden death – in the case of Christopher Marlowe and Josiah Gurdin. And perhaps also Esau Miller. Or in the case of Roderigo Lopez, a sham trial, because he was a notable figure, and a public outcry served a purpose. It demonstrated how carefully the safety of Her Majesty and the realm is guarded by the Cecils.'

'But it was the Earl of Essex,' he objected, 'who made the accusation against Lopez in the first place, that Lopez planned to assassinate the Queen and start a rebellion against the government. Although I agree with you that the entire case was fabricated.'

'Essex initiated the accusation,' I said dryly, 'but you will note that it was the Cecils' man, Sir Edward Coke, as Solicitor General, who conducted the trial of Oyer and Terminer.'

'It fell to his office.'

'Indeed. So in the end, more credit accrued to the Cecils than to Essex, though in the whole matter of Ruy Lopez, I think both parties found it in their interests to work together for once.'

'So you believe,' Mylles said slowly, 'that the deaths of Marlowe, Gurdin, Miller, and Lopez are in some way linked?'

'It can never be proven,' I said, 'but it seems to me that there is, as I said, a pattern.'

We were silent as the serving man brought our food, but when he left, I spoke again.

'One other man has never answered for his actions.'

Mylles raised his eyebrows, his spoon halfway to his mouth.

'Let us not forget,' I said, 'the murderer of Esau Miller. Robert Poley. Vanished quite from sight. Another man of the Cecils. One of those, you will recall, also present at the killing of Christopher Marlowe.'

'He never suffered any punishment for that affair,' Mylles said. 'None of them did. It was ruled an accident.'

'Aye,' I said. 'It is surprising the number of accidents which occur around Poley. I have no doubt he will emerge one day, shining and innocent as a newborn babe. But let us forget these unhappy matters. The Lady Elizabeth is with you still? How does she fare?'

'Very well indeed.' He smiled. 'And the Countess of Essex has come to spend some time with us during the unhealthy simmer weather here in London, bringing her son Lord Robert and the new baby, Lady Dorothy.'

'Oh,' I exclaimed, 'I am glad to hear that! I know that the Countess missed her daughter, although she was happy that Lady Elizabeth was with you.'

I could not have asked for better news. As Essex had not been granted a second son, I hoped he would also deal more carefully with the one he had.

The severe storm of the previous summer, which had destroyed so much of the grain crop shortly before the harvest, meant that the cost of food had risen steeply this year, as all the stores of food in London had been gradually exhausted. Rumour had it that conditions were, if anything, even worse in some parts of England, where in addition to food shortages there had been recent flooding. In accordance with regular practice, bakers must make their penny loaves to conform with the current weight laid down by the government, and that meant that the standard legal loaf, the basic foodstuff of the poor, had grown smaller and smaller as the supply of wheat dwindled and the price rose. Nor could the poor drown their misery and ease the ache in their empty bellies by means of a drink, for the barley harvest had been as poor as the wheat, and the price of ale accordingly went up.

What were the poor to eat? Even the vegetables grown to the north of London and in the small farms dotted about between Southwark and Lambeth had suffered last year. This year constant rain meant that onions and leeks rotted in the fields, peas and beans began to sprout, grew a few inches, then collapsed and lay in mouldy rows, spurned even by the slugs and birds. There were tales abroad of folk eating grass, and the city's population of rats fell prey to the desperate.

Meat made up little of the diet of the poor, even in the good years. And even could they have afforded it, more than the usual lack of winter feed had meant a great slaughter of beasts the previous Michaelmas. Fewer beasts kept over the winter meant fewer young animals this year, so that even the more well to do must pay higher prices for their meat or else tighten their belts. Meals served at the inns grew smaller. My supper with Mylles was barely half the quantity it would have been a couple of years earlier.

The dearth meant starvation, and starvation meant rising deaths amongst the citizens of London. Our almshouses at St Thomas's were packed, not only with the old and feeble, but with whole families seeking help in their desperate need.

'I do not know how long we can feed them,' Superintendent Ailmer said to me one day. He looked worn down with worry. 'The governors have granted us more funds, but with the cost of food rising, so it seems, every day, it will not suffice to feed all these extra mouths.'

When I encountered Peter Lambert one day in the City, he said that St Bartholomew's was suffering as well.

'My troubles of last year seem as nothing,' he said, 'compared with what these people must endure. We find them every morning, huddling in the old cloisters, like walking skeletons, some already having died in the night.'

I nodded. 'It is the same in Southwark. And with the terrible weather this year, I fear it can only grow worse.'

As well as the care of malnourished children and mothers whose babies were born weak and small, I had all my usual illnesses to treat in my two wards. In the early weeks following the execution of Ruy Lopez, there was

241

much ill feeling against Strangers, and especially against those of us who, like Ruy, had come from Portugal. I had to endure shouted insults in the streets, and even the thrown stone or two. In the hospital, where I had now worked for nearly five years, I was mostly accepted by my English colleagues, although one or two grew more reserved, or seemed to avoid me.

I was quite widely known and liked amongst the people of Southwark, but, it seemed, not with everyone. One day, something happened at the hospital to bring the anti-Jewish fever much closer to me.

'I do not want that Portingall to treat my son,' the woman said.

She stood, braced on widespread legs and with her arms akimbo, blocking my way to the cot where a sickly child had been laid by one of the nursing sisters. As far as I could tell from my limited sight of him, it was at least a severe case of rickets together with a fever.

Dr Edwards, one of my older English colleague, had been checking in the new patients with me, for the almoner, John Haddon, had sent up more children than usual. Normally he worked in the men's wards, but had volunteered his help that morning.

'Why, mistress,' he said, 'Dr Alvarez is particularly skilled in the care of children. He has brought many a one back from the brink of death.'

It was generous of him, and I gave him a smile, which he did not return. I could see he was troubled.

'With a name like that, he is surely a Portingall,' she said stubbornly. 'And see his hair, black as soot. He is a Portingall, and all Portingalls are known to be poisoners.'

She had a stupid, flabby face, like a half-risen crock of bread dough. For one brief moment I felt an urge to punch it, as one punches down rising dough.

'Mistress,' I said civilly, but with great difficulty, 'I assure you I have never poisoned anyone in my life.'

I nearly added, *Not knowingly, at any rate*, but did not think she would appreciate the jest.

The woman shook her head and would not move aside.

'If it is the Portingall who is to treat him, I will take him home again. I want no filthy Jew to touch him.'

The child looked very sick. He needed treatment urgently. I inclined my head to my colleague.

'Do you take the case then, Dr Edwards,' I said. I knew my cheeks were burning. 'It is more important to care for a sick child than to argue with a parent who possesses a sick mind.'

With that, I turned and walked away, glad that my long gown hid my shaking knees. I should not have spoken thus to the woman. It would not be forgotten, or forgiven. But I could not endure such an attack on my professional skill in silence.

Once she had left, Dr Edwards urged me to take over the case, for he was needed in his own wards. The child not only had rickets and a high fever, but showed the unmistakable signs of starvation which we were seeing more and more every day. He joined the other patients in the children's ward, who were unusually quiet these days. I told Goodwife Watson and Alice to warn me if the hostile woman appeared again, so that I could retreat to the lying-in ward or my office.

It was a few days later that I was checking the newest babies in the Whittington ward. Many bore the signs of their mothers' malnourishment, born underweight and weak. The quiet of the ward, without the usual hearty wails of healthy babies was suddenly broken by the sounds of shouting and skirmishing coming from the top of the stairs.

'What is this?' I said, confronted by the angry countenance of one of the hospital servants, who had grasped an intruder by the arm.

The intruder, whose back was toward me, did not possess the height or build to threaten the servant, who was one of the burly men who did the heavy work about the hospital. In fact the intruder would barely have reached my shoulder, even had he not been hunched over with a smaller child upon his back, a barefoot grubby girl, whose thin arms were clasped about his neck. Her stranglehold did not seem to be impeding his shouted protests.

'I'll not wait to see no almoner!' he said. 'Dr Alvarez is going to see to my sister, whatever the devil almoner says.'

'Tommy Atgate,' I said, 'that is no way to speak of Master Haddon.'

The fierce intruder broke free from the servant's grip and swung round, impeded by the burden on his back.

'Do not concern yourself, Jos,' I said, 'I know this young man. If he has slipped round the almoner's office, I am sure it was with good reason.'

The servant glowered at Tommy, muttered something inaudible, and stamped away down the stairs.

'Put your sister down, Tommy,' I said. 'I think she is somewhat too heavy for you.'

He leaned over and tried to slide the child off his back, but her arms were twined so tightly about his neck that I needs must prise her off. Her whole body throbbed with heat, and her eyes were glazed with fever, yet in spite of all, she retained a frantic strength. I picked her up and turned toward the children's ward.

'Open the door for me, Tommy,' I said. 'We will have your sister into bed first, then you may tell me everything. What is her name?'

'Eliza,' he said, opening the door for me.

Of course.

Alice was surprised and pleased to see Tommy again, and even Goodwife Watson seemed to have forgotten his antics. Alice ran to fetch warm water, soap, and one of the simple night shifts we keep in the hospital, while Goodwife Watson led us to the far end of the ward, where just one bed remained unoccupied, next to the child whose mother who did not trust Portingalls.

Relieved of responsibility, Tommy relaxed and squatted down on the floor beside the bed. While Alice bathed Eliza and dressed her in the clean shift, I fetched a tincture of febrifuge herbs, a cup, and a bottle of the raspberry cordial I add to make medicines more palatable for children.

The girl's breathing was rapid and shallow, and when I laid my ear against her chest, I could hear a rustling in her lungs – a sound like dried leaves heaped up in autumn.

'How long has she been ill, Tommy?' I asked.

'More'n a week, doctor,' he said. 'I *told* him she should be brought here, but he wouldn't. Just told me to shut my gob.'

More than told, I thought, for there was an ugly bruise across Tommy's mouth.

'Your father?'

'Aye.'

'Could your mother not have brought her?' I remembered that Tommy's mother had not been afraid to come to St Thomas's in the past, whatever her husband might say or do.

'Ma died, two months gone,' he said. He tried to sound indifferent, but was betrayed by the tremble in his lower lip.

'Oh, Tommy, I am so sorry.'

As I propped Eliza up on my arm and helped her to drink the febrifuge tincture, I wondered whether Tommy's father had gone too far at last in his violence toward his wife, but before I could think of a way to ask indirectly, Tommy gave me my answer.

'We a'nt got enough to eat. Ma died of the hunger, and so did the two littlest ones. My big brother Al has gone for a wherryman, and Mary has moved to live with her man, so there's just me and Eliza left at home. I tried to look after her, but she got sick. Is she going to die, doctor?'

'I hope not, Tommy,' I said. 'You did right to bring her here. It is the lung sickness and she isn't very strong, but you know that we will do our best. The almoner would have admitted you, you know. There was no need to try to creep in without seeing him.'

'I wasn't going to waste no time. She's much worse today.'

'Well, you can leave her safely with us and go home now.'

He shook his head. 'I a'nt going anywhere till I sees she's better. I'll just get a lamming from Him. Besides,' he looked up at me sideways and grinned. 'Besides, I thought maybe I'd get something to eat here.'

I laughed. 'Very well, you may stay, provided you behave yourself and help Goodwife Watson and Goodwife Alice. You will need to sleep on the floor, I am afraid.'

'That's no bother,' he said, grinning again. 'That's where I sleep at home.'

With that grin I noticed that he had gained more of his second teeth since I had last seen him.

Eliza's eyes were drooping, although she was still very flushed. It would be some while before the tincture would take effect.

'Come on,' I said to Tommy. 'We will leave her to sleep. I am sure we can find you some work to do. You can see that we have more children than ever in the ward today. Goodwife Watson will tell you how she needs you to help.'

He scrambled to his feet, then leaned over the bed and patted Eliza's shoulder.

'I a'nt leaving you, Eliza,' he said. 'I'se staying right here, but I got work to do. You go to sleep now.'

The little girl opened her eyes, which looked up at him, unfocused, but a faint smile played over her lips, then she closed her eyes again.

We walked away quietly, in search of Goodwife Watson.

Tommy settled in remarkably quickly and quietly, as a sort of servant in the children's ward. Jesu knew we needed help, for those were the busiest days there I could remember at St Thomas's. With the sickly babies coming into the world in the ward next door, I was grateful to the little scamp. True to his word, he played none of his past tricks, although he had not lost his impudent tongue. I wondered at first whether we should have his father storming in, wrathful that Tommy had disobeyed his orders, but there was no sign of him. I supposed that if he was now alone at home, he need not even provide what little food he had given to these two waifs, but could spend all his earnings from the brickworks on food and drink for himself.

We did send word to Tommy's elder brother and sister, to let them know where he and Eliza were, but we heard nothing back. Perhaps they were too anxious to break with their unhappy past to want to reply, or perhaps they were amongst the many overtaken by the famine which had so much of London in its grip.

Eliza was very ill. Already weakened by starvation, her body had little strength to fight off the lung disease, which grew worse for several days, so that I spent one night at the hospital, fearing I should lose her before the morning. Near dawn, with Tommy asleep on a pile of blankets on the floor beside her bed, she broke into a terrible sweating fever, but when it passed she was drenched but cooler. Alice and I quietly changed her bedding and her shift, tiptoeing around her sleeping brother.

'Will she recover now, doctor?' Alice whispered. She was observant, and was becoming quite skilled in recognising the stages of illness.

'Aye,' I said, 'I think there is good hope that she will. Now we must persuade her to eat, for she has taken nothing but fluids since she came, has she not? Gentle food, little and often, until we build up her strength.'

Tommy must have heard us speaking, for he stirred and sat up.

'Eliza?' he said anxiously. 'She a'nt worse, is she?'

'Nay, Tommy,' I said. 'Go back to sleep. I think that now she is going to get better.'

The banns had been read for Mellie White's marriage to Edwyn Somers, and she had sent me a letter, carefully written by herself, with very few mistakes, begging me to come, along with Goodwife Margaret Appledean, who had helped me to care for her after Hannah's birth.

And if it plees you Master Hethering who come with you to Christs one wintertym, she ended.

Both Goodwife Appledean and Simon were glad to come with me, for there is no happier time than a summer's wedding, if the sun shine and the couple be in love, and not tied together to suit the needs of family and property. Mellie had no family of her own, but had found a new family at Christ's Hospital, and she had told me that Edwyn had a mother and an older married sister. The wedding was to be held at Christ's the following Friday.

The three of us took a two man wherry to save our wedding finery from the dust of the summer streets. Margaret Appledean was resplendent in a new gown of bright green, or at any rate a gown I had never seen before, because in the hospital all the nursing sisters wore plain gowns of brown, grey, or black which would take no harm from the many accidents which may occur when caring for the sick.

Simon had donned one of the expensive doublets which had cost him so dear in the days when he had tried to emulate the gaudy finery favoured by Christopher Marlowe. I supposed by now he was able to suppress the memory of his past debt to Ingram Friser and the beating it had earned him. Secretly, I thought it a little too fine, and hoped it would not outshine the clothes of the bridal couple, but that Mellie would take it as a compliment.

As for myself, I had not so many clothes to choose from, but I wore my best doublet and hose, with a new shirt trimmed with a ruffled collar. I decided to leave my physician's gown behind, for the day had dawned warm and was growing warmer. Rikki I decided to leave with Tom, for I feared the wedding feast, laid out on trestle tables, might prove too much for his self control.

We walked up from the river to Newgate Market, Goodwife Appledean holding her skirts high out of the dust, and found that even the gatehouse of Christ's Hospital had been garlanded for the festivities. Although we had set out early, the tide had been against us and we arrived only just in time for the wedding procession. Whereas this would normally proceed through the streets from the bride's and groom's homes to the church, here both homes and church were clustered together in the extensive grounds of the orphanage, so the procession formed up at the foot of the stairs leading up to Mistress Wedderbury's room, where Mellie now lived.

There was a group of musicians, with drums, pipes, a shawm, and a lute, tuning up in a confusion of notes, and a crowd of children, clean and shining, dressed in their blue and yellow uniforms, from the petties of three or four up to the largest boys and girls, on the point of taking up an apprenticeship, or even, in the case of a few clever boys, leaving for Oxford and Cambridge. The youngest babies were mostly sent out to wet nurses in the country, although a few remained here. Amongst the crowd I could pick out the familiar faces of children I had brought here, including little Jamey, once one of the beggar children, now almost unrecognisable.

Then the musicians grew quiet and everyone turned to the stairs as Mellie came shyly down to the courtyard. She wore a simple gown of soft yellow, but it had been embellished with a small white ruff, probably the first she had ever worn, and her hair, usually tucked into a cap, hung glossy and shining to her shoulders. In her hands she carried a garland of rosemary and white roses.

It was almost impossible to believe that this was the raped and frightened child I had first cared for at St Thomas's, her face bruised, her hair lank and matted, and the baby she carried swelling her child's body grotesquely. She had grown into a very lovely young woman. And behind her, plump and excited, came Hannah, carrying her own small garland, already crushed in the fierce grip of her hands.

The musicians began to play a lively dance, and we moved off in procession round the perimeter of the quadrangle, where we stopped outside the steward's office. The young man who emerged looked as shy as Mellie, but he beamed at her with pride. He was a little older – I remembered that she had said he would be one and twenty this summer. A slight young man, but wiry, with fair hair and dark blue eyes. The bones of his face were strong, and I thought that, in time, he would grow sturdier. He held out his hand to Mellie and she laid her hand in his.

On around the quadrangle we went, and back to Christ Church, which had been the church of Greyfriars Monastery, before it was converted into an orphanage. At the church door the young couple went forward to stand in front of the rector, while the rest of use clustered behind.

The familiar words of the wedding service rang out over the sunny quadrangle, and I thought how appropriate in this case was the promise to cherish each other. Mellie, sadly orphaned and abused, had come at last to this loving fulfilment. When the rector pronounced Mellie and Edwyn man and wife, Edwyn took the garland from her and placed it on her head. And all the children, who had been dutifully quiet until now, burst out into cheering. I saw that Margaret Appledean was openly weeping.

The wedding ceremony at the church door was followed by a service inside, then we all tumbled out and the young couple led us to the trestle tables set out in the centre of the grass. Servants removed the cloths which had been laid over the food to keep away the wasps and began filling cups of ale that we might toast the health and happy future of the bride and groom.

I had lost sight of both Simon and Goodwife Appledean, but now found myself beside Mistress Wedderbury, who smiled at me warmly.

'Well, doctor,' she said, 'we could hardly have foreseen this, could we, when you brought Mellie and Hannah to me?'

'Indeed,' I said, 'but I remember that you told me then that the most important thing Christ's Hospital offered these children was love. Mellie seems to have found it in abundance.'

'She deserves it,' Mistress Wedderbury said seriously. 'I have great hopes of both Mellie and Edwyn.'

'You have found them somewhere to live?'

'Aye, three rooms on the ground floor just next the stairs to my rooms. Mellie will be close to her work, Edwyn will need to walk only along the side of the quadrangle to the steward's office, and Hannah will have her lessons at the petty school. They may take their meals in the refectory, or if she wishes Mellie may cook over her own fire.'

'And should there be more children?' I said.

'Oh, we shall manage,' she said comfortably. 'They are young, I am sure they will want children. And there is always room for children here.'

The crowds around the table were thinning a little, so we made our way there and helped ourselves. The steward, who was acting as the bride's father might have done, called for silence and asked us to drink a toast to Mellie and Edwyn, then the musicians, who had been refreshing themselves liberally, struck up a merry dance, so that soon the grass was hidden in a whirlpool of dancers.

Across by the gatehouse I caught sight of Simon, who was talking to a man who had just stepped through, and who seemed familiar, although I could not place him. They began to make their way toward me, though they must needs stop and sidestep the dancers, so that it took some time for them to reach me.

'Kit,' Simon said, 'I thought we should never reach you. This good fellow has been seeking you.'

The man pulled off his woollen cap and bowed. Then I realised where I had seen him before, although not for many months now. He was one of the house servants at the Nuñez home. His name I could not remember.

'I beg your forgiveness, doctor,' he said, 'for interrupting.'

'Nay,' I said, 'no need to apologise. Dame Beatriz is not ill, is she? Or one of the household?' I was thankful I had brought my medicine satchel with me, although I had left it with the gatekeeper, so that it would not be an impediment during the wedding. I took a step toward the gatehouse.

The man shook his head. 'Nay, 'tis nothing like that. A letter came to the mistress's house, addressed to Dr Alvarez at the home of Dr Nuñez of London. Although my master is long gone, it reached us safely, although 'tis quite worn and must have travelled far.'

He delved into his scrip and drew something out, but I could not see it clearly.

'So,' he went on, 'the mistress tells me to go over to Southwark to St Thomas's and find you. "Give it to Dr Alvarez," she says, "and no one else." So over I go to St Thomas's, but when I get there, they tell me you were gone to a marriage at Christ's Hospital. I dare not leave the letter for you there, after what the mistress said, so I make my way back over the Bridge.'

I held out my hand for the letter, but he wasn't prepared to hand it over yet, being determined to tell his whole story.

'Then I sets out to come here, but my shoe comes adrift, sole from body as 'twere.'

He looked at us expectantly to see whether we appreciated his jest. Simon and I both smiled politely. I wondered how much of this Simon had already heard.

'Well, I must have the shoe mended, didn't I?' he said reasonably. 'I could not walk halfway across the City with my shoe flapping loose.'

He held up his foot so we could admire his newly stitched shoe.

'Excellent,' I said, wondering when this would end. 'And now you have found me, so you may give me the letter.'

252

I had no idea what it could be, for who would send me a letter at the home of Dr Nuñez? Surely everyone who knew me would also know that he had been dead nearly these three years.

Finally, the man held out the letter to me, and I took it.

He had the right of it. The paper was creased and dirty, the edges frayed, as though it had passed through many hands, over many miles. He handed it to me with the seal uppermost. The wax bore no imprint and was cracked, but the letter had not been opened.

I turned it over.

To be directed to Dr Alvarez
At the home of Dr Hector Nuñez
London

I stared at it and my hand began to shake. The sound of the musicians and the shouts and laughter of the dancers faded away, until they were no more than the boom of the distant ocean.

I knew the hand, although I had not seen it for many years. It was as round and childish as it had been then.

It was the writing of my sister Isabel.

Historical Note

The trial and execution of Dr Roderigo Lopez was one of the greatest scandals to occur during the reign of Queen Elizabeth I, a period not unfamiliar with plots, counter plots, and crooked dealings.

Roderigo Lopez was one of a number of Marranos who escaped from Portugal to England during the late sixteenth century. Like the others he was of Jewish descent but was a baptised Christian. Just how far the Marranos retained their Jewish faith, and how far they had converted to Christianity, is a moot point. Certainly the younger generations mostly became Christians (like Aemilia Bassano), but Lopez belonged to the transitional generation. In theory, there were no Jews in England between their expulsion in 1290 by Edward I and the relaxation of the ban during the Commonwealth in the mid seventeenth century, but this sixteenth century group of refugees, fleeing increasing persecution by the Inquisition, were received in England without question. Many came from the professional classes and often combined the exercise of their professions with mercantile activity, having relatives and friends scattered throughout Europe and the Mediterranean, including the Ottoman Empire.

On the whole, there was relatively little anti-Semitism in England, but – as so often happens – when times were hard, employment scarce, and food prices high, prejudice reared its head against immigrants ('Strangers' is the contemporary term). In early 1593, the attacks on Strangers, both verbal and physical, were not particularly directed against those of Jewish descent, but against foreigners in general, as we meet in *That Time May Cease*. Who was responsible for posting up the placards vilifying Strangers will probably never be known, though it was also clearly connected to an attempt to implicate Christopher Marlowe.

However, as time progressed and conditions in England became more difficult for the poor, anti-Semitism grew more pronounced (aggravated by performances of Marlowe's *The Jew of Malta*), and this anti-Semitism was exploited during the Lopez trial, amongst others by Sir Robert Cecil who, from his seat amongst the jury, openly accused Lopez, calling out 'By our Souls' witness, the vile Jew is lying'.

Ever since the death of Sir Francis Walsingham, and the subsequent collapse of his intelligence service, there had been a struggle for power between the Earl of Essex and the Cecils (Lord Burghley and his son, Sir Robert Cecil). Control of the intelligence network was a major part of their bid for power, which would not end until the final and most treacherous act of Essex in 1601.

Roderigo Lopez was clearly an exceptionally fine doctor and served the Queen as her personal and trusted physician for many years. Like other well-to-do Marranos, he was also a merchant, and as such was able to serve Walsingham by gathering information and sometimes intercepting enemy despatches. He was a substantial property owner and had taken English citizenship.

However, Lopez had a weakness. Like many who have lost their homeland, he was anxious for security and a position in society. He also dabbled, dangerously, in politics. As Kit says in this novel, he was his own worst enemy. When the opportunity arose of backing Dom Antonio's claim to the throne of Portugal, Lopez became deeply involved in the campaign, with hopes of returning to Portugal in glory, foreseeing an assured future as the new king's right-hand man. When disaster overwhelmed the Portuguese expedition, Lopez did not give up hope.

Having greater belief in his own skills in diplomacy than was justified, he appears to have carried on with some late scheme of Walsingham's after the spymaster's death, which seems to have involved a movement towards a truce with Spain. Lopez's mistake was to act on his own, from a misguided and arrogant assumption that he did not need the support of one of the great men of the time. In the struggle between Essex and the Cecils, he belonged to the Cecil faction, but did not tell them of his scheme until far too late. He also used as his agents and collaborators several men of very dubious character, some of whom were double agents, betraying him to Essex.

Despite intensive investigation, we shall probably never know the truth, for the interested parties took great care at the time to cover their tracks. It is certain, as is now generally agreed, that Lopez was never involved in a plot to assassinate the Queen, nor did she ever believe he was. It is possible that he was at least party to some plot against the convicted murderer Antonio Perez, but we cannot know for sure.

Essex had come to hate Lopez, no doubt partly because he spread rumours that Essex suffered from syphilis. Moreover, Essex reckoned that by accusing Lopez of planning to poison the Queen, he could severely damage the Cecils, whose man Lopez now was. Thus Lopez was trapped in the middle of the deadly rivalry between the two factions. The Cecils could have saved him. They chose not to. It was a callous, self-serving decision, but they must have felt themselves seriously threatened, and so agreed to support the trumped-up charges against Lopez.

It was not a solitary case. If someone became what we would now call 'a loose cannon', the Cecils would rid themselves of him. In my own mind, I am certain that this was the case with Christopher Marlowe, though any evidence to that effect will have been destroyed long ago.

If we consider what we know from our own times, this scenario is not unfamiliar. In countries where there is a lawless struggle for power between ruthless men, those who become 'inconvenient' may well find themselves the victims of rigged trials. The outcome is inevitable.

Once Roderigo Lopez was brought before a court of Oyer and Terminer, whatever his innocence, his fate was sealed.

The Author

Ann Swinfen spent her childhood partly in England and partly on the east coast of America. She was educated at Somerville College, Oxford, where she read Classics and Mathematics and married a fellow undergraduate, the historian David Swinfen. While bringing up their five children and studying for a postgraduate MSc in Mathematics and a BA and PhD in English Literature, she had a variety of jobs, including university lecturer, translator, freelance journalist and software designer. She served for nine years on the governing council of the Open University and for five years worked as a manager and editor in the technical author division of an international computer company, but gave up her full-time job to concentrate on her writing, while continuing part-time university teaching in English Literature. In 1995 she founded Dundee Book Events, a voluntary organisation promoting books and authors to the general public, which ran for fifteen years.

She is the author of the highly acclaimed series, *The Chronicles of Christoval Alvarez*. Set in the late sixteenth century, it features a young Marrano physician recruited as a code-breaker and spy in Walsingham's secret service. In order, the books are: ***The Secret World of Christoval Alvarez, The Enterprise of England, The Portuguese Affair, Bartholomew Fair, Suffer the Little Children, Voyage to Muscovy, The Play's the Thing, That Time May Cease*** and ***The Lopez Affair***.

Her *Fenland Series* takes place in East Anglia during the seventeenth century. In the first book, ***Flood***, both men and women fight desperately to save their land from greedy and unscrupulous speculators. The second, ***Betrayal***, continues the story of the dangerous search for legal redress and security for the embattled villagers, at a time when few could be trusted.

Her latest series, the bestselling *Oxford Medieval Mysteries*, is set in the fourteenth century and features bookseller Nicholas Elyot, a young widower with two small children, and his university friend Jordain Brinkylsworth, who are faced with crime in the troubled world following the Black Death. In order, the books are: ***The Bookseller's Tale, The Novice's Tale, The***

Huntsman's Tale and *The Merchant's Tale.* Both this series and the Christoval Alvarez series are being recorded as unabridged audiobooks.

She has also written two standalone historical novels. *The Testament of Mariam*, set in the first century, recounts, from an unusual perspective, one of the most famous and yet ambiguous stories in human history, while exploring life under a foreign occupying force, in lands still torn by conflict to this day. *This Rough Ocean* is based on the real-life experiences of the Swinfen family during the 1640s, at the time of the English Civil War, when John Swynfen was imprisoned for opposing the killing of the king, and his wife Anne had to fight for the survival of her children and dependents.

Ann Swinfen now lives on the northeast coast of Scotland, with her husband, formerly vice-principal of the University of Dundee, a rescue cat called Maxi, and a cocker spaniel called Suki.

You can receive notifications of new books and audios by signing up to the mailing list at www.annswinfen.com/sign-up/ and follow her monthly blog by subscribing at www. http://annswinfen.com/blog/

Learn more at her website www.annswinfen.com

Printed in Great Britain
by Amazon